SOMETHING
UNEXPECTED

Something Unexpected
Edited by: Jessica Royer Ocken
Proofreading by: Elaine York, Julia Griffins
Cover Model: David J. Harman
Photographer: Marq Mendez
Cover designer: Sommer Stein, Perfect Pear Creative
Formatting by: Elaine York, Allusion Publishing
www.allusionpublishing.com

SOMETHING
UNEXPECTED

VI KEELAND

For my Sarah, and her unwavering love
of her grandmother and Harry Styles.

CHAPTER 1
Nora

"**Y**ou've got to be kidding me..." I mumbled and turned, shouting over my shoulder. "Oh, and thanks for sticking me with the tab!"

The bartender walked over. "Everything okay, ma'am?"

I sighed. "Yeah. Guy I met on Tinder just turned out to be nothing like I expected."

A deep voice came from the other end of the bar. "Shocker. Maybe you should try looking somewhere a little more respectable..."

I squinted down at him. "*Excuse me?*"

The guy rattled the ice in his glass without looking up. "What's the matter? He wasn't as good-looking as his picture made him out to be? You gotta give a guy some leeway. You women are the queens of hiding shit. Lord knows we go to bed with someone with long hair, a great tan, and full lips. In the morning, we wake up next to a person we don't recognize because of all the makeup, hair extensions, and plumping crap you use."

Seriously? "Perhaps if you weren't so rude and *looked* at a person when you were speaking to them, you might have noticed that I don't have hair extensions, wear very little makeup, and I'm *naturally* plumped in *all* the right places."

That seemed to get his attention. The guy's head lifted, and he did a quick sweep over my face before his eyes snagged on my cleavage. It gave me my first good look at him. The face that came with that attitude was *nothing* like I would've expected. Based on how defensive he was about my would-be date's looks not being up to par, I thought maybe he had some experience disappointing women. But this guy definitely didn't let down anyone. He was younger than his grumbly voice hinted at, with dark brown hair that could use a cut. Yet I would've enjoyed running my fingers through it had *he* been my Tinder date. He had a strong, masculine jaw peppered with stubble, a Roman-esque nose, tanned skin, and aquamarine eyes lined with the thickest black lashes I'd ever seen.

Too bad he was also *a jerk.*

When his eyes finally met mine, I arched a brow. "Which one of us is the shallow one again?"

His lip twitched. "Never said I didn't appreciate beautiful things. Just that you should give a guy a chance."

I shook my head. "Not that it's any of your business, but the reason that guy wasn't what I expected was because he had an indent from his wedding band on his finger. Probably slipped it off two seconds before he walked in. It had nothing to do with his looks."

"I apologize then." He motioned to the bartender. "Her next round is on me."

I pointed to the half-drunk expensive scotch Tinder guy had left behind—without any cash. "How about that one is on you instead?"

He chuckled. "You got it."

I sipped my wine, still stewing over the jerk I'd wasted three days talking to. Eventually I yelled over to Mr. Attitude again. "Hey, so what do you use?"

"Pardon?"

"What dating app? You said I should use a more respectable dating app."

"Oh." He shrugged. "I don't use any."

"Married?"

"Nope."

"Girlfriend?"

"Nope."

"So you just what...troll the supermarket pretending to shop?"

"Something like that." He smirked. "Is Tinder your go-to?"

"It depends on what I'm looking for."

"What were you looking for tonight?"

I thought about the question. Let's face it, I found the guy on Tinder three days ago and met him in the bar in the lobby of my hotel. I think it was clear what both of us expected to happen. But it wasn't really about the physical—at least for me. "To forget," I answered.

The guy's mask of superiority might have slipped, just a little. Then his phone rang, and he swiped to answer.

"Tell them I'll join in five minutes," he said. "I need to get up to my room where the prospectus and my notes are." He said nothing more before swiping off and lifting his chin to the bartender. "I need to run. Can I sign the tab to my room?"

The bartender nodded. "Sure thing."

"Room two twelve." Arrogant guy reached into his pocket and took out a wad of cash. Tossing a few bills on

3

the bar, he motioned to me. "Put her bill for the night on my room, too, please."

"You got it."

I lifted my wine. "Shame you have to go. Maybe you aren't such a jerk after all."

His lip twitched. "I called the meeting, so I can't miss it. But it's definitely my loss."

I grinned. "Sure is..."

Though as I watched him stand and realized he was well over six-feet tall and his dress shirt hugged him *very* nicely, I wondered if it was my loss after all. Nonetheless, he disappeared with only a nod.

Forty-five minutes later, I told the bartender to save my seat—even though I was the only person in the bar—and went to the ladies' room. Yawning as I washed my hands, I figured it was time to call it a night. But when I returned, a man sat in the chair next to mine. And not just any man—the arrogant, incredibly handsome guy from earlier.

I took my seat, which now had a fresh glass of wine in front of it. "How was your meeting?" I asked.

"Do you really care?"

"No, but I was being polite. Something you should try once in a while." I turned to face him and tried to ignore that he was even better looking this close up. I'd never used the word *smoldering* to describe eyes before, but that's what his were. *Smoldering bedroom eyes.* He smelled damn good, too. "You know, just because you're hot doesn't mean you can be rude. Maybe that works for you in the supermarket, but it won't work with me."

He raised a brow. "You think I'm hot?"

I rolled my eyes. "You should've focused on the part about being rude. Figures all you heard was good-looking."

4

"Is that why you picked Tinder guy? He was polite?"

"He was nice, yes. He was also funny and made me laugh."

He lifted his drink. "Nice and funny got you a married guy who stuck you with the tab. Maybe you should try hot and rude?"

I chuckled. He had a point. "Do you have a name? Or do you prefer to be referred to as Mr. Arrogant? Because that's what I've been saying in my head."

Mr. Arrogant extended his hand. "Beck."

When I put mine into his, he lifted it to his lips and kissed the top. It caused a tingle all over me. Though I wasn't about to tell him that.

"Is this how they do it in the supermarket? Kiss a stranger's hand and invite her back to your place?"

"My place is three-thousand miles away."

"Oh. So you aren't looking to replace the guy I kicked to the curb earlier?"

He grinned. "If you're actively seeking a replacement, I mean, *I am* right here. But I'd like your name first, at least."

I laughed. "Nora."

He nodded. "Nice to meet you, Nora."

"What brings you out to the middle of nowhere, Beck?"

"I came to see family. You?"

"Girls' trip. We're just passing through for a few days."

Beck's phone buzzed on the bar. He leaned forward to check the screen and shook his head. "I'm gone a half a day and all hell breaks loose at the office."

"Not going to answer it?"

"It can wait till tomorrow."

"What is it you do that makes you such a popular man?"

"I'm in mergers and acquisitions."

"Sounds fancy, but I have no idea what that actually means."

"It varies. Some days my company helps companies around the same size consolidate and become one big powerhouse. Other days we help a powerful company take over a weaker one."

"Does the smaller company want to be taken over?"

"Not always. There are friendly transactions and hostile ones. The one all the calls have been about tonight is not a friendly takeover." He sipped his drink. "What do you do?"

"I make coffee table books."

"Like the thick ones with travel photos or fashion through the years or whatever that people leave out?"

"One and the same."

"So are you an author or a photographer?"

I shrugged. "Both, I guess. Though it still seems surreal that I can make a living doing something so much fun. I went to school for journalism with aspirations to be a writer. Photography was always my hobby, but now I write the copy and take the photos for my books."

"How did you get into that?"

"After college, I queried an agent with hopes of selling a thriller novel I was writing. Back then, I had a blog for fun. I used to take photos of people living on the streets of New York, and underneath each one, I wrote a little story about the person. I had a link to it in the signature block of my email. The agent I'd sent the chapters to didn't love the story, but she noticed the link to my blog and checked it out. She asked if I'd be interested in pitching a coffee-table-type book instead. I said sure, and over the next eight years I created twenty-five coffee table books about the people who live on the streets in different cities. Last year I started a new collection about graffiti and graffiti artists in different cities."

"That sounds a hell of a lot more fun than mergers and acquisitions."

I smiled. "I'm sure it is. I consider myself very lucky, career-wise. I make a good living doing something I love and get to travel all over the place. Plus, I've met some amazing people along the way, and I donate a percentage of all book sales to support housing for those who need it."

Beck's eyes roamed my face. "What are you trying to forget, Nora?"

It took me a second to realize what he meant. That's what I'd told him I was trying to do with the Tinder guy. "Doesn't everyone want to forget life once in a while?"

"Maybe." He rubbed his bottom lip. "But usually there's something in particular, like a difficult relationship, stress on the job, financial struggles, or family troubles."

I traced my finger through the condensation on the bottom of my glass while Beck quietly waited for my response. I turned to face him. "Do you want to know why I like Tinder instead of meeting people in the supermarket or a bar?"

"Why?"

"Because it's easy to find men who are happy to make me forget, yet don't care enough to ask *why* all I want from them is sex."

Beck tipped his glass to me before raising it to his lips. "Got it."

As he drank, I noticed the chunky watch on his wrist—Audemars Piguet, not Rolex. I'd always felt the type of watch a man wears says a lot about him. Most men use a Rolex as a status symbol, showing off that they can afford to spend the price of a car to decorate their wrist. And they know others know it too, since it's one of the world's most popular luxury brands. On the other hand, Audemars Piguet is not particularly well known to a non-watch person, and it's generally more expensive. Most men wear a Rolex for other people, but an Audemars Piguet is worn for yourself. Mr. Attitude moved up a notch in my book.

The second thing I often used to gauge a man was the drink he ordered. Beck's glass had been full when I came back from the ladies' room, so I wasn't sure what the amber liquid was. I presumed some sort of whiskey.

"Is that scotch?" I motioned to the tumbler in front of him.

He held it out to me. "Whiskey. Would you like to taste it?"

"No, but I'm curious what kind it is."

He tilted his head. "Why?"

"I don't know. I've just always found a certain type of man orders a certain type of drink." My eyes pointed to his wrist. "Watches can tell a lot about a person, too."

"So my watch and telling you what brand of whiskey I'm drinking is going to help you figure out who I am?"

I shrugged. "Maybe."

He finished what was left in his glass and signaled the bartender, who walked right over.

"What brand did you say this was?" he asked.

"It's called Hillcrest Reserve. Made about ten miles away from here by a third-generation distiller."

Beck pushed his glass forward on the bar. "Thank you. I'll take another when you get a chance."

Once the bartender walked away, Beck looked to me. "Apparently it's called Hillcrest Reserve."

My brows furrowed. "Did you not know that when you ordered it?"

He shook his head. "Nope. I asked if they had any locally made, small-batch whiskey. I like to try local foods and whiskey when I travel. I live in Manhattan. I can walk into any bar and get two-hundred-dollar-a-nip Macallan. But I can't get Hillcrest Reserve."

I smiled. "I like that."

"But you look surprised. I take it my selection doesn't match the type of man you'd assumed I was."

"Not really."

"What did you think I was drinking?"

My smile broadened. "The two-hundred-dollar-a-nip Macallan you can get anywhere."

Beck chuckled. "And what type of man orders that?"

I took a drink of my wine and set it down. "The kind who lives in Manhattan, works in mergers and acquisitions, and wears a fancy suit and Rolex. Basically every Wall Street douchebag standing outside Cipriani for happy hour on a Friday afternoon."

Beck threw his head back in laughter. I'd just insulted the guy, and he was amused. "I guess I made a pretty shitty first impression."

I deadpanned. "You told me I should look someplace more *respectable* for my dates."

"I thought you deserved better."

"I think you're full of shit. You're only being nice now because you know I was looking for a night of no strings attached, and you think you have a shot at being my replacement."

"Am I out of the running?"

I took a moment to check him out again. *Damn, he's pretty*. "You're only hanging on by a thread because you're gorgeous."

A slow, sexy smile spread across his face. "I like your honesty."

"I like your jawline."

His eyes gleamed. "You'll like my big dick even better."

I bit my bottom lip. The conversation had just taken a turn toward most of my Tinder messages—definitely a place I was more comfortable than talking about why I wanted to forget my life for a while. "How do I know you're not a serial killer?"

"How did you know the Tinder loser wasn't?"

Good point. I sipped my wine. "How old are you?"

"Old enough that I know what to do with you, and young enough that I don't have to take a pill to do it."

I smirked. "Is that so? You know what to do with me?"

He smiled self-assuredly. "I do, yes."

The air crackled between us. For some reason, I knew this guy could deliver on his promise. Maybe it was his quiet confidence, or maybe it was that a man who looked the way he did got lots of practice. The latter would've been a turnoff if I was looking for more than one night, but it didn't much matter if it served my purposes for a one-time deal.

I looked into his too-blue eyes. "Tell me then."

"Tell you what?"

"What you would do with me."

The wicked grin that slid across his face almost made me want to take back what I'd asked. *Almost.*

Beck lifted his glass and gulped his drink before leaning over to my ear. "I'd start by burying my face in your pussy until you came all over my tongue. Then I'd fuck you like I hate you."

Oh God. My toes actually curled. *Sold!*

He pulled back to look at me and raised a brow.

I teetered on the edge, debating whether I was crazy for considering taking this man up to my room. While I deliberated, I happened to look down.

Holy shit. His slacks had pulled tight around the top of one thigh, and there was a distinct bulge running down his leg. A *very long*, *very thick* bulge.

I was a woman who believed in signs, and *that* one I couldn't miss. So I knocked back the remainder of my wine and slipped one of my two hotel keycards from my purse, sliding it over in front of the man next to me.

"Room two nineteen. Give me a ten-minute head start so I can freshen up."

CHAPTER 2
Beck

"Where are you? I just went by your office and it's dark. The Franklin meeting starts in ten minutes."

I pressed the button to put my cell on speakerphone and set it on the vanity in the bathroom so I could finish shaving. "I'm in Idaho."

"Idaho?" Jake said. "What the hell are you doing there?"

"Apparently, Sun Valley is a popular place for jumping off cliffs. I came to talk some sense into our grandmother since she blocked me and I can't call her."

"Oh Jesus Christ. Leave the woman alone. She's living her life, doing what she wants to do."

"Has she ever mentioned to you that she wanted to go *wingsuit diving*?"

"No, but I probably didn't mention to her that I wanted to go muff diving on that nurse she had when she was in the hospital last year. We don't announce everything at family get-togethers."

My brother didn't worry about anything. Maybe because he was only twenty-three and still thought he was invincible. Ten years and one marriage ago, I probably had a lot fewer worries, too. "I think the friend she's traveling with may be a little unstable and is pushing her into doing some of these crazy things."

"What makes you say that?"

"Well for one, yesterday this woman texted that I should bend over and pull on my ankles really hard so maybe I could see my own head up my ass."

"Gram's friend texts you?"

"Gram gave me her number for emergencies, right before she blocked me."

"Let me guess, you've been using it to harass this nice old lady since you can't reach Gram?"

"Nice old lady?" I pulled the skin on my neck taut and shaved a clean line. When I traced the curve of my chin, I nicked it. *Shit. Damn cheap hotel razor.* I got a piece of toilet paper to stop the bleeding. "That nice old lady also told me I was a gray sprinkle on a rainbow cupcake."

Jake chuckled. "Man, she has you pegged and she's never even met you. You need to relax a little. Gram is just trying to have fun. If I were in her place, I'd rather have three months of living than a year of waiting to die."

I frowned. I wasn't getting into this debate again. Three weeks ago, our grandmother had been told that her pancreatic cancer was back. It was the third time in ten years, and it now had metastasized to her lungs and esophagus. The doctors said another round of chemo and radiation would likely only extend her life expectancy from three months to nine. Though they'd also said there was a one percent chance that treatment could send the cancer back into remission and she could be around a lot longer.

Gram had chosen not to have treatment this time, which we'd all supported, even though I'd selfishly wanted her to take the chance to be around in ten years.

But then she'd decided to take a crazy trip with a woman none of us had even met, and lately it felt like she was on a suicide mission.

"I gotta go. I don't know what time they're leaving, and I need to get a cup of coffee before I go argue with Gram."

"What do you want me to do about the meeting?"

"Handle it."

"You usually hate the way I handle things."

"Surprise me. Goodbye." I swiped my phone off and finished shaving. A little while later, I went down to the hotel lobby in search of caffeine. After pouring a cup of coffee, I turned to look for the cream and sugar, and my eyes meet a gorgeous pair of green ones. They were currently shooting daggers at me.

Shit.

Nora. The beautiful blonde from last night.

She was sitting at a table not more than five feet away.

"I see you found your way to the coffee," she said. "Yet you somehow got lost last night on your way to the second floor?"

I shoved my hands into my pockets, feeling like an idiot. "About that…"

A familiar woman's voice from behind me interrupted our conversation. "Good morning, my dear."

I turned to find my grandmother. I'd assumed she was speaking to me, but her forehead wrinkled when she saw me.

"Beckham? What are you doing here?"

"I came to talk some sense into you."

"Wait..." Nora's mouth dropped open. "Beck as in Beckham, Louise's grumpy grandson?"

I turned to her. "You know my grandmother?"

"Ummm... We've been traveling together for the last two weeks."

"You're Eleanor Sutton? I thought you said your name was—" *Shit. You've got to be kidding me.* I shook my head. "Nora...short for Eleanor?"

I'd assumed Eleanor was seventy years old, not a blond bombshell in her mid-twenties.

Gram motioned between the two of us. "You know each other?"

I wasn't about to explain to my grandmother that I'd told her friend I wanted to fuck her like I hated her, then didn't show up to close the deal. So I wasn't sure how to respond. Luckily, Nora was better on her feet than I was.

She put on a smile even I knew was forced. "We just met at the coffee bar."

My grandmother stepped forward and kissed my cheek. "Hello, sweetheart. It's always lovely to see you. But if you've come to give me a lecture, I'm afraid you've wasted a trip, and you can turn your cute little derrière around and not let the door hit it on the way out."

I couldn't help but smile. "I see your sparkling personality is intact. How are you feeling, Gram?"

"If the dumb doctors hadn't gone and told me the devil was back, I wouldn't even know it. Maybe a little more tired than usual, but then again, we're on the go a lot."

"That makes me happy to hear. Can I get you some coffee?"

"I think we need to hit the road."

"Actually..." Nora frowned. "I texted you earlier, Louise. I guess you haven't read it yet. They canceled the jump for this morning due to high winds. The company said they'd give me an update by lunchtime to let us know if there'll be an afternoon jump, but if there is, it wouldn't be until four."

"Well then..." Gram turned to me. "I'm breathing, and I've got a full face of makeup on. So you can take us out to breakfast, preferably someplace that has Kahlua for my coffee."

I smiled. "You got it."

"I think I'll stay behind," Nora said. "I have some work to catch up on."

"You've gotta eat. Might as well let my grandson foot the bill. Besides, maybe he can show you he's not as much of a jackass as he seems over text."

It looked like Nora was going to try to bow out again, but my grandmother was a hard woman to say no to.

"Come on." Gram motioned toward the lobby. "We were supposed to be on our jump, so there's nothing you have to do that can't wait an hour."

Nora forced a smile. "Sure. Let's go."

~

"I'll take an eggs benedict and a coffee with a shot of Kahlua," Gram said to the waiter.

He smiled. "I'm afraid we don't have Kahlua. We don't have any liquor, actually."

"That's fine." My grandmother patted her purse. "Got some in here. You can pretend you don't see me spiking our drinks. I wouldn't take the sale away from you, but I don't expect you to take the happiness from me, either."

The waiter chuckled. "I won't see anything."

Nora was next to place her order. While she spoke, I zoned in on her lips moving—the lips I'd imagined wrapped around my cock while I took care of myself in the shower this morning. It hadn't been easy to behave last night, especially after I realized my room was right down the hall from hers. But when I'd paid the bar tab and saw how many glasses of wine Nora had consumed, I couldn't do it. I might be a man some women regretted, but it was never going to be because they hadn't had the capacity to say no.

"Sir?" I looked up to find the waiter with an expectant face.

Nora's sly grin made me think she knew where my head had just been.

I cleared my throat. "I'll have the eggs benedict and a coffee with cream, please." After the waiter walked away, I laid my napkin across my lap. "So how do you two know each other? I don't remember you mentioning Nora before this trip."

Gram patted Nora's hand. "She lives in my building."

"At least the blog makes sense now." Gram's partner in crime had been blogging about their trip since the beginning, taking videos of my grandmother doing all kinds of crazy shit. The page was called *Live Like You're Dying*.

"What do you mean?" Nora asked.

"Well, I had assumed you were older. I don't know too many people my grandmother's age who blog." I looked at Gram. "No offense."

Nora folded her arms across her chest. "Well, if she's not offended, I am. There isn't a certain age for women to do things. Why is it only a young person can blog or go skydiving?"

Oh Jesus. Now *this* was the woman I'd been texting with.

"I didn't say older people couldn't do those things. I just said I don't know too many who do."

"Did you ever stop to think that's because narrow-minded younger people are ageist and discourage their family members from living their lives to the fullest? When they should be encouraging them? Believe it or not, your grandmother didn't have to go to the library for a technology class in order to figure out how to block you."

I looked at my grandmother.

She grinned. "Don't look at me for help. You've been digging your grave with Eleanor ever since I gave you her number to use in an emergency."

"Speaking of those wonderful texts we've exchanged," Nora said. "The next time you're rude to me or demand I pass along a message to your grandmother—particularly one that you know damn well will upset her—I'm going to block you, too."

Normally if someone spoke to me like that, I'd be salivating, waiting for my turn to rip them a new asshole. But for some crazy reason, all I could imagine was arguing with this woman in private—then fucking the attitude right out of her.

I smirked. "Noted. Thanks for the warning."

My acquiescence seemed to diffuse her anger, and for a half a second I considered bringing up how many deaths had occurred while *wing diving* the last few years, just to get into it with her again. But then Gram started talking about a snorkeling trip they were planning, and the way her eyes lit up made the inside of my chest warm. Snorkeling seemed harmless enough...

"And then once we get the hang of it," she said, "they start chumming."

"Chumming?"

Gram nodded. "For the sharks."

And there goes the harmless snorkeling trip. "Seriously, Gram? Swimming with sharks? Why can't you just snorkel and look at the colorful fish?"

"Why would I do that when I can watch a giant monster with five rows of teeth *eat* all the colorful fish?"

"I completely understand wanting to travel and do things, but why do they all have to be dangerous? You never had a desire to do any of these things before you found out..."

Gram frowned. "Found out that *I'm dying*. It's okay to say it, Beckham. I'm dying. Chances are, in a few months I won't be around anymore. So why not do things that give me an adrenaline rush and make me fear my own mortality? Lord knows sitting around at home, I'm not afraid of anything. I mean, what's the worst that can happen? I cross against the light and get hit by a cab? I want to feel alive. And hell, if I go a little earlier than expected because the wings on my wingsuit don't flap enough, or a shark thinks I'd make a good dessert, at least I'll have one hell of an obituary."

I was smart enough to know when to shut my mouth. I'd talk to my grandmother when she was alone and not feeling so ornery. Right now I changed the subject and tried to enjoy listening to her explain all the things they'd done so far. That made for a peaceful remainder of our meal.

After we got back to the hotel, Gram said she was going to lie down for a while. She claimed she'd been too excited about the impending wingsuit dive to sleep well last night. So I walked her to her room and asked if we could have lunch together, just the two of us.

She kissed my cheek at her door. "I'm happy to spend as much time with you as possible. But you're not going to change my mind, Beck."

"I'll come by and get you around noon?"

On my way back to my room, I decided to knock on Nora's door. I appreciated her keeping what had gone down between us to herself. And I owed her an apology. I also recognized that I'd have a better shot of getting through to Gram if Nora were on my team. As odd a couple as they made, they seemed pretty tight.

Nora's face fell when she answered. "I hope you don't think you're getting a rain check from last night. You lost your opportunity when you stood me up."

"About that..."

She started to shut the door. "I don't need an explanation. It's your loss."

I stuck my foot in the doorway. "Hang on a second. You might not need one, but I'd like to give you one anyway."

She rolled her eyes. "Say what you need to say and go."

"You had six glasses of wine. I saw it when I paid the bill."

Nora shrugged. "Was that too many for you to pay for? I'm not reimbursing you."

"I'm not complaining about the cost. But the six glasses are why I didn't come up, as much as I wanted to. And trust me, I *really, really* wanted to. I might've even stood outside your door for ten minutes trying to convince myself I wouldn't be a piece of shit for knocking since you'd invited me. But in the end, I couldn't take advantage of a woman who'd had too much to drink."

"Only two of those wines were mine. Louise and I met two ladies for drinks before I met the Tinder Loser. I told her I'd pick up the tab. I was perfectly sober, especially considering I'd been sitting there a couple of hours." She tilted her head. "And by the way, *I was looking to be taken advantage of.*"

I dropped my head. "*Fuck.*"

20

"Worked out just as well, anyway. Obviously I didn't know you were Louise's grandson—the one who's been barking at me like I work for him."

I raked a hand through my hair. "She's my grandmother. I'm worried about her."

Nora put her hands on her hips. "Because she's doing dangerous things for the first time in her life, right?"

"That's right."

"Did you know your grandmother is a certified scuba diver? She was one of the first women to take the certification course in nineteen sixty-seven. Her favorite kind of dive was exploring deep-sea wreckage."

"What are you talking about?"

"Did you know that when she was twenty-three she navigated Lava Falls, one of the most difficult whitewater runs in the world?"

"Really?"

She nodded. "Your grandmother is not the shrinking violet you think she is. She's a badass. Maybe if you stopped looking at her as someone old and frail who needs to be taken care of, you could see that."

"Why didn't she ever say anything?"

Nora shook her head. "Maybe it's because you never *asked*. Do you know how she and your grandfather met? Or why we're going to a ranch in Utah to visit a man she hasn't seen in sixty years?"

She'd made her point. Now she was just pissing me off. "Do you know who sat by her side every single day after her first pancreas surgery? Or after the cancer came back and she was sick for months during her treatment?"

"I'm not questioning whether you care about your grandmother. I'm saying you need to support her in her choices now, whatever they are."

I was quiet for a moment. "Why are you doing this?"

"Because you knocked on my door."

I shook my head. "No. Why are you traveling with a woman three times your age? What's in it for you?"

Nora's nostrils flared. "What's *in it* for me? Go screw yourself."

"People don't usually do things without there being something in it for them."

"What are you implying?"

"I'm not implying anything. I'm simply asking why you're taking this trip."

Her answer was to growl at me. *Literally growl.* Right before she slammed the door in my face.

I blinked a few times and then a smile crept up on my face, surprising even me. I probably needed my head examined, but Nora Sutton was *sexy as shit* when she was angry.

CHAPTER 3
Beck

"I really hope you didn't come down here expecting a repeat of last night," Nora said.

I took the seat at the bar next to her and shook my head. "Time change is screwing with me."

She nodded and turned her attention to her wine.

"How was your *wing dive* this afternoon?" I asked.

Nora's brows knitted. "Louise told you we went?"

I shook my head. "I happened to be looking out the window around three this afternoon and saw you two sneaking out to the car. Two minutes later, Gram called to say she hadn't napped yet, but was going to probably sleep for a few hours. I put two and two together. Plus, I saw the photo you posted on your blog. By the way, that's the first picture of yourself you've posted. Why is that?"

"I didn't realize it was. But I suppose because the blog is about Louise's journey."

"Well, how was your afternoon?"

Nora grinned. "It was incredible. Though you wouldn't have liked it. You seem to be fun adverse."

The bartender came over, so I ordered the same whiskey I had last night.

"You don't like me very much, do you?" I asked.

"Not really. I think you're arrogant."

I waited until my drink arrived and I'd gulped a mouthful. It burned as it went down, but felt good. "I'm not particularly fond of you either. I think you're righteous and annoying."

Nora smiled as she brought her wine to her lips. "You seem fond of *parts* of me. I caught your eyes wandering a few times this morning at breakfast."

"I also stared at the picture you posted on your blog. But you were wearing a skin-tight, rubber unitard. The fucking birds were staring. Doesn't mean I like you."

She shook her head and laughed. "Well, seems like we're going to have to find a way to tolerate each other, since we both care for your grandmother. Maybe we should shake hands and make peace."

"Or..." I waited until she looked at me. "We can hate-fuck each other and get it out of our systems."

"Hate-fucking seems to be a theme with you. Is that your thing?"

"Never has been before. But you piss me off, and it makes me want to rip your clothes off."

Nora looked down at my crotch and sighed. "Such a shame you're Louise's grandson. Because I'm rather fond of part of you, too."

I smirked. "Maybe you should see that part up close. Right in your face works for me."

She laughed and finished her wine before turning to me and extending a hand.

"Friends?"

I took her hand, but rather than shake, I lifted it to my lips and nipped her finger.

"Oww!"

I kissed the area and grinned. "If you insist. Though I like my idea better."

"I bet you do..."

Not wanting to be a complete pig, I refocused on a safer topic. "So...I've never seen you around. How long have you lived at Vestry?"

"Vestry?"

"Vestry Towers. My grandmother said you lived in her building."

"Oh, yeah." She shook her head. "Right. Not too long. About a year, maybe. I'm moving back to California soon. That's where I'm from. I moved to New York for college and never went back."

We were quiet for a minute. "Can I ask you something without you getting pissed?"

She smiled. "Probably not. But go ahead anyway."

"I asked you earlier why you were taking this trip—"

"Actually," she interrupted. "You asked me what I was *getting out of it*, like I was playing some sort of an angle."

"Right." I nodded. "Perhaps my delivery wasn't so pleasant. I'm sure my staff would attest that I have a habit of speaking bluntly, which can occasionally be off-putting."

"I'm guessing it's more than occasionally."

"How about if I ask my question this way: When you found out my grandmother was planning this trip, what made you decide to join her?"

Nora stared into her wine glass. "My mother passed away at a young age, only a few years older than I am now. Thinking about that has made me consider things differently. Instead of asking why should I go, I now ask myself why *shouldn't* I go? Life is short."

"I'm sorry for your loss."

"Thank you."

"Do you mind if I ask how she died?"

Her face went tight, full of pain, and I immediately regretted the question.

"I'm sorry." I held up a hand. "I shouldn't have asked that."

"It's fine. It's called rhabdomyosarcoma, a malignant cardiac tumor. It's rare."

"It couldn't be treated?"

"Some can be removed, some can't. She wasn't one of the lucky ones."

I nodded. "Thank you for sharing that."

She finished off her wine. "Is it my turn now? I don't have a question, but what I have to say will probably piss you off."

I smiled. "Shoot."

"Stop bitching at your grandmother about her choices. They're hers to make, and she's enjoying herself."

"I saw that. Her smile was huge when you two snuck back into the hotel after the jump."

"It's scary to know you're going to lose someone. I get that. But I promise, your grandmother doesn't have a death wish. She just wants to feel alive, and getting close to death *on her own terms* gives her that."

"I'll work on it."

"She talks about you all the time, you know?"

"*Uh-oh.*"

Nora smiled. "Most of it is good. Though she did want to smack you when you told her you *forbid* her from doing the wingsuit jump. Haven't you figured out that when you tell a certain type of woman they can't do something, it only makes them want to do it more?"

I rubbed my lip. "A certain type of woman, huh? I have a feeling my grandmother isn't the only one who falls into that category on this trip."

"Maybe not." She smiled.

I leaned to her. "I forbid you from having sex with me."

Nora's head bent back in laughter. It was a pretty damn spectacular sight.

"Your grandmother says you're a whip," she said, shaking her head. "I can see why."

"What else does my grandmother say about me?"

"Lots of things. She says you're smart, first in your class at Princeton. Successful—you started your own company one year out of college and have invested wisely in Manhattan real estate. You work too much, and apparently that comes from your grandfather. You're divorced and have an adorable little girl who I think is six?"

I nodded. "Go on..."

"You're close to your brother—who is ten years younger and pretty much the opposite of you and drives you nuts, yet you hired him to work for you anyway because you're extremely loyal. Oh, and you once went with your grandmother to pick up your little brother from daycare. You insisted you should hold the infant carrier, instead of her. And neither one of you noticed until you got home that you'd grabbed the wrong baby. When you went back, the police were there because the mother thought someone had stolen her child."

I hung my head. "Jesus Christ, did she have to tell you that? She was selling me so well with the beginning stuff."

She grinned. "Another time, when you two were on the subway, a mouse ran through the car. You asked how it got in, and your grandmother told you the skeleton of a mouse allows them to get through small cracks. You slept on your back for a month before she found out you were afraid to turn over for fear one would get into your butt."

"Seriously? Why would she tell you that?"

Nora shrugged. "We were standing on the subway platform one night waiting for a train, and a mouse ran across the tracks. Louise went hysterical laughing, and then she explained why. She didn't mention how old you were, so I'm hoping it wasn't too recently."

"Wiseass." I finished my drink and raised a hand for the bartender. "I'm at an unfair disadvantage here. I don't have any stories about you."

"And we'll be keeping it that way." She laughed.

The bartender came over. He pointed to my drink. "The same?"

"Please." I looked to Nora. "Another wine?"

She shook her head. "No, thank you."

"Have another. I'm leaving in the morning, and I'm not even pissing you off at the moment."

"I actually have some work to do, edits for my next book I need to approve. They're due today."

I was disappointed. Even with the chance of going back to her room all but gone, Nora was spirited. I enjoyed listening to what came out of those full lips, even if I still wanted to slip something between them.

She pulled out her wallet.

I stopped her. "On me, please. It's the least I can do for everything you're doing with my grandmother."

She smiled sadly. "You still don't understand. I'm getting as much as I'm giving from Louise. It's not a favor or a burden. We only do things we both want to do." Slipping her wallet back into her purse, she stood. "But thank you for the drink anyway. It was nice to meet you, Beck. At least I think it was?"

I chuckled. "I still have your room key, you know. I could let you finish your work and then finish what we almost started last night?"

Nora leaned down and kissed my cheek. "Probably not a good idea now that I know you're Louise's grandson. I was going to use you."

"I'm good with being used..."

She laughed. "Goodnight, Beck. Maybe I'll see you around someday."

CHAPTER 4

Beck

"Just when I was getting comfy giving the orders around here..." My brother leaned against the doorframe of my office. "...the ogre is back."

"You gave the orders around here? Do I need to file for bankruptcy?"

Jake pushed off and welcomed himself into my office. He leaned on the back of one of my guest chairs, tilting it so the front legs came off the ground. His eyes zoned in on the multiple Band-Aids on my hands. "What the hell happened to you?"

"*Bitsy* happened," I grumbled.

Jake's brows shot up. "Gram's dog? She bit you?"

"That dog hates me. The little shit waits until I fall asleep, and then climbs up on the bed to wake me by biting my fingers. Every damn night."

My brother laughed.

"It's not funny. You know, you can take her, too. I had to have the neighbor's kid watch her while I was away."

"Gram asked you. Besides, sometimes I don't make it home at night."

I shook my head. "Did you want something? I have a lot to catch up on."

"How's Gram?"

"Stubborn. Opinionated. Obstinate."

Jake grinned. "So she's still acting normal? No signs the cancer is affecting her yet?"

I took off my suit jacket and hung it on the back of my chair before pulling it out to sit. "I think she might be the first person cancer is too scared of to attack a third time."

"Did you meet the woman she's traveling with? The one who's been such a bitch to you?"

"Oh, I met her alright."

"That bad? Did you have another fight?"

"Something like that..."

I didn't offer that while Gram's friend might be a pain in my ass, she'd also been the object of my dreams the last few nights. If my brother knew, I wouldn't put it past him to hop on a plane and go visit our grandmother. Jake could charm the pants off any woman he met with his boyish ways and our father's bone structure and dimpled smile. It helped that he wears five-thousand-dollar suits and a flashy watch. On that note, my eyes dropped to my brother's wrist. *A Rolex.* On second thought, maybe he wouldn't have such an easy time with Nora...

"So what did I miss around here?" I asked, rolling up my shirtsleeves.

My brother sat down. "I didn't want to tell you this while you were traveling, but our auditors caught someone stealing."

My brows drew tight. "Who?"

"Ginny Atelier, in accounts payable. While they were reviewing the books, they noticed a few of the petty-cash checks didn't have receipts to back them up. When they questioned her, she started to cry and admitted she took the money."

Fuck. Of all the people I employed, it had to be her? "Did she give a reason?"

My brother nodded. "She claims she has a sick mother and needed the extra cash for medicine her insurance doesn't cover. I already spoke to HR. They're just waiting for your nod to terminate her."

I blew out a deep breath and shook my head. "Maybe we shouldn't fire her."

My brother's eyes widened. "Are you kidding me? It's a tug-at-your-heartstrings story, but not firing her is the last thing I expected you to say."

"Why? I have a heart..."

My brother squinted at me. "No, you don't. You've fired people for looking at you wrong. So something is up. What's the deal?"

I raked a hand through my hair and sighed. "Fucking Christmas party and those stupid peppermint martinis. There's a reason I stick to sipping whiskey and keep away from vodka."

Jake laughed. "Oh my God, you hooked up with an employee? You're such a dick. How many lectures have you given me about dipping my pen in the company ink?"

"You're an employee."

"So? Does only the boss get to pilfer the pink-collar employees?"

"You're the dick."

"Maybe." My brother leaned back, grinning from ear to ear. "But at least I haven't fucked any of the staff."

I sighed. "Let me talk to legal before we make a decision on how to handle it."

"You got it, big brother."

I opened my laptop, hoping my brother would take the hint that the conversation was over. Of course, he didn't.

I frowned. "What? Is there anything else we need to discuss? If not, I have a lot of work to do."

"Nope. Just basking in the warmth of your flames. Your fuckups are so rare."

I pointed to the door. "Get out. Or you'll be taking Ginny's place in the unemployment line."

∽

I didn't usually check texts during a meeting. But this one was boring as shit, and it was Nora's name that popped up. So I swiped to open. A picture of my grandmother riding a dolphin filled my screen. She looked like Rose from *Titanic*, holding her arms out as the animal propelled her forward. I smiled and typed back.

Beck: Now that's more my grandmother's speed.

A response came as quick as her wit.

Nora: Be nice, or I won't send you any more pictures. Your grandmother is enjoying life. Maybe you should try it sometime. What are you doing right now? Sitting in some stuffy, boring meeting?

I chuckled to myself.

The analyst making her presentation stopped speaking, and all heads swung in my direction. Must have been louder than I thought. I shook my head and pointed to the numbers projected on the screen. "Pay attention."

Nora had said she and my grandmother only did things they both wanted to do. So she must've swam with the dolphins, too.

Beck: I assume you partook in today's swim as well?

I continued to ignore the meeting in favor of watching dots jump around.

Nora: First off...partook? Are you ninety? Maybe if you spoke like a young person, you might act like one and have some fun. But yes, I did swim with the dolphins today, and it was amazing.

Beck: Can I see a picture?

Nora: You just want to see me in a bathing suit...

I smiled down at my phone.

Beck: Just wanted to see what I missed by being a gentleman.

Nora: A lot. Trust me.

I had no doubt she was telling the truth.

Beck: What's on tap next?

Nora: We're here for another few days and then next week we're going to the Bahamas for some gambling and sun. After that, Montana for a wilderness trip.

Beck: Wilderness trip?

Nora: Custer-Gallatin National Forest. We're doing two nights at a ranch with some day riding and an overnight camping trip on horseback through the mountains.

That gave me pause.

Beck: My grandmother was born and raised in Manhattan. I don't think she's an experienced cowgirl.

Nora: Hence the two nights at the ranch to practice our riding before we set off.

Beck: Whose idea was this jaunt?

Nora: Mine.

Beck: Are you an experienced rider?

Nora: Yes, but not horses...

She ended that with a little winky face.

Nora: Gotta run! Louise just walked in. We're driving an hour and a half for a dinner show.

At least that sounded nice for Gram.

Beck: Enjoy, and tell my grandmother the same, please.

Nora: We will! I've got enough one dollar bills to make it more than enjoyable. ☺

I rolled my eyes. And here I'd been thinking they were going to see an off-Broadway version of *Jersey Boys* or something.

A few minutes later, my boring meeting ended, and I packed up the presentations I'd been given—as if there was a chance in hell I was going to read them when they couldn't even keep my attention during the actual meeting. As I stood, my phone chimed. It was Nora again, so I swiped to read before leaving the conference room.

Nora: Here's your consolation prize. Try to find some fun tonight, Mr. Stuffy.

Beneath it was a photo of Nora in a yellow bikini, riding the dolphin.

Damn. The woman had curves. Full, perky tits that looked about two seconds away from slipping out, nipples pointing right at the camera, a tiny waist, and the type of hips and thighs I liked on a woman—curves that felt good in the dark.

I thought about writing back, but there was nothing clean I could say. Instead, I saved the picture to my camera roll and thought to myself, *Oh, I'll be doing something fun tonight—with your picture.*

⌒

"We might have a slight problem."

Yates Bradley. It wasn't the first time he'd sat down on the other side of my desk and said those words. When

35

I'd taken him on as a client eighteen months ago, with plans to sell his global baby-food conglomerate, I'd had no idea what I was getting myself into. The guy was a walking, talking PR nightmare, and two deals had already fallen through because of shit uncovered during due diligence. We were now ten days from closing on the sale with a third buyer, and I hadn't thought there were any more skeletons in the closet. I should've known better.

I leaned back in my chair and tented my fingers. "What's going on now?"

"My wife cheated on me."

"I'm sorry to hear that, but it shouldn't be relevant to your sale, if that's what you're worried about."

"Things could...come out."

Oh fuck. What now? "What kind of things?"

"She was screwing her yoga instructor."

It felt like we were playing twenty questions, and I had to guess what was going to blow up in my face. "Mrs. Bradley isn't an employee or shareholder of your company, so while that's unfortunate, I'm not seeing how it's a problem for your sale."

"Well..." he said. "She cheated first."

And here we go... "First? So does that mean you cheated as well?"

"Only because she deserved it."

I knew from our background investigation before taking on a client that the current Mrs. Bradley wasn't his first wife. He'd had two others before her, and both marriages had ended in payoffs, even though he'd had prenups.

"Are you concerned about finances? You had a prenup this time, correct?"

"Yes, I never get married without a prenup. It's like going on a rowboat in the middle of a storm without a life jacket."

"Well, then you should be fine."

"Unless she leaks the pictures..."

Fuck my life. "What pictures?"

"The ones of me and Miss Pain."

I shut my eyes. "Please tell me that's spelled P-A-Y-N-E and it's not what I think it is."

He had the nerve to look indignant. "What I chose to do in my personal life is not relevant. Alternative lifestyles are becoming more and more accepted these days. Maybe it won't be a problem."

"Mr. Bradley, you own a *baby food* company. Your buyers are new moms, most of whom are family-oriented at the time of purchase. A cheating scandal would have some impact on your brand, but photos of you involved in BDSM or some other situation could jeopardize your sale." I leaned forward. "What exactly are we talking about here?"

Mr. Bradley got his phone out and punched in a code. He held it out to me.

I took it, though I had a feeling I didn't want to see.

He pointed. "There's a folder called Miss Pain in there."

Great. I scrolled until I found it. "There are more than a thousand pictures in here. Does your wife have all of these?"

"I didn't realize they were backing up to the cloud."

Taking a deep breath, I opened the folder. The first few weren't terrible. The woman, whom I assumed was Miss Pain, wore a leather outfit. Yates wasn't even in the pictures...until he was.

I shook my head and mumbled a string of curses. If I had thought up the worst, most compromising thing related to BDSM for a man who was the face of a baby-food company, I couldn't have imagined this.

I cleared my throat. "You're on your knees wearing a bonnet and a diaper while a woman clad in leather pierces your skin with her stiletto, and you walk into my office and say we *might* have a slight problem? That's like saying a sinking ship has a slight hole, Mr. Bradley."

His shoulders slumped. "What do I do?"

I slid the phone across the desk. "You go home to your wife and offer her whatever amount of money it will take to make this go away."

"She's already moved out and won't speak to me. Her lawyer wants to meet."

"Well, then set up a meeting."

"I did. He'll be here in an hour."

"Here? Why is he coming here?"

"Because I didn't know who else to turn to, and you've fixed all the other things that popped up."

"I'm in the business of buying and selling companies, Mr. Bradley. Not playing Whac-A-Mole."

"Please..."

I huffed. "Fine. But I'm speaking to him alone. Go home, and I'll call you after I'm done."

"Okay."

"And I'm taking another point on the sale for the shit you've put me through."

CHAPTER 5

Nora

"I've never gone skinny dipping, you know..."

The following week, Louise and I were sitting on a beach in the Bahamas, watching the sunset. I sucked the rest of my piña colada through the paper straw and turned to her with a grin.

"We should fix that..."

My friend's eyes widened. She looked around. There was only one other couple on the beach now. It seemed most people cleared out to shower and change for dinner before the best part of the day. "Let's see if they leave soon."

I shrugged. "Who cares if they see?"

"My body doesn't look like yours, dear. I'm going to have to use one hand to keep my breasts from dragging in the sand, and the other to cover my hooha."

"Why are you covering your hooha? We just got it buffed out. Show that thing off."

Louise and I had gone for massages and a wax yesterday afternoon when we'd arrived. After, she'd told me it was the first experience she regretted so far.

"I'm like Bob Ross, better with a happy little bush."

I laughed. "You want another drink?"

She held up her margarita glass. "If we're stripping, you'd better tell that cute bartender I need a tequila floater on top."

"You got it."

I went to the bar and came back with two drinks, as well as two tequila shots. It looked like the last couple who had been watching the sunset were packing up to go.

"We're going to have the beach to ourselves in a few minutes." I handed Louise a shot. "I thought we could use these, too."

She and I clinked shot glasses before knocking them back, then sat on the beach finishing our drinks until the sun ducked below the horizon.

"You ready?" I asked.

She stood. "You only live once."

As we stripped out of our clothes, my camera fell from my bag. I picked it up and wiped off the sand. "I guess this is going to be the first activity I'm not recording for my blog."

"Will you get shut down if you post something like this?"

"I don't think so. Are you saying you want me to record it?"

"Maybe you can put some of those black bars over my nooks and crannies? But let's film it. We're trying to inspire other people not to sit home and wait for their last days to come. We told them we'd share the good, the bad, and the ugly. This will be the latter."

I smiled. "Whatever you want."

Once we were both undressed and I'd set up my camera on the beach chair, I held out my hand to Louise. "You ready?"

"I was born ready, and I'm gonna die the same way. Let's go."

We squealed when we entered the water. It wasn't cold, but it hit the parts that were normally covered with a shock. Once we were neck deep, we floated on our backs.

"This feels incredible!" Louise exclaimed.

"I know. It's so freeing."

"I can't believe I'm going to say this, but this might be my favorite thing we've done so far."

I sighed. "Sometimes the simple things can be the most rewarding."

"We should keep that in mind as we plan the rest of our itinerary. It doesn't always have to be about things that scare the bejesus out of us."

"You'd probably make your grandson happy if we had some activities that weren't risking your life."

"Oh, that's true. Maybe we could not tell him about the more subdued activities. Otherwise he might think I listened to him about calming things down."

I laughed. "God forbid."

Louise and I floated for a long time, staring up at the stars. It made me feel free, yet at the same time, connected to the elements in a way I'd never been. When we started getting pruney, we decided it was time to get out. Except when we looked at the shore, we weren't alone anymore.

I squinted. "Are those people at our chairs, or did we float down the beach?"

Louise covered her breasts as we moved closer to get a better look. "I think that girl is wearing my hat!"

Three teenagers, two girls and a boy, were rummaging through our shit. I yelled and pushed forward in the water as fast as I could. "Hey! That's our stuff. Get away from there!"

41

One of the girls pointed to us, and the other two hood-lums scooped up everything we'd left on the chairs.

"Let's go!" one yelled.

"No way," the boy said. "I want to see their tits."

The girl tugged at his arm. "Let's go, you jerk! Or we're gonna get in trouble."

Before I could reach the shore, all three were running down the beach. About a hundred yards away, a jetty of rocks jutted out, which was what made the area where we were swimming so calm and private. The teens sprinted along the sand until they got to the rocks, then ran into the water, holding the clothes and bags they'd just stolen from us over their heads. I was a good fifty yards behind them, so once they turned the corner and got on the other side of the rocks, I lost sight of them.

Cursing, I dove back into the water and swam as fast as I could. I'd always been a solid swimmer, so I figured that would work better than trying to run in water that was chest deep. I maneuvered around the rocks, managing to hug close and not come up for air until I felt my knees hit the bottom on the other side. Then I climbed to my feet, ready to resume chasing the three asshole teenagers on foot.

Only, it wasn't the three asshole teenagers I saw when I stood.

It was *the bride*.

Oh. My. God.

Please tell me I'm imagining this?

But I wasn't. And I had no choice but to keep going now.

I stepped onto the sand.

The heads of fifty people wearing suits and dresses swung my way.

The steel drums playing screeched to a halt like a needle on a record.

Two large men wearing matching polos and dockers ran toward me. I was pretty sure they were security.

I had to make a split-second decision—turn and attempt to swim back around the rocks, or bolt and try to make a run for it on land. Out of the corner of my eye, I saw the three teenagers exiting the water on the other side of the wedding. I guess they'd been smart enough to pay attention to what was going on before getting out. Since security didn't have any clothes for me to wear and didn't look too happy, I made a run for the teenagers.

"Sorry!" I yelled to the wedding guests. The people seated in chairs continued watching me instead of the ceremony. When I reached the bride and groom, I waved, buck-ass naked. "Congratulations!"

A little farther down the beach, a dozen round tables had been set up for what looked like the couple's reception. Each had a basket of flowers in the middle, keeping the tablecloths blowing in the breeze anchored in place. I tugged one of the cloths out and wrapped it around my shoulders as I glanced back to check if security was still hot on my tail. Luckily, they'd stopped. One was bent over with his hands on his knees, while the other was barking into a walkie-talkie.

I was going to kick the asses of the little fuckers' who stole our stuff, if I ever caught them.

Up ahead, the teenagers made a run for some stairs, so I kept going, though I fell more and more behind with each stride. My lungs were also starting to burn. When I reached the concrete landing at the resort, I looked right and left. The kids were nowhere to be found, but three more security guys were now coming toward me from the left, so I ran the other direction.

The tablecloth didn't cover much as I sprinted, and the men chasing me were getting closer, so when I turned a corner and saw a door open, I ducked inside.

It looked like a supply closet, but I wasn't about to turn on the light and find out. My hand shook as I felt around the door in the dark, trying to find a lock. Locating it, I twisted it right and leaned over in an attempt to catch my breath. Twenty seconds later, voices were right on the other side of the door, and someone turned the doorknob back and forth.

I slapped my hand over my mouth to muffle the sound of my breathing.

"She must've gone into the hotel through that entrance," one of the men yelled. "There's a bathroom before you get into the main lobby. She's probably in there!"

I listened with my ear pressed against the door until I could no longer hear footsteps or voices. My heart rate slowed. I felt around on the wall for a light switch and flicked it on. As I'd suspected, I was in a supply closet. It had shelves filled with pool chemicals, cleaning supplies, and gardening equipment. Tucked away on the top shelf in one corner was a stack of black material. I yanked the pile down and was relieved to find what appeared to be uniform pants. Behind that was a pile of red fabric, which I couldn't reach. But I pulled over a bucket of pool chemicals and stood on top of it.

Polos with the hotel logo embroidered on them. I closed my eyes. *Thank God.*

The pants were all a few sizes too big, so I yanked the hair tie from my hair and used it to gather the excess material of the pants and tie it into a knot. After, I tugged on a polo and grabbed an extra of each for Louise. Then I quietly unlocked the door and peeked outside. With the coast clear, I slipped out and power-walked back to the beach through the hotel grounds with my head down.

I'd just started to think maybe this naked nightmare was coming to an end when I arrived back at the entrance to the beach where I'd left Louise and found her with the police.

Crap. I ran down to the chairs we'd been using earlier. Louise sat wrapped in a blanket, while a cop stood with a flashlight shining in her face.

"What's going on here?" I demanded. "Louise, are you okay?"

"They're arresting me for lewd conduct."

I looked at the cop. "Are you joking? Some kids stole our clothes, and you're going to arrest *her*?"

He looked me up and down, zeroing in on the logo on my shirt. "Do you work here?"

Oh shit. "No. I had to borrow a uniform to walk back after chasing the brats who committed the real crime."

"So you're the one who streaked through the wedding?"

"Streaked? No. I had no idea they were even there. I didn't do it intentionally. I tried to stay in the water, but—"

The other cop interrupted. "Ma'am, the wedding you just ran by naked? The father of the bride is the *mayor of this island*. He wants to press charges." He lifted his chin. "I'd keep my mouth shut, unless you also want to be charged with stealing that uniform."

"*Stealing the uniform*? I borrowed it because three teenagers stole our clothes. Why aren't you chasing them?"

The first cop shrugged. "If you had kept your clothes on, like the law says you need to do here in the Bahamas, everyone would be happy right now."

Louise pursed her lips. "I'm sure *your wife* would be happy if you kept your clothes on."

Uh-oh. He'd pissed off Louise now.

The cop raised his brows. "Excuse me?"

"Clearly if you got laid once in a while, you'd be more relaxed about seeing a little skin."

I closed my eyes. The chances of talking our way out of this were already slim, but that sealed the deal. A half hour later, we were being booked at the police station.

"What happens after you're done filling out your report?" I asked one of the cops who'd brought us in. "Do we pay a fine or something?"

"You'll see the Bahamas court magistrate. They'll set your bail. Then we'll bring you back here, and you can make a phone call to get someone to post whatever amount they assign. If no one comes..." He thumbed to a door without looking up from his computer. "You'll spend the night down the hall in the holding tank."

"But we can post it ourselves, right? Like with a credit card or something?"

"You can use your own money to post bail. But it gets posted down the road at the clerk's office, so you can't post it yourself. Someone will have to go in and do it for you."

"We're here by ourselves."

The officer shrugged. "You can try your country's embassy. But they're not that fast, especially on a weekend."

Over the next two hours, Louise and I were shuttled to appear before a night court judge and then brought back to the station. Bail was set at five-hundred dollars each. I called the US Embassy to see if they could help with posting bail, but the person who answered the phone said they'd reach out to someone and get back to me. They couldn't tell me when. Then the policeman was kind enough to let us make a second call—one I did *not* want to make.

Louise phoned her grandson. I cringed to think about how he'd take the news. But she said he had business in the Bahamas and could probably find someone to help us.

In the meantime, they escorted me back to a packed holding cell. Women sat on the floor around most of the perimeter, while one older lady laid across the only bench in the cell. The group looked me up and down as the officer unlocked the door and guided me inside. None of them seemed very happy to see me. There was an open spot in one corner, but when I went to sit, the two women on either side shifted over, silently suggesting I find someplace else to park my ass. That happened twice before I figured out that the woman currently snoring couldn't object, so I sat near her.

Twenty minutes went by before the guard came back with Louise.

"Hey." I climbed to my feet from the floor. "You doing okay?"

She nodded. "Not my first time in the clinker. You?"

"Actually, it is."

"Back in the sixties, I got arrested for dancing in a vulgar manner. I think today you young people would call it twerking."

"Louise, are you telling me you can throw that ass back?"

"My best friend was from Egypt. She's gone now. God rest her soul. But her mother taught her how to belly dance, and she taught me. Except I liked to shake my ass more than my belly."

The woman hogging the entire bench all by herself suddenly sat up. She lifted her chin. "Let's see."

"That's probably not a good idea," I said.

"Sure it is." Louise walked to the center of the cell. Most of the ladies sitting around were in various stages of passed out or asleep, but all open eyes shifted to the seventy-eight-year-old jailbird. Louise held her arms out and shook her hips back and forth. The police-issued orange jumpsuit she had on was baggy, but you could see she knew how to move.

"So this is what you start with when you're belly dancing," she explained. "You go side to side." After thirty seconds or so, she stopped and widened her stance, leaning forward. "Now you do the same movement, except instead of side to side, you go front to rear."

"Holy shit!" One of the ladies pointed and laughed. "Baby got back!"

I didn't know why anything to do with Louise Aster surprised me anymore. But sure as shit, she thumped her butt up and down, putting even Miley Cyrus to shame.

When she was done, the packed cell hooted and hollered, and an officer came back, looking unhappy to have had to get up from his desk.

"What's going on here?"

One of the ladies winked. "Just talking about you, Officer Burrows. You know seeing your handsome face makes us girls rowdy."

He shook his head. "Yeah, well, keep it down."

The woman fluttered her false eyelashes. "Yes, sir, Georgie Porgie, Pudding and Pie."

Officer Burrows frowned but walked back out.

Fortunately, Louise's dance recital seemed to have won us some new friends. The woman hogging the bench moved over and patted the seat next to her.

"Come sit here, big momma. Queens don't sit on the floor."

After that, the vibe in the holding cell changed. Even the snoring woman next to me woke up once Louise told everyone she'd been arrested for indecent exposure. Frieda, the bench hog, seemed almost in charge of the place, and the other ladies seemed to know it.

"What are you in for, Frieda?" Louise asked.

"I hosted a card game at my house."

"It's illegal to play cards in the Bahamas?"

"Not for you. But gambling is illegal for residents."

"That's ridiculous."

She shrugged. "It is what it is. They usually leave me alone, but every once in a while, they shut me down when they need money for extra expenses in the department. They confiscate all the cash on the tables and don't arrest any of my players. They know none of them will make a stink about their money going missing, so no one comes in to claim it, and the department gets to keep it after a while."

I made friends with a young girl who had been brought in a few minutes after Louise. Our cellmates all called her Mad Dog, and I found out it was because she collected the island's stray dogs. Mad Dog had recently lost her job, and she could no longer afford dog food. She'd been arrested for stealing kibble. Another woman had been arrested for breaking into a house. She'd suspected her husband was cheating and followed him, then broke in and caught him in the act. The other woman involved had insisted on pressing charges.

I had no idea how long we were in there, because there wasn't a clock and the police had taken my watch, but it seemed like it had to be morning by the time a guard came back.

Officer Burrows unlocked the cell door. "Eleanor Sutton and Louise Aster, you're free to go."

I climbed to my feet. "Did the embassy post our bail?"

"Nope. Some rich dude with an attitude."

Louise rolled her eyes. "Sounds like one of my grand-son's friends."

However it had happened, I was thrilled to get out. Louise and I said goodbye to our newfound friends and were taken to the property room where we picked up what was left of our belongings. It seems the little thieves had dropped my thong and Louise's phone. I wasn't sure if the person who had posted our bail would also stop at the po-lice station, but it turned out he had. And the man respon-sible did *not* look happy.

Louise stopped short as we entered the lobby. "Beck, what are you doing here?"

CHAPTER 6

Beck

"**S**eriously, Gram? What the hell?"

"Don't you use that language with me—or any woman, for that matter." She turned to her partner in crime and smirked. "Except maybe in the bedroom. I like a little dirty talk."

I closed my eyes. "Where's a hot poker to stick in my ears when I need it?"

"Oh, don't be so uptight. What the heck are you doing here, anyway?"

"You called and told me you got arrested."

Gram shrugged. "So? I asked you to see if you could get someone to bring bail to the clerk, not hop on a plane."

"I'm concerned about you."

"Well, that's a waste of energy. You don't need to be."

I held my hands out, motioning to the room full of police officers. "Look where we are, at the police precinct in a foreign country."

"It's the Bahamas, not North Korea," Gram protested.

I turned to Nora. "Can you help me out here, please?"

"How? She's right. It's not North Korea."

"I should've gotten drunk on the plane," I mumbled.

Outside, I directed Bonnie and Clyde to my rental car, where my grandmother got in the front seat and Nora slid into the back.

Gram clicked her seatbelt. "We need to make a stop on the way to the hotel."

"Where?" I asked.

"At the clerk's office. The place you posted the bail."

"I already posted your bail."

"This is for Frieda."

Nora leaned up from the backseat. "And Mad Dog. I'd like to spring her, too. Oh, and do you think we could also stop for some dog food?"

I squinted. "What the hell are the two of you talking about?"

"Language!" they answered in unison.

I scrubbed my hands up and down my face. "I feel like I'm in a Three Stooges skit and we're all having different conversations. Who is Frieda, and why do we need to pay her bail?"

"And Mad Dog," Nora once again chimed in.

"Of course." I rolled my eyes. "We can't forget Mad Dog."

It was only six thirty in the morning, yet it had to be at least eighty-five degrees out. I needed to turn the car on to run the air conditioning. I'd traveled half the night and was running on no sleep, so I started the engine and decided it would be faster to just do as they said.

When we arrived at the clerk's office, Moe and Larry got out of the car and marched inside. I followed to make sure they didn't get themselves into any more trouble. If I hadn't been so exhausted and pissed off, the sight of them together would've been comical. Nora was wearing pants that looked like they would've been too big for me, tied up in the front, and an oversized polo with the name of a hotel embroidered on it. And my almost-eighty-year-old grandmother was sporting an orange inmate jumpsuit. Neither seemed to notice or care.

"Hi," Nora said to the clerk. "We'd like to post bail for our two friends."

The man behind the desk looked them over. "Okay... What are the names?"

"Frieda," my grandmother said emphatically.

"And Mad Dog," Nora yet again chimed in.

The guy looked to me. I shrugged. "Not a clue."

As crazy as it was, it only took about five minutes for the clerk to figure out Frieda was Frieda Ellington—a woman frequently arrested for illegal gambling, and Mad Dog was Elona Bethel, picked up for shoplifting dog food. Once that was squared away, the clerk told them bail was seven fifty for Mad Dog and fifteen hundred for Frieda. They looked at each other before turning to me.

Nora bit her lip. "Could I borrow a little money until we get back to the hotel? I forgot I don't have my purse."

"And I need some cash, too," Gram announced. "But I'm not paying you back. You're going to be getting plenty from me soon enough."

I shook my head, more at myself than these two, as I got out my wallet. When we were finally done, we piled back into the car.

"Thank you, Beck," Nora said. "For bailing us out and for loaning me the money to help the lady I met."

I looked in the rearview mirror. "Where did you meet this Mad Dog?"

She smirked. "In the clinker."

I laughed. "You just bailed out a woman you didn't know before getting locked up?"

Nora shrugged. "She was really nice. And she rescues dogs."

I had no idea what the fuck to do with that, so I started the car.

"What hotel are you at?"

"Paradise Found. Sorry, I can't even look up the address for you since my phone is gone."

"Gone?"

"Stolen. By rotten teenagers."

My lip twitched. "Of course."

Paradise Found was a fifteen-minute ride from the police station. I figured I'd get a room and decide what I was doing after I crashed for a few hours. But when we walked into the resort, and Nora and my grandmother asked the front desk for new keys to their rooms, the guy behind the desk disappeared and came back with a man wearing a suit.

"Hello, Ms. Sutton, Ms. Aster. I'm the manager, Alan Harmon. I'm sorry to inform you that we can no longer allow you to stay at this property. We'll refund any charges that we've advanced for the remaining nights."

Gram's hands flew to her hips. "Why can't we stay here?"

"Because of the incident." The manager's eyes dropped to Nora's uniform—the one she'd apparently stolen from the hotel. "We've taken the liberty of packing your things for you. We have them in the back. Just give me a minute to get them."

"I cannot believe this," Nora said.

"I can't say I blame them." I shook my head. "You were arrested for public indecency on their grounds, and

54

you're currently wearing evidence that you stole from their property."

"No." Nora shook her head. "I don't mean that. I get that they have a reason to toss us out, but they packed our stuff for us? That means someone touched my vibrator."

"Mine too," my grandmother added.

I shut my eyes. *First dirty talk and now a vibrator.* It was shaping up to be a great day after traveling all night. I shook it off, taking out my cell to text my assistant. Except I only had one bar. Thinking it probably wasn't a great idea to ask for the hotel's Wi-Fi password, I excused myself and stepped outside.

The service there wasn't much better, but at least I was able to shoot off a text asking Gwen to find a decent hotel somewhere. When I returned to the front desk, the manager was wheeling two bags around the counter.

"We also have two glass jars," he said. "We didn't want them to break, so they weren't packed into the suitcases. Let me grab those."

He came back out carrying two Mason jars. Both were filled with little pieces of paper.

"Are those yours?" I looked to Nora.

She nodded. "One is mine and one is Louise's."

"What are they?"

"Our gratitude jars."

"What the heck is that?"

"Every day we find fifteen minutes to close our eyes and reflect on the good things that have happened. We write down at least one on a slip of paper and put it in the jar. That way, when life gets us down, we can take out the slips to reflect on how much good there has been in our lives."

I stared at Nora.

She turned to the manager. "*You* will not be making it into our jars."

Gram raised her pointer finger into the air. "But we should write about our prison friends!"

Jesus Christ, it felt like I was in some sort of bizarro world with these two. Shaking my head, I grabbed the handles to both pieces of luggage. "Is this everything?"

"I don't know," Nora said. "How do we know they packed everything?"

The manager put his hand on his chest. "I took the liberty of inspecting the rooms after the bellman was done. I can assure you, there was nothing left."

"Did you check the end table?" Gram asked.

The man sighed. "Yes, ma'am."

Feeling like we were about two seconds away from these ladies opening their bags in the lobby and taking inventory, I intervened. "Do you have a card, Mr. Harmon? In case there's anything missing once we get to a place where they can check?"

He reached over the counter, extending it to me. "I'm sure you'll find everything in order. But just in case, here you go."

"We also have a rental car here," Nora said.

"Did you sleep last night?" I asked her.

She shook her head.

"Is it parked in the lot?"

"Yes."

I looked at the manager. "Can you keep the car until tomorrow?"

"Of course."

"Thank you."

I looked between Nora and Gram. "We'll deal with it then."

Outside, I stowed the luggage in the trunk of my rental car and slipped behind the wheel, just as my phone buzzed.

Gwen: Three rooms booked at The Four Seasons. Let me know if you'd like me to make any other plans.

At least something had gone right today.

⁓

Later that evening, I was sitting in the bar answering emails on my phone as I downed my second whiskey, when Nora walked in. She slid into the seat next to me and smiled. I didn't return the sentiment.

"I'm sorry about today," she said.

"What the hell were you thinking?"

She shook a finger at me. "Your grandmother wouldn't like that language."

"Her, I have to respect. You...not so much."

Her jaw dropped. "Why not?"

"Well, for starters, you're not my grandmother. Everyone else has to earn it."

She frowned. "I really am sorry you felt you had to come all this way."

"So you're not sorry you did what you did, just sorry you got caught and I had to make the trip?"

"Well... Yes, that's right."

I shifted in my seat to face her. "My grandmother is seventy-eight years old. Did you really think it was a great idea for her to strip naked in public in the Bahamas?"

"Oh my God. You're such a jerk."

"*I'm* a jerk?"

"Yes. You have a problem with an older woman taking off her clothes, but not a younger one."

"I didn't say that..."

"So if I told you I wanted to find a quiet little area of the beach and take off all my clothes, you'd be okay with that?"

"It might be the only thing that could change my mood right now."

Nora pursed her lips. "Well, then I guess you should get comfortable with your mood. It's going to be around for a while."

The bartender walked over and motioned to my drink. "You want another?"

"Double, please." I shook my thumb at Nora. "Put it on her tab."

She rolled her eyes. "Fine. And I'll take a cabernet, please. Whatever you have open is great."

"You got it." He walked away.

"Have you ever tried skinny dipping?" Nora asked.

"Not since becoming an adult."

"Maybe that's your problem. You need to have a little fun."

"I wasn't aware I had a problem."

"Oh, you definitely do. You're an uptight ageist with a stick up his ass who acts like a dick whenever your grandmother wants to have a little fun."

"Very nice. Do you kiss your mother with that mouth?"

She squinted at me. "My mother's *dead*. But I do give really good head with it."

Her comment caused a twitch in my pants, though I was still pissed off. "I'd ask you to demonstrate, but I don't want whatever you picked up in prison."

Nora's pouty mouth formed a solid line of *fuck you*. I waited for the comeback, but instead, her eyes dropped to my lips.

Is she fucking with me? Trying to knock me off my game by pretending she was interested, or was our arguing working for her? Or maybe I was seeing things. I had no damn idea, but I knew one way to find out.

I leaned closer. "You're a giant pain in my ass."

Her eyes widened, then narrowed to pissed-off slits. She glared at me for a solid ten seconds before she leaned over and crushed her lips to mine.

It took me a heartbeat or two to get over the shock, but when I did, I sucked her bottom lip into my mouth and bit down. Hard.

"Oww..." She tried to pull back, but I had a pretty good hold on her with my teeth. "That's for the name calling," I growled, not letting go. "Now give me your fucking tongue."

She definitely liked that. Fisting two handfuls of my shirt, she got out of her chair and pushed her big tits up against me, the same big tits I might've jerked off to, thinking about the bathing suit shots she'd sent me. And she also gave me her tongue.

Damn, who knew lust and rage combined into Viagra. I was hard as a rock, sitting in the middle of a damn bar. Somewhere deep down, I knew I should pull back, be the voice of reason, but I was incapable. Instead, I slid my fingers into her hair and wrapped a clump of it around my fist. She moaned through our joined mouths when I tugged.

Fuck me.

I needed more.

More of her.

All of her.

I was just about to toss her over my shoulder and drag her back to my room, when the sound of someone clearing their throat interrupted. Dazed, I tried to pull back, but Nora bit my lip this time. *Hard.*

Oh fuck.

She liked pissed off. Well, that I could do...

"You're so infuriating," I grumbled.

"Yet you want to fuck me anyway."

"I'd like to put you over my knee first."

"Oh, I like the sound of that."

I considered trying to fuck her right here. It was probably just the bartender interrupting anyway. Let him watch. I jumped back into the moment, ignoring everything around us. Never in my life had the chemistry with someone been so strong.

But then came another throat clearing. And this time it was followed by a voice, a man's voice.

"Jesus Christ, Nora. You're going to get arrested for public indecency again."

That snapped me out of it. Nora too.

We turned the direction of the voice, and Nora blinked a few times. "Richard. What are you doing here?"

"Watching you dry hump, apparently."

"Seriously, what the hell?"

I really hoped this guy wasn't her boyfriend, or husband even. Because getting into a fight with a hard-on wasn't going to be fun.

"You called me, remember? To bail you out of jail?"

"And you told me to go fuck myself."

"Yet I showed up anyway...like I always do for you." The guy looked at me for the first time. He lifted his chin. "Who are you?"

"Beck Cross. And you are..."

He motioned to Nora. "Her *fiancé*."

"*Ex*-fiancé," Nora clarified.

Perfect. Just fucking perfect.

CHAPTER 7
Beck

Two hours later, I was still sitting at the bar when the guy from earlier strolled back in. He and Nora had disappeared after he'd interrupted us sucking face.

"Mind if I sit down?" he asked.

I shrugged. "I'm not looking for any trouble."

The guy grinned and took the seat. "Looks like you found her anyway." He surprised me by extending his hand. "Richard Logan."

This was fucked up, yet I shook.

The bartender walked over and set a napkin in front of Richard. "What can I get you?"

"I'll take a vodka tonic. Make it a double."

"You got it." The bartender looked to me. "You want another?"

"I'm good," I told him. "Thanks." Keeping my head screwed on straight might be important with the guy currently sitting next to me.

Nora's fiancé, *or ex-fiancé*—whichever it was—sat quietly to my left until after he'd gotten his drink and lifted it to his lips.

"You ever hear of aconitum?" he asked.

I shook my head. "Don't think so."

"It's a plant. Gorgeous. Tall, deep purple or blue usually. The flowers are helmet shaped, and there's a shitload of them on a single stem. They grow wild and sort of billow in the wind, giving you that free feeling when you look at them. Chinese medicine uses the extract to take away pain, but if you eat too much of it, you die." He gulped some of his drink and pointed to me. "That's Nora. Gorgeous and able to take away all your aches and pains. But try to take too much of her, and it'll kill you inside."

I held up a hand. "We're not together."

He smiled halfheartedly. "She told me the same thing for a long time, too."

"It's not like that."

Richard shrugged. "Whatever you say. But remember, I warned you."

A few minutes went by. Since the guy hadn't slugged me yet, I figured it was safe to poke around—not that I was interested in more than what was about to happen between Nora and me, but she was traveling with my grandmother, after all.

"What's her story?"

"You got a month or two?"

"Complicated, huh?"

"Like having a chocolate teapot to make your hot tea."

I chuckled. "You were engaged, I take it?"

"Split up eighteen months ago."

"Yet she called you when she got arrested..."

"I'm a lawyer. Probably the only one whose number she knows by heart. It was the first time I've heard from her in over a year."

I nodded.

He shook his head. "Finally just moved on a month ago, too. New girlfriend's not going to be too happy when she finds out I hopped on a plane the minute my ex called and said she needed help."

"Sorry..."

"So what's your deal? Nora said she's traveling with your grandmother?"

"They're friends. Odd, I know. But they seem pretty tight. My grandmother isn't well. Cancer. Third recurrence. She decided not to treat it anymore and enjoy her time left. They've been traveling together doing crazy shit."

"I'm sorry she's sick."

"Thank you. She feels good, though. If you met her, you wouldn't have any clue she wasn't healthy."

"I actually did meet her a little while ago. Nora and I went to her room to talk. Your grandmother's is right next door. When she heard us in the hall, she popped her head out, and Nora introduced her. I wondered why she was traveling with an old lady." He held his hand up. "No offense."

"None taken."

"Nora being Nora, didn't mention the woman was sick. Just insisted it was her friend. But their traveling together makes sense now."

"How so?"

Richard sipped his drink. "Because of what Nora went through."

I looked over. "What did Nora go through?"

"Shit. I figured you knew. Nora had some pretty serious health issues a few years back." He smiled sadly. "She said you two weren't a thing. Guess she wasn't lying."

"Because I didn't know?"

He took a billfold from his front pocket and tossed two twenties on the bar. Then he knocked back the rest of his drink and stood. "Because if you had seen her naked, you would've seen the scars and asked questions." Richard stuck out his hand. "I'm going to catch the afternoon flight back to New York. Good luck with your grandmother, and remember, the aconitum will kill you."

~

"Hey."

"What's going on, big bro?" Jake let out a big *ahhh* after he spoke, and I visualized him sitting at my desk with his feet kicked up.

"Where are you?"

"It's eight in the morning. I'm at the office."

"Right, but where exactly?"

"In your office. I came in to get the prospectus I need to cover the meeting you asked me to cover."

"Get your feet off my desk, dickhead."

"How the hell did you know my feet are up on your desk?"

"You're an easy read. You enjoy playing king of the castle too much."

Jake laughed. "It is fun. But how's Gram doing? I had to listen to your message twice because I was sure I'd misheard and you said Gram was *congested*, not arrested. What the hell happened?"

"She went *skinny dipping* the night before last."

"And that's illegal?"

"It was on the beach attached to the resort where she was staying."

"I can't believe she got arrested for having a little fun."

I frowned. "She broke the law."

"Lighten up, bro. We can't all be as perfect as you."

"Anyway, I'm calling to tell you I'm not going to be back tonight like I originally thought."

"Oh good. More days sitting in the ivory tower for me."

I sighed. "I'll have Gwen reschedule everything for the next few days, so you won't have to cover much."

"Even better. I make a much better figurehead than actual boss. It's probably because my head is so pretty."

"Or because your head is empty... Anyway, Gram has a hearing in a few days, and I want to stick around and make sure everything goes okay. She refuses to let me hire a lawyer, so someone has to keep her from telling the judge to go screw himself. Plus, I thought maybe I could talk some sense into her while I'm here."

"And see her travel buddy in a bikini."

Better yet, suck her face... I kept that to myself. "Goodbye, Jake."

"Later, pumpkin."

After I hung up, I shot off a few emails and went in search of some breakfast. The hotel restaurant was empty, except for one table where a certain gorgeous blonde wearing a sheer headscarf was sitting alone. As I approached, I realized she had on a matching sheer beach coverup with a bathing suit top underneath. *Maybe four days won't be so bad after all.*

Reaching the table, I looked around for her partner in crime.

"Is my grandmother here?"

"No. She's been sleeping in a little. Her lower back is bothering her. I think it's kidney pain. It started a few days ago. She called her doctor, and he said it's to be expected and prescribed something that seems to help. But it also makes her tired, so she started taking them at night."

I pointed to the empty seat across from her. "Do you mind if I join you?"

"Help yourself. I'm going to beach yoga at eight fifteen, but I have a few minutes to keep you company."

The waitress walked over, so I ordered a coffee in exchange for a menu. "Your fiancé didn't stay?" I asked, though I already knew the answer.

"*Ex*-fiancé, and no. Though he did suggest I should let him share my room for a night for his troubles. When I said no, we had a fight, and *I* suggested he catch a flight home."

"You argued? Does that mean you wound up sucking face?"

Nora laughed. "No. But that's funny."

"See? I'm not always a jerk."

Her eyes twinkled. "Just most of the time."

Her ex had given me a pretty stern warning to keep my distance, so I was curious what she had to say about him.

"So why is there an ex in front of fiancé, if you don't mind my asking?"

"I don't mind. I guess the main reason is that he was overbearing and possessive. Richard had a long-term girlfriend who cheated on him and got pregnant by the other man. It made him certain all women were the same. I travel a lot for work, and at first he would call me a few times a day to check where I was. Eventually he stopped doing it, and I thought he'd finally started to trust me. Then I found an Apple AirTag hidden in the lining of my purse. I checked his phone, and he'd been tracking me."

"Shit."

"He blamed it on me, said I'd forced him to stoop to that level because I didn't spend enough time reassuring him I wasn't cheating." She shrugged. "The way I see it, if you need reassurance from someone who has never done anything to make you doubt them, it's your issue, not mine."

She had a good point.

The waitress came back and took my order. When she left, Nora forked a piece of cantaloupe and pointed it at me. "What about your love life? Any luck trolling the supermarket aisles these days?"

"I've been a little busy chasing my grandmother and her beautiful, yet mildly infuriating friend, all over the country."

"Just mildly infuriating? I'll have to try harder."

I smiled. "So what's on the agenda for today? You two sticking your heads in a shark's mouth or letting a blind man shoot an apple off the top of your heads with a rifle?"

"We actually don't have anything lined up since we were supposed to leave soon. Obviously there's been a change of plans since we have to stick around a few more days for the hearing. But Louise loves the steel drums, and I saw a sign in the lobby about a beach party the hotel's having this afternoon with music, so I thought maybe we'd do that and catch a little sun."

"Think you can manage to keep your clothes on while you're on the beach?"

"It won't be as much fun, but I can handle that. What about you? What time is your flight?"

"I hate to disappoint you, but I'm not leaving today. I'm also sticking around until after the hearing. I want to make sure my grandmother doesn't give the judge a piece of her mind and get locked up again."

"I'd say that's ridiculous and would never happen so you can go home and not worry, but I wouldn't put it past her. It's probably good that you stay. Plus, between us, I think she likes having you around."

I nodded, quiet for a minute.

"So..." Nora nibbled on her plump bottom lip. "About last night—what happened before Richard showed up."

I rubbed my lip. "You mean when you told me you give great head, or when you kissed me?"

She blushed. The alcohol had definitely made her bolder. "Both."

"What about it?"

"Well, I just wanted to say, I don't think it's a good idea if we pick up where we left off, especially with you staying a few days."

That was deflating, though I didn't let it show. "Why not?"

"Because I'm not looking for a relationship."

"Neither am I." I tilted my head. "Sounds like we're on the same page, and it might be a *very good* idea if we pick up where we left off. Actually, scratch that. I wasn't a gentleman. Maybe we should start over. You told me you gave good head, but I didn't share that I would love to bury my face between your legs until you scream."

Nora's eyes widened briefly, but then she looked away and cleared her throat. "While that's a generous offer, I think it's best if we stay friends."

I smirked. "We're not friends. We don't like each other enough."

"We don't like each other enough to be friends, but we like each other enough to have sex?"

I nodded. "That's right. People can be physically attracted to each other without liking each other's personalities."

"So you don't like my personality?"

"Not particularly. You like to lecture me. The only part of that I enjoy is imagining the different ways I might shut you up by sticking something in your mouth." I leaned forward. "And I think you like the thought of that, too. Am I wrong?"

Nora's chest rose a little higher, and her eyes darkened. *I'm definitely not wrong.* But then she looked away again, and when her gaze returned, she'd gotten control of herself. "I like sex, but I don't like messy. And I don't mean that in the literal sense," she said. "If I didn't care about things becoming tangled, I would have accepted Richard's offer to stay the night. We had decent-enough chemistry when we were together."

My jaw clenched. I wasn't a jealous guy. In fact, in most of my casual relationships, I adopted the old Clinton military position—*Don't ask. Don't tell.* I supposed the fact that it irked me to think of her with another guy should've been a red flag, though Nora was the kind of woman who was worth a little risk. But I already knew she wasn't the type who wanted to be coaxed into anything—only she decided what she was up for.

Nevertheless, we'd met twice now and almost wound up in bed as many times, so I liked the odds of leaving the ball in her court.

"I'll be around if you change your mind," I told her.

Nora drank the last of her coffee, wiped her mouth, and tossed her napkin on her empty plate. "I should get going for yoga. Will I see you at the beach later for the party?"

"Probably not. I have a lot of work to do."

She stood. "Shame. I was kind of looking forward to seeing what's under those crisp dress shirts you seem to like so much."

"Three-one-nine," I said.

"Is that the exercise regimen you do or something?"

I winked. "It's my room number. Stop by whenever you'd like, and I'm happy to show you what's underneath anything I'm wearing."

CHAPTER 8

Nora

"Well, well, well." I slid my sunglasses to the edge of my nose to get a better look at the man approaching my beach chair. "Whadda you know? The suit owns a pair of shorts. I never would have guessed."

Beck's lip twitched. "I just bought them at the gift shop. The only shorts I own are for running."

"What do you wear when you go to the beach?"

He raised a brow. "The beach?"

"Oh my gosh. When was the last time you were at a beach?"

Beck put his hands on his hips and looked out to the ocean. "Not sure. A long time ago."

"You don't know what you're missing."

This time Beck pushed his sunglasses down the bridge of his nose. His eyes dropped down to my body and slowly skimmed their way from my toes to my neck, lingering at my breasts for a while, before he pushed his glasses back up using one finger. "It might've been easier if I didn't."

I smiled. "Finish all your work?"

"The critical things." He looked around. "Where's my grandmother?"

I pointed down the beach. "She's taking a calypso dance lesson."

He nodded. "Sounds about right. Mind if I sit?"

"Are you going to take off that T-shirt?"

"It's hot. I was planning on it. Is that a problem?"

"Nope." I motioned to his torso. "Go ahead. Just do it before you sit so I get a good look. What's fair is fair."

Beck chuckled. But he also reached back to the collar of his T-shirt and yanked it over his head.

Oh my. Damn, he was pretty all over. Tanned skin, bulging biceps, washboard abs, a V that made my mouth water, and pecs I had the craziest urge to lick. He held his arms out. "Well?"

I downplayed my approval. "Not bad."

He grinned and suddenly his pecs were dancing, the muscles bouncing at a rapid speed.

I covered my mouth. "Oh my God. You're one of *those* guys."

Beck laughed. "Actually, I wasn't sure if I could pull it off anymore. I haven't done that since I was sixteen. I taught myself in an attempt to get my buddy's older sister to notice me."

"Did it work?"

"She was twenty-three and dating a guy in med school. I was getting my how-to-attract-women advice from Ronnie on *Jersey Shore*. What do you think?"

I chuckled.

Beck sat down in Louise's lounge chair next to me. His eyes dropped to my cleavage, and his face changed, so I knew he'd noticed my scar. When his eyes rose, I could see he was deliberating mentioning it, so I saved him the struggle.

"I had heart surgery a few years back."

"Your ex mentioned something about that. When I told him about my grandmother and the reason for the trip, he said it made sense considering the health scare you'd had. Could I ask why you needed surgery?"

"Rhabdomyosarcoma."

"The same thing your mother died of?"

I nodded.

"I'm sorry. Everything good now?"

I hated talking about cancer, especially while on a beautiful beach, so I gave Beck my standard answer whenever a stranger noticed my scar. "It's perfect. I was one of the lucky ones." I pointed to the activities shack not too far away. "I was thinking about going jet skiing. You up for it?"

Beck frowned. "No thanks."

"Louise wasn't into it either."

"That's not surprising, considering that's how her daughter died."

My eyes bulged. I ripped the sunglasses from my face and sat up. "What did you just say?"

"My mother died in a jet-skiing accident when I was eleven."

I covered my heart with my hand. "Oh my God. I had no idea. This was the second time I asked Louise to go. Today I *bock-bock*ed her, too—you know, flapping my arms like a chicken."

"That's very mature."

"Well, how the heck was I supposed to know? She'd mentioned that her daughter died years ago in an accident, but I automatically thought car."

Beck shook his head. "My parents were away on vacation for their fifteen-year wedding anniversary. My father was driving the jet ski, and they collided with a boat. He didn't have a scratch on him, but my mother suffered a traumatic brain injury."

"Jesus. So she died on vacation?"

"She actually lived three months after that. They flew her back to the US, but she never regained consciousness. I was only a kid, and it was a horrible few months."

"I'm so sorry."

Beck nodded. "Thank you. I didn't mean to bring your head down. Just figured I'd let you know. That's probably the one bucket-list-type thing my grandmother won't be checking off."

"Of course. Who could blame her?" I shook my head. "Can I ask you a nosy question?"

"What?"

"Did your father pass away after that? I know Louise raised you and your brother after your mom died. I assumed it was because your dad was killed, too. But you just said your father wasn't injured."

"He wasn't. But he had a lot of guilt. Apparently he'd had a few drinks before they got on the jet ski that day. Not enough that he failed the breathalyzer when they tested him a few hours after the accident, but he was never able to move past it. He started drinking heavily, and my grandmother took my brother and me to her place for a few days. He disappeared after that for a while, and we never went back. Last I heard, he was on his fourth wife and still a drunk. He lives down in Florida, I think."

"I'm sorry you went through that."

"My grandmother gave us a good life."

"I guess I can understand why you're overprotective of Louise now. She's been so many things to you."

"Does that mean you're going to stop these crazy trips?"

"No, because while what you just shared helps me understand your concerns, it doesn't change the fact that what Louise is doing is not about you. It's about her."

"I don't have to like it."

"No, you certainly don't. But you should show her enough respect to accept her decisions."

Beck frowned. "How about we go back to checking out each other's bodies? That's a lot more fun than talking to you."

I glared at him.

He glared back.

"You know what I think your problem is?" I asked.

"Nope. But I'm guessing you're going to enlighten me."

"You're a control freak, and you hate that you don't have control of what your grandmother is doing."

"You say that like it's a bad thing. Control freaks make good leaders. They're perfectionists, and hard workers."

"They're uncompromising and bad listeners."

Beck cupped his hand to his ear. "I'm sorry. What did you say?"

"Ugh. Just shut up and look pretty, will you? That's what you're good for."

"I'm good for a lot more than that. How about I show you?"

I felt like punching him. But at the same time, I had to fight my arousal. Why *the hell* did I feel such a stir from arguing with this guy? The more tense the moment, the more overwhelming the physical effect seemed to be.

And I wasn't alone. Beck's eyes dropped to my mouth, and he licked his lips. He looked like a hungry lion about to pounce. And I was a willing antelope. Luckily, my phone interrupted my ridiculous thoughts. I pulled it out of my bag and swiped to answer.

"Hey, Louise."

"There's a handsome Bahamian calypso dancer up here without a partner," she said. "And they're giving out free Bahama Mama drinks."

My eyes lifted and met Beck's. "A handsome dancer and free drinks? That sounds like just what I need. I'll be there in a few minutes."

When I was done, I spent a minute doing some quick research on Google. All the while, Beck kept quiet and watched me.

"Ha!" I turned my cell to show him the screen. "It has nothing to do with you."

Beck squinted and leaned closer to read. "The human brain releases testosterone, cortisol, and adrenaline when under stress, such as during a fight. To counteract those hormones, the human body craves the pleasure hormones sex can provide."

His brows drew together. "What the hell did you Google?"

"Why am I getting horny arguing with an asshole."

His lip twitched, yet again. It did that a lot when we spoke.

"You know what I have to say to that?" he asked.

"What?"

He lifted his hands and locked them behind his head, elbows out, making his pecs dance again. "I bet your handsome Bahamian calypso dancer can't do this."

I got up with a huff. "Enjoy your company for the rest of the afternoon."

He smirked and leaned back, keeping his hands behind his head as he settled into the lounger. "Oh I will. I'll be with my favorite person."

CHAPTER 9

Nora

Later that evening, I went down to the lobby to meet Louise for dinner. She'd texted and told me she made reservations at a fancy place, but I hadn't asked if Beck was joining. When I asked the dress code, she told me to wear the royal blue dress I'd bought at a cute little boutique the other night. It was a slinky, one-shoulder number with a curve-hugging bodice and slit that probably could've used two-sided tape so I didn't get arrested again. I paired it with the set of heels I'd brought that matched anything—four-inch silver stilettos with a thin strap that wrapped around the ankle. A few heads turned as I waited, and it made me feel good after the last week in grungy beach and travel wear. Sometimes I forgot how much I enjoyed indulging my feminine side.

I'd told myself I'd gotten all dressed up for me, but when Beck stepped off the elevator and saw me standing there, he walked smack into the person in front of him. Maybe it wasn't *all* for me.

He didn't even pretend to hide his admiration as he approached. Oddly, I appreciated that he didn't mask his physical attraction. Too many men pretended their interests were virtuous when they only wanted to get laid.

Beck wore a three-piece, definitely custom suit. It checked more than a few of the boxes on my Christmas list. Knowing there was a chiseled body underneath made me want to unwrap it even more. So I was definitely glad Louise was joining us. A girl only has so much willpower, especially one who hasn't been laid in forever.

"You're wearing my favorite color," Beck said. "Maybe I should say it looks horrible on you so we can argue. But I'm not a liar. You look beautiful."

I blushed. "Thank you. You don't look so bad yourself."

He lifted an arm and pushed back his shirtsleeve, revealing a set of expensive-looking cufflinks and his even more expensive chunky watch. "Am I early?"

I shook my head. "Right on time. Louise should be down soon."

He nodded. "When she texted me to wear a suit for dinner, I thought about telling her I was just going to order room service. I'm glad I didn't, or I would've missed that dress."

My phone buzzed from my purse at the same time Beck's did from somewhere inside his suit jacket. We looked at each other.

"Is that a coincidence?" I said.

"Don't know."

We took our cells out and read at the same time. It was one text written to both of us.

> **Louise: Sorry for the late notice. I'm going to skip dinner tonight. Feeling a bit tired. I'll order room service if I get hungry. You two enjoy. The reservation is at the Royal Bahamian here in the hotel.**

Shoot. I shook my head. "I'm going to call her. Just to make sure it's only that she's tired and not anything more."

"Good idea."

Louise answered on the second ring. "Hello, darling. I'm fine. It's my age, not the cancer."

I smiled. "How did you know why I was calling?"

"Because you act happy-go-lucky, but deep down you're a worrywart, just like my grandson."

I lifted my eyes to meet Beck's. "I am nothing like your grandson."

Louise chuckled. "Maybe you two can make friends over dinner. I adjusted the reservation. It's under my name. Try to enjoy it."

I sighed. "Get some sleep. I'll text you in the morning."

"Goodnight, dear."

I swiped off.

"She's okay?" he asked.

"I think so. She sounds fine."

He nodded. "Why did you say we are nothing alike?"

"Oh. Because she said I was a worrywart like you."

"I'm glad you are. Before I came, I thought you were someone very different."

I gripped my hips. "Who did you think I was?"

He put his hand at the small of my back. "Why don't we head to dinner and save the argument for dessert. Where is the restaurant?"

"It's here. The Royal Bahamian. I saw a sign for it on my way to the beach this morning."

He held his other hand out. "Lead the way."

The restaurant was at the back of the hotel, with open windows and some tables facing the water. We gave Louise's name to the maître d' at the podium, and he smiled.

"Ah yes, our special guests for the evening."

Beck and I looked at each other. Before I could ask what that meant, we were directed to follow. We walked toward the back of the restaurant, so I thought we were going to be seated at an ocean-view table. But then the maître d' turned and led us down a hidden set of stairs. When we got to the bottom, he opened a door, and we were outside on the beach.

A table for two had been set up along the water's edge, under a rustling palm tree that the trade winds had bent to form an arch. White linens blew in the light breeze, while a glass hurricane lamp protected the candle in the middle from going out. I looked around. There wasn't another table anywhere on the beach.

"This is for us?"

"Yes, madam. Is it not to your satisfaction?"

"Oh no. It's amazing. I just... It's very romantic."

He smiled and looked between Beck and me. "Yes, it is."

"Wasn't our reservation supposed to be for three?"

The maître d's brows drew together. "For three?"

I looked to Beck. "Are you getting the feeling I'm getting?"

He raised an eyebrow. "That my grandmother is upstairs in her room practicing calypso and not tired at all?"

"She also told me to wear this blue dress, which I now know is *your favorite color*, when I mentioned I was going to wear a pink one, *my* favorite color."

"I'll have to remember to thank her for that part."

I looked to the maître d'. "Would you have another table? Maybe something inside?"

He frowned. "I'm afraid not. We're fully booked this evening. Your reservation is for the Taste of the Sea Experience. It's a seven-course tasting menu at this table only."

"Maybe someone wants to swap with us. The couple by the stairs with the woman in the red dress looked lovey-dovey. I could ask them if they'd like to switch?"

The poor guy looked horrified.

Beck pulled his billfold from his pants pocket and peeled off some bills, handing them to the man. "This table is fine. I'll take it from here. Thank you."

The maître d' couldn't get away fast enough.

I raised my hands in confusion. "Why did you do that?"

"Because you're being ridiculous."

My lips pursed. "How am I being ridiculous?"

"Can we just sit and eat? It's not going to kill you."

"Whatever." I rolled my eyes. "Let's get it over with."

Beck and I took our seats, and a waiter stopped by almost immediately with the wine list.

"Are you getting your usual whiskey?" I asked him.

"I'll have wine. Whatever you pick is fine."

I ordered a bottle of the red I'd been enjoying by the glass since we'd arrived. Once we were alone again, the only sound was the gentle lapping of waves against the shore less than five feet away. I watched the tide pull in and out a few times, mesmerized.

"It really is beautiful," I said.

"It is." Beck's voice was soft, but I caught a touch of something in it. So I looked up to figure out what it was and found him looking at me in *that* way. He hadn't been talking about the island.

"How about if we make peace for the evening?" I suggested. "A truce, perhaps. No arguing."

"What fun will that be?"

I extended my hand. "Are you up for the challenge?"

Beck took my hand, but brought it to his lips with a smirk and kissed the top. The warmth of his lips spread through me.

"Sure." He winked. "There's more than one way to skin a cat."

"You won't be skinning anything, trust me."

His grin widened. "I love a challenge."

The waiter came back and opened our wine. After a taste, he filled our glasses and departed. Beck looked over the candle at me while he rubbed his bottom lip with his thumb—something I'd noticed he did often.

"What are you pondering?" I asked.

"Who says I'm pondering? Maybe I'm just quietly enjoying the company."

I pointed to his hand, which was now on his wine glass. "You rub your mouth with your finger when you're debating asking something. You're not exactly a hard read."

"I suppose that's because I don't usually find it necessary to hide what's on my mind."

"So?" I held my hand out, palm up. "Spill then. Why start now?"

"I was trying to keep within your pact to not argue."

"Oh…" I nodded. "So whatever you're thinking is going to piss me off?"

He shook his head. "I'm still trying to figure out why you're taking this trip."

I rolled my eyes. "Again with that?"

"There has to be fifty years between you. Even you have to see that it's an unusual pairing."

"Forty-nine, and I wasn't aware of an age limit on friendships. Besides, you act like I'm doing your grandmother a favor by traveling with her, like she needs a chaperone or something,"

"She *did* get arrested just two days ago..."

"Whatever. She doesn't need a chaperone, and some days I think she's the one doing *me* a favor. Not the other way around. Some of the things we're doing together are things I want to do, you know."

"Like what?"

"Well, for example, we're here in the Bahamas because I want to go to Exuma. We were supposed to be spending a few nights on this island to gamble a little and have some fun, and then we were going to take a boat over to another island this morning."

"To do what?"

"To see my father."

"He's on vacation there?"

I shook my head. "He lives there. He owns a small hotel in Georgetown. I've never met him before."

Beck's brows puckered. "What do you mean, you've never met him?"

"Well, like you, my mother died when I was young. I was only three when she got sick. I don't even remember her, only from pictures. She was married to William, who I thought was my biological father until I was eighteen. Turned out the man who raised me by himself was my stepfather. He'd met my mother when she was five months pregnant with another man's baby and never cared that I wasn't his child. William was madly in love with my mother. Still is. Never remarried. He's the most amazing human I've ever met. When he told me the truth, he said he and my mother had never planned to keep it a secret, but after she died, he didn't want to take away the only other parent I'd ever known."

"Wow. Does your biological father know you exist?"

I shrugged. "I suppose. He did at one time, at least. My mother told him she was pregnant, and he sent some checks to help out when I was born. But William told him if he wasn't going to be involved in my life, the checks weren't necessary. He could take care of his family without a stranger's assistance. That was the last they heard from Alex Stewart. About five years ago, I did one of those 23andMe tests, and I got a few hits on my father's side. But no first-degree relatives like siblings or my father or anything. Then one day last year, I received an email saying I had new relatives. That happens frequently when you're on that site. Usually it's like a fifth-degree cousin or a great-great aunt. But that time when I went in to check, it said my father's name and the relationship was parent. He must've been notified of it, too. So I assume he knows I'm still kicking around."

"Did you ever make contact?"

"Nope. And neither did he. But I did research him online. That's how I found out he lives in the Bahamas now. Apparently he became an executive for a large hotel chain, and when he retired early, he bought a run-down hotel here and brought it back to life. I found an article when I was looking into him."

"If you got the email a year ago, what took you so long to come see him?"

"I'm not sure. I don't have that feeling of abandonment like some people do who never got to know their parents. I don't have questions I need answered or blame to hit him with. I guess I never had a sense of urgency."

"Why now then?"

I shrugged. "It just feels like the right time, I guess."

Beck nodded. "So what's your plan? Walk up to him and tell him you're his daughter?"

I sighed. "I don't have one."

"Sounds about right."

I chuckled. "Shut up."

Beck smiled. "You know your eyes lit up when you talked about your stepfather."

"He's truly an amazing man. Some women have issues because their father left or wasn't a stand-up guy who set a good example of how a woman should be treated, and it causes dysfunctional relationships with men. My daddy issue is that no one can live up to the standard William set. He's wise and fair, tough when he needs to be, but also a big teddy bear."

"If my daughter grows up and describes me half as good as that, I'll feel like I did my job in life."

My eyes roamed Beck's face as I sipped my wine. "I bet you're a really good dad."

"I try. I had a good parenting example to follow in Gram, and while my ex wasn't the greatest wife, she's a pretty good mom. But it sounds like we both got lucky that the right people jumped in to take over when we needed them."

My eyes welled up unexpectedly, and I took a deep breath, fighting tears and searching for something to say. "I'm sorry Louise is dying. I can't even imagine William..."

Beck reached across the table and swiped his thumb across my cheek, catching a tear. "Well, this evening took a turn for the depressing pretty quick, didn't it?"

I laughed and blotted my eyes with my napkin. "Let's talk about something more fun. Tell me about your brother, Jake. Your grandmother said you two are nothing alike."

Beck shook his head. "That's a compliment. Jake is ten years younger than me, but it often feels like he's my child. He works for me."

"What does he do?"

"I'm not really sure. I'll let you know when I figure it out."

I laughed. "No, really."

"He does marketing and public relations. He's actually pretty good at it. But don't tell him I said so. He came on board right out of college. I'm good at in-person stuff. Get me a meeting, and I can land most clients. But I'm not great at the non-in-person presentation prospective clients see—websites, prospectus design, getting articles printed in magazines. Jake has a boyish quality to him. He's never not smiling and always needs his shirt ironed. But it works for him."

"That's funny. Meanwhile you're brooding, impeccably groomed, and there's nothing boyish about you."

Beck's eyes glinted in the candlelight. "I'm glad you noticed. I'm all man, sweetheart."

I felt my cheeks heat. Luckily, the waiter arrived with our first tasting course, a single homemade potato chip with caviar atop. Absolutely delicious.

I wiped my mouth with my napkin. "So tell me, Beck. Why are you divorced?"

He sat back in his chair. "That's a big question."

I tilted my head. "I told you what happened between Richard and me. I think it's only fair that I get to hear why you're divorced."

"Alright. It's not pretty, but I would imagine most divorce stories aren't. Married a woman I met while I was in grad school. She was from Nevada and didn't have much family on the East Coast, except for an uncle who was a professor where we went to school. A few months after we started dating, a friend of mine told me he saw Carrie making out with Professor Burton. Carrie and I actually had a good laugh over it, because Professor Burton was her uncle. A few months after I graduated, Carrie got pregnant. I wasn't ready to be a dad, if I'm being honest, but it was coming whether I liked it or not, so I figured I might as well go all in. Six months after Maddie was born, I came home early from work and found Carrie in bed with Professor Burton."

My eyes went wide. "She was sleeping with her uncle?"

"That's of course what I thought, too. Turned out the guy wasn't her uncle. He wasn't related to Carrie at all. But they'd been caught a few times together, him driving her around and stuff. So they'd told people he was her uncle so it wouldn't raise suspicion. He's thirty-one years older, so it made sense. She'd been sleeping with him since freshman year, and he'd been promising he was going to leave his wife for her. When he didn't, she broke things off. Once we got married, the guy changed his tune and finally left his wife. Then Carrie was torn between the cushy life I was giving her and the guy she'd always wanted but could never have. When he started coming around again, she thought maybe she could have both. Ironically, I filed for divorce on our one-year wedding anniversary."

"Holy crap. What happened between her and the professor?"

"They're married now. He just turned sixty, and she's twenty-nine."

"Wow. That's a crazy story. Makes Richard tracking me seem normal."

He chuckled. "I'm glad my life can make you feel normal by comparison."

The waiter came with our second course, and after we finished that, the plates kept coming every five or ten minutes for the next hour.

Each portion was so small—just a taste—yet I was stuffed by the end. I leaned back and patted my stomach.

"I'm so full. But everything was delicious."

"It was. And I enjoyed the company. We seemed to have managed to keep to our pact."

"We did." I smiled. "Who knew you could be pleasant for that long?"

"Wiseass."

When the waiter came back the next time, Beck asked for the check, but apparently Louise had pre-paid the bill. We walked back through the restaurant and down the hall toward the elevator banks. As we passed the lobby bar, I heard a familiar, robust laugh.

Beck and I looked at each other before turning toward the far end of the bar where the sound had come from. A woman and two older gentlemen were sitting together, all three of them and the bartender laughing loudly.

"Apparently Louise is feeling better," I said.

Beck shook his head. "Why am I not the least bit surprised?"

We walked over together. When Louise saw us, her already-big smile widened. "There you are. How was dinner?"

Beck narrowed his eyes. "You would know if you hadn't been too exhausted to show up. Speaking of which, you seem to have gotten a miraculous second wind."

Louise didn't seem to give two shits whether we knew what she'd done. "I did. Come join us. Meet my new friends."

I took a seat, but Beck looked at his watch. "I actually have to run. I have a call with a business partner in China in a few minutes."

"Oh, okay." I forced a smile, but I was disappointed. As much as I didn't want to, I'd enjoyed Beck's company. He also wasn't bad to look at across the table. "Have a good night."

"You too."

After he left, Louise and I had a glass of wine with the two men she'd met at the bar. It turned out they were a couple on their honeymoon. They'd both been married to women for most of their lives and had only come out in recent years. After we finished, they said goodnight and headed out to take a walk on the beach.

"Make sure you keep your clothes on down there," Louise said. "We got ourselves in a bit of a pickle taking an evening skinny dip. Apparently that's illegal here."

The men chuckled. "Good to know."

I watched them walk off. "God, imagine spending your life not living your truth like that. I'm glad they found a way to be who they are before it was too late."

"So am I. Life is too short for regrets. Speaking of which, did you enjoy your dinner?"

I smiled. "Your grandson is very handsome, and tonight he was even good company. But I don't think pairing is wise, for more than one reason."

Louise waved me off. "I think you two could do each other some good. He needs to relax a little, and you could use someone to take care of you."

"He lives in New York. I'm moving back to California at the end of the summer. Plus, it's not the right time, Louise."

"Sometimes we find the right person at the wrong time. And we just have to trust fate."

CHAPTER 10
Beck

Two days later, we went to the courthouse for Gram and Nora's scheduled hearing. I was happily surprised when things went smoothly. They both pleaded no contest, and we paid a fine and were out the door fifteen minutes later. But I noticed Gram coughing a lot. Last night at dinner I'd noticed it once or twice, but it was more frequent today and had turned into a dry hack.

"You okay?" I asked her when we emerged from the courthouse. "Maybe we should go see a doctor?"

Gram cleared her throat and shook her head. "What for? We know what's wrong with me."

I pursed my lips. "Because there might be something they can give you to help. I know you don't want treatment, but that doesn't mean you can't take some medicine to ward off an infection or something."

Nora nodded. "Beck is right. You have a little wheeze going on, too. They might be able to give you a nebulizer treatment or an inhaler. Maybe even a cough suppressant or something."

"Fine. But we're going to a clinic here and not some hospital back home."

Nora shrugged. "Works for me."

I looked at my grandmother. "I say something, and you immediately fight me on it." I thumbed at Nora. "She says it, and it's a good idea."

"I'm sure it's because your grandmother is used to you trying to control her, so she automatically gets defensive."

My eyes narrowed. "I wasn't asking you."

Nora rolled her eyes. "Let's just go find a clinic."

Two hours later, Nora and I were in the waiting room of a packed urgent care. They'd taken Gram back almost a half hour ago.

The receptionist slid the glass window open and leaned to the opening. "Eleanor Sutton!"

Nora stood and went to the window. I followed.

"The doctor and your grandmother would like you to come back."

"It's not her grandmother," I said. "It's mine."

The woman looked me up and down. "You don't look like an Eleanor Sutton."

"I'm not. But the patient is my grandmother, not hers."

The woman shrugged. "Well, they asked for her. Not you."

"Maybe she's not dressed or something," Nora said, putting her hand on my arm. "Let me go back and see what's going on."

Left with no choice, I nodded.

Fifteen minutes later, I was growing impatient when Gram and Nora came out from the back. I stood. "I thought you were going to come get me?"

My grandmother rolled her eyes. "Oh, take a chill pill, Beck. The doctor just wanted to make sure Nora knew the

Heimlich maneuver in case food gets stuck. The tumor in my esophagus likes to catch things. It's why I'm coughing. Little pieces get stuck and irritate my throat."

"Can they shrink it?"

Gram frowned. "You know I'm not getting treatment."

"But...if it will help your quality of life..."

She sighed and held up a white paper bag. "He gave me some Alka-Seltzer and something called simethicone that will help my stomach produce gas. Gas increases the pressure on the esophagus and can help push the food loose. Now let's get out of here."

I stayed quiet as I drove Bonnie and Clyde back to the hotel. If I was going to try to talk my grandmother into some preventative treatment, I wasn't dumb enough to do it when I was being double-teamed. So I waited, and when I walked her to her room, I asked if we could talk for a few minutes. She said she needed to use the bathroom but would meet me down in the lobby for some coffee in fifteen minutes.

But it wasn't Gram who showed up.

"She's not coming," Nora said when she emerged from the elevator.

"Why not? She told me to meet her here."

Nora took the seat across from me. "I believe her exact words were 'Love that boy, but he's more stubborn than a mule sometimes.'"

"So she sent you?"

"No. I came on my own so you wouldn't worry about her when you lost your patience and inevitably went up to her room to look for her. She's not there."

My heart clenched. "Where'd she go?"

"I don't think you want to know."

I shook my head. "Where is she?"

"She went to Frieda's to play cards."

"Frieda?"

"One of the women we met in jail. She has an afternoon game and told Louise to stop in any time."

"How'd she get there?"

"She said the concierge would grab her a cab."

I blew out a deep breath. "She's a piece of work. Thanks for telling me."

Nora covered my hand with hers. "I promise I will keep an eye on her."

I scoffed. "Great. Will that be from two-thousand feet while you both have parachutes on?"

"I'll watch her then, too." She smiled and stood. "I'm going to go join them and play some cards."

"At the illegal gambling house where you met the proprietor in prison?"

"Quit being such a buzzkill. Would you like to come?"

I shook my head. "I think I'll pass. I have work to do anyway."

She shrugged. "Well, I'm not missing out on an opportunity to enjoy myself with Louise while I can."

Nora walked off. It only took about ten seconds for me to realize what she'd said. *"While I can."* My heart squeezed. *Fuck.* She was right. Work could wait. I was the boss anyway.

I stood and yelled to Nora. "Wait up!"

∽

"Who brought the Bahamian sunshine?" A woman with a heavy island accent stopped dealing cards and looked up at us. She had on a colorful headwrap and a bright shade of peach lipstick.

I looked behind me, trying to figure out what she was referring to. Nora chuckled. "Pretty sure that's you, Beck."

"That's my grandson." Gram leaned back in her chair with a smile. Not to be outdone by the colorful headwrap lady, she'd worn a sparkly shirt and matching sparkling eyeshadow. "Handsome but bossy."

One of the ladies at the table wiggled her brows. She had to be close to seventy. "I like 'em bossy."

I guess my face showed I wasn't so sure what to make of the crew, because they all laughed. "Lighten up, boy. Come on in. Any friend of Big Momma is a friend of ours."

"Big Momma?"

Nora leaned over. "That's what they call Louise. It works, right?"

This was going to be one hell of an afternoon.

Nora and I joined the group at the table. Aside from Frieda, the owner, there was a guy they called Sugar. The lady who liked 'em bossy was Rowan, and last there was another man they called Slim, who was anything but. My grandmother was seated at the end, smoking a cigar.

When she saw my eyes on it, she shrugged. "Give me a break, kid. What's it gonna do? Give me cancer?"

I shook my head but managed to bite my tongue. They seemed to be playing blackjack. "Mind if we join?" I asked.

"Sure thing. I'm not gonna complain about looking at that pretty face up close, sunshine." The woman extended her hand and leaned over the table. "Frieda Ellington. Good to meet you."

I guess Vegas-style card rules didn't apply here. A patron could never touch hands with the dealer. I shook. "Beck Cross."

Nora smiled. "Hi, Frieda. It's nice to see you."

"You're looking a little better than the last time I saw you."

Nora laughed. "I hope so. We got arrested after a long swim in the ocean, and I was wearing a uniform four sizes too big that I'd stolen."

Nora and I took the two open seats. They were opposite each other, which worked for me. Frieda wasn't the only one who would enjoy the view today.

I pulled my wallet from my pocket and opened it, but Frieda motioned no with her hand. "Day games are for fun with friends. We only take live action at night."

"Oh. Okay."

She gathered two stacks of chips and pushed them across the table to me. "But we do have a jackpot at the end. Big winner for the day gets to pick one thing from anyone at the table. Can be the shirt you're wearing or a ride home. We keep it simple."

I looked down at my watch. "They can pick anything?"

She smiled. "Don't worry about that fancy thing on your wrist. We have a twenty-five-dollar max value. But you better hope Rowan here doesn't win. She's been known to take a kiss."

Rowan flashed a yellow-toothy smile. I might've preferred to give up my watch.

CHAPTER 11

Nora

I was a nervous wreck when we arrived on Exuma the next day. I'd booked a different hotel than the one my father owned, not wanting to be stuck there if things didn't go well. I still didn't have a plan for what the heck I was going to say when I saw him—assuming he was even at the hotel today. But it seemed like one of those things in life you couldn't plan. Whatever was going to happen would happen.

Louise had offered to come with me, but I needed to do this alone. So after we checked into our hotel, she went to relax at the pool. Beck wasn't able to get a flight home until tomorrow, so he'd decided to join us on our boat trip to Exuma. He was in his room doing some work, and I was supposed to be heading four miles down the road to the Sunset Hotel. But I'd made a pit stop at our hotel bar about an hour and a half ago, and I hadn't worked up the courage to go any farther just yet.

I was on my second glass of wine when a deep voice startled me.

"Back so soon?"

Beck.

I let out an exaggerated sigh. "I haven't left yet."

"You need a ride?"

I shook my head. "No. There're cabs sitting around out front waiting for people who need rides. And the concierge said if for some reason there aren't any, he can call and have one here in five minutes or less."

Beck eyed my almost-drained wine glass. "Working on liquid courage?"

"Are you going to make fun of me if I say yes?"

"Nah. I had two fingers of scotch in my room before I got the balls to come back down to the bar after my Zoom call the night we met. You can be a little intimidating."

My eyebrows climbed toward my hairline. "*You* were intimidated by *me*? You're lying."

He motioned to the open seat next to me. "You want some company?"

"Sure."

Beck sat down. The bartender walked over. "What can I get you?"

"Can I have a sparkling water, please?"

"Coming right up."

The bartender pointed to me. "You want a refill?"

"What the hell. Why not?"

When he walked away, Beck looked me over. "You're wearing your favorite color today instead of mine."

I glanced down. I'd completely forgotten what I had on—a pale pink sundress. "I'm actually more of a hot pink fan than light pink. But that doesn't wear so well. You have a good memory though."

Beck tapped his pointer to his temple. "Hard to forget. I won't be getting the image of you in that blue dress out of my head anytime soon."

I hid my blush by finishing off the last drops in my glass before the bartender brought my refill. "You finished your work already?"

"Not yet. I was heading to the business center to pick up some documents my assistant emailed over for me to sign. The bar is on the way."

"Oh. Well, don't let me keep you. I'll be fine."

"You want to role play?"

"Pardon?"

He gave me a slow, sexy smile. "Believe it or not, that wasn't meant to be dirty. You're nervous. So pretend I'm your father and say whatever you're planning on saying to him. We'll do a little dry run."

I bit my lip. "That's the problem. I don't have anything planned."

Beck shrugged. "We'll freestyle then. Improvise." He lifted his chin. "Close your eyes for a minute. Take a few deep breaths, maybe shake out your arms and roll your shoulders, and then just shoot from the hip."

I nodded. Why not? So I did as Beck suggested and let myself relax as much as possible. Then I turned to face him head on.

"Hi." I smiled. "Are you Alex Stewart?"

Beck kept a straight face. "I am. How can I help you?"

I drew a complete blank and stared at him. "Holy shit, Beck. What the hell am I going to say to this man?"

"I don't know. How about starting by asking him if he remembers your mother?"

"Oh. Yeah...that's a good idea. It's an icebreaker."

Beck held his hand out. "Go ahead. Try it out."

I straightened in my chair. "Hi. Are you Alex Stewart?"

"I am. How can I help you?"

I took a deep breath. "This might be a strange question, but do you remember a woman named Erica Sutton?" I shook my head. "Sorry. Erica Kerrigan. Kerrigan is her maiden name."

"Yes. What about her?"

"Well, she's...*my mom*."

"Okay..."

"Oh gosh. Do you think he won't get it when I say that, and I'll have to say more?"

Beck shrugged. "No idea. But might as well prepare for the worst."

"You're right. Okay. Let me back up a question then. Do you remember a woman named Erica Kerrigan?"

"No."

I blinked a few times. "What do you mean, no?"

"I don't remember her."

"No, Beck. You were supposed to say you do, like you did the first time."

"This is improv. You gotta go with the flow. I'm guessing what he's going to say."

"Alright. Let's just continue then."

Beck went back into character. "I don't remember any Erica Kerrigan."

"How could you not remember her? You got her pregnant." I covered my mouth. "Oh shit. Should I not say that?"

"I think you should say whatever you want to say. If it upsets you that he doesn't remember a woman he got pregnant, let him know that."

"Okay. What's he going to say after I remind him he got her pregnant?"

"I'm not sure."

"Well, what would you say if a girl walked up to you and said you got her mom pregnant?"

"I guess I'd be curious why the hell I was finding out only after the child was old enough to talk. But in your case, it's different because your mother did tell him about you. So it shouldn't come as a total shock."

The bartender came over with my wine and Beck's sparkling water. I knew my limits. Two glasses helped me relax. Well, at least normally it did. But the third one would put me over the edge and impair my judgment.

I sighed and motioned to my drink. "I think I'm going to skip that after all. One more glass and I either won't go or shouldn't go."

Beck slid my glass back and moved his in front of me. "Have some water."

"Thanks."

"How about I drive you there?"

"Oh, no. That's not necessary. It's only a few miles away. I can take a cab."

"Yes, but the cab driver isn't going to talk you down off the ledge when you pull up."

I smiled sadly. "That's a good point. You sure you don't mind?"

Beck shook his head. "Not at all."

The Sunset Hotel looked just like the pictures on its website. Painted in Caribbean green, with bright white shutters and trim, it had that laid-back, island vibe. Two employees in floral uniforms danced to overhead reggae music as we pulled up. The taller of the two men opened my door with a smile.

"Welcome to the Sunset Hotel." He offered a hand to help me out of the car. "Are you checking in today?"

"Umm... No. There's a bar here, right? I just came to have a drink."

"Our bar is the place to be for the sunset." He gestured to the open-air lobby. "You just go straight through to the back and down the stairs. You can't miss it."

Beck walked around the car. "You want me to come with you?"

"Oh no. I've interrupted your day enough. You have work to do."

"It can wait."

"I can't ask you to do this with me..."

"You didn't ask. I offered. I'll just stick in the background in case you need me. Let you do your own thing."

My palms were sweating, and I felt a little lightheaded. The thought of having someone I knew nearby did bring me comfort. So I nodded. "Okay. Thank you."

Beck tossed the keys to the valet. "Keep it for a little while?"

"Sure thing, mister."

My heart raced as I walked into the hotel. I probably looked like a criminal, the way my eyes darted from person to person. Beck wrapped a hand around my hip and gently squeezed as he leaned in and whispered, "Breathe, sweetheart."

I nodded and inhaled deeply. Once we were through the lobby, steps led down to an outside patio. The beach bar was visible below.

Beck and I stopped. "No one has looked old enough to be your father so far. So I take it we haven't passed him yet?"

I shook my head.

"What does he look like?"

"Oh." I pulled out my cell. "I can show you." I typed into my phone and scrolled around the hotel's website. "He looks like an aging beach bum—sun-bleached, sandy colored, shoulder-length hair. Tan. Sunglasses that hang around his neck from a Croakie." I found the picture I was looking for under the *About Us* tab and turned my phone to show Beck.

He smiled. "Exactly how I would've pictured him from your description. Thanks. At least now I can help you keep an eye out." He looked down at the bar below. "Did you really want to go to the bar, or did you want to take a look around first?"

"His bio says he can often be found working behind the beach bar, barefoot."

"Alright then. You ready?"

I shook my head. "No."

Beck chuckled. "Let's go anyway."

We walked side by side down the stairs to the beach. The bar had a thatched-palm roof that rustled in the breeze and bright blue seating around three sides. A few tables were off to one side, one of which was occupied by a couple in bathing suits.

I stopped as we reached the wooden path, less than a hundred feet away. "I think that's him."

Beck's eyes zoned in on the man behind the bar. Sunglasses on top of his head held shaggy hair back, and he had a cigarette between his teeth as he opened a beer bottle. Beck nodded. "Certainly didn't do any false advertising. I think that's the same shirt he had on in the picture on the website."

I couldn't stop staring. "He's nothing like William."

"No?"

I shook my head. "William is clean-cut. He gets up at the crack of dawn and runs five miles a day—wearing shorts and a shirt with a reflective stripe for safety."

"You going to be okay?" he asked.

I swallowed and nodded.

"Why don't you sit at the bar, and I'll take a seat at one of the tables, give you some privacy."

I took a deep breath. "Okay."

Beck smiled. "You got this."

The short path that led to the bar felt more like a gangplank. When we reached the bar area, Beck winked at me and kept walking toward an empty table. I took the closest seat to him, which happened to be the farthest from the bartender.

I thought I'd get a minute to pull myself together, but my butt cheeks were barely on the stool when the man behind the bar walked over. The sunglasses that had been on top of his head now covered his eyes. He flashed a welcoming smile.

"Hey, beautiful. What can I get you?"

Oh God. I felt queasy, like I might throw up. But apparently, whatever was going on internally didn't show on the outside. Or at least the bartender didn't seem to notice. Because he waited, as if I was supposed to respond rather than puke all over his bar.

"Umm... I'll take a piña colada."

"You got it."

My eyes followed as he walked to the other end of the bar and tossed some things into a blender. I searched his profile for any resemblance.

Maybe we have the same chin? Though it was hard to tell with all that scruff on his face.

His cheekbones were high, but so were my mom's, and no one but her was ever going to get credit for any of my good features. When he pressed the button and the blender whirred to life, I nearly jumped out of my seat. I needed to get a hold of myself.

Too soon, the man—*my father*—walked back to my end of the bar. He set the drink in front of me, and I hoped he would just go back to whatever he'd been doing before I sat down. But no such luck. He lifted a knee onto something behind the bar and leaned.

"Haven't seen you around before. You just check in today?"

My hands were shaking. "Oh... I'm not staying here. I just came to have a drink."

He covered his heart with his hand. "Not staying here? That hurts. There's no better place to stay than the Sunset." He pushed the sunglasses back on top of his head and revealed a set of familiar bright green eyes that popped from his tanned skin. "What does your hotel have that the Sunset doesn't?"

Looking into his eyes was like looking in the mirror. Our eyes were identical in color. If you asked ten people who met me what color my eyes were, you'd get five different answers. They weren't blue. They weren't green. They were somewhere in between. On a cloudy day, some might even call them gray. When I was younger, I'd never been certain what box to check when a form asked for eye color—though I'd settled on green as a teenager and made it official with my license and passport. I couldn't tell you how many times I'd heard someone say they'd never seen eyes my color. And honestly, I hadn't either. Until now.

But I was the only one who'd noticed. Because while I was stupefied and unable to do anything but stare, the man with my eyes seemed to be waiting for something.

Shit. What did he ask?

Something about the sunset?

"I'm sorry, what did you ask?"

"I asked what your hotel has that this one doesn't? But let me tell you what this one has that yours doesn't instead."

"Okay..."

He pointed two thumbs at himself. "Alex Stewart."

Confirmation of this man's identity hit me hard. "Alex...Stewart?" For some reason, it came out like a question.

"It has a nice ring to it on your tongue. And you are?"

My heart pounded, and a sheen of sweat formed on my forehead. Did he know what my mother had named me? Should I make up a fake name?

He stood so close, just on the other side of the narrow bar, and watched me so intently, there wasn't a lot of time for deliberation. So I went with the truth, which might be telling him without telling him.

"My name is Nora Sutton."

I held my breath and waited for something to register on his face—surprise, shock, confusion, even a vague sense of familiarity. But...nothing. So I pushed a little more.

"Actually, my name is Eleanor Sutton. I was named after my grandmother. Though no one calls me Eleanor. Not since my mom passed. Well, except my friend Louise sometimes. But I go by Nora."

Not a batted eyelash.

Not a squint.

Definitely no jaw dropping in shock.

Nothing...

It made my insides feel hollow.

My own father didn't recognize me. Not by face. Or by name. Even if you've had no contact with your child for nearly thirty years, how do you forget her name once you've been told?

"So you here by yourself, Eleanor—Nora Sutton?" he asked.

I shook my head. "I'm traveling with a friend."

"Is she as pretty as you?"

Oh Jesus. Is he flirting with me? When I walked up, he called me beautiful. But I'd chalked it up to an island bartender being friendly. But now, the hollow I'd felt inside started to fill—with anger.

"She is," I said. "And she's closer to your age, too."

I had one hand casually resting on the bar. Alex reached across and stroked his finger along the top. My anger bubbled to rage.

"Are you married, Alex?"

"Let's not spoil the moment, babe."

Ugh. Yet I managed to smile. It was an evil one with clenched teeth, but a man who didn't recognize his own daughter's name surely was too oblivious to notice.

"Have any children?" I asked.

"Nope."

"Why not?"

"Never wanted any."

That was a kick in the gut. My emotions swung from sad to angry and back to sad again like a ping-pong match.

"How long are you in town for?" he asked.

"Just the night."

"How about if I show you the island?"

I narrowed my eyes. "Is that a service you offer? Every person who passes through this place gets a free tour of the island?"

The asshole seemed to be enjoying our banter. He flashed a smarmy smile.

"Only the beautiful ones. So whadda you say? I can get someone to cover me. I've got an open-air Jeep parked right out front."

"No thanks." I stood. This had been a mistake. A giant one.

"Where you going? You haven't even touched your drink."

"Somewhere there's better company." I turned away, but stopped and looked back. "You know what? You should learn to have more respect for women. A man your age should be keeping an eye on a lady sitting at the bar by herself, not eyeing who he can take advantage of."

Alex's face twisted. "You're all the same. Pretty girls who expect free drinks for nothing in return. That's not the way the world works, babe."

My eyes widened. There was so much anger and disappointment inside me. So I expressed it the only way I could at the moment. I picked up the piña colada I hadn't touched and tossed the contents of the glass in his face. "Nice to meet you, Alex Stewart."

Before he could wipe the frosty drink from his eyes, Beck was up and over the bar with my father's shirt in his grip.

Oh shit.

He looked like he was about to kill.

"Beck, no!"

Anger seeped from his pores. "What the fuck did this guy do to you?"

I waved my hands. "He didn't do anything. Let's just go."

When Beck didn't loosen his grip on Alex, I leaned across the bar and touched his shoulder.

"Beck, please. It's fine. I just want to get out of here."

He let go, lifting his chin to my unsuspecting father. "You're fucking lucky, buddy."

My father just stood there, wiping the drink from his face, as Beck hopped back over the bar.

"You sure you're alright?" Beck asked.

I shook my head. "I just want to get out of here."

He wrapped an arm around my waist and navigated us back through the hotel. Neither of us said a word as we walked up the stairs, into the lobby, and waited for the valet to bring Beck's rental car. The silence continued as we got in, and Beck drove white-knuckled down the road. We'd gone about a mile when he pulled into the parking lot of a boarded-up laundromat.

He slammed the gear shifter into park and turned to face me. His jaw was hard and rigid. "What happened? Are you sure you're okay?"

I'd managed to stuff down the emotions of the last hour. But now they all rushed to the surface at once. My mouth trembled as I spoke. "He...hit on me."

Beck's face was positively murderous. He mumbled a string of curses under his breath.

I fought the burn of tears. "I said my name—he didn't even recognize it. How does a person not recognize the name of their child? Even if he'd only heard it once in his life. My name is Eleanor. It's not like it's Katelyn or Ashley." Tears welled in my eyes. "How many Eleanors do you know?"

Beck didn't say a word. His eyes followed a tear as it streaked down my face. Then he abruptly got out of the car and walked around to my side. He opened the passenger door and held out a hand for me. Once I was standing, he wrapped me in his arms. It shocked the shit out of me, but it was also exactly what I needed. The independent part of me wanted to wiggle out, tell him I was fine and it wasn't a big deal. But the part of me that few had ever seen needed this so much.

Every hurt I'd felt over the last eleven years about a father who didn't want me bubbled to the surface. And I cried. And cried. Ugly, snot-leaking, breath-catching cries. Beck held me so tightly, there was a good chance I'd be bruised tomorrow. But I didn't care. When the sobs finally subsided, he pulled back to look at me.

"Did you get it out?"

I laughed through the last of my emotions. "I did. And it's all over your shirt."

Beck smiled. "It's okay. I have another one."

He loosened his hold, but didn't let go until my breathing returned to normal.

"You want to talk about it?"

I shook my head. "Not really. There's not much more than I told you."

"The offer isn't limited to talking about what happened just now."

I forced a smile. "Thanks. But I think I'm okay."

Beck put his hands on his hips. "What do you want to do? You want to go back to the hotel?"

I shook my head. "Let's go get drunk at some hole-in-the-wall local place."

A smile spread across Beck's face. "Now you're talking..."

CHAPTER 12

Beck

"We should probably set some ground rules before I get drunk." Nora hiccupped and covered her mouth.

I arched a brow. "Before?"

She shrugged. "Whatever. Drunker? Is that a word? It sounds funny. Druuunkerrrrrr. Drunk-her. Wait, if you drink more after you're already drunk, are you drunk-him?"

I chuckled. Nora and I had found a local bar, though it wasn't a hole-in-the-wall like she'd requested. Actually, there weren't even any walls. About a mile down the road from where we'd stopped, there had been a painted wooden sign for a beach bar. I followed it down a bumpy dirt road until we arrived at a place that was little more than a metal awning covering a local guy with a dozen bottles of liquor. He had a bunch of old beach chairs set up on the sand and played music from what looked like a thirty-year-old boombox. It was perfect. I'd had one drink to Nora's two, and since she was half the size of me, she was feeling no pain right about now.

"What rules did you want to set, Drunker?"

She hiccupped again and waved her pointer in my face. "No hanky panky. Sometimes when I get tipsy, I get horny."

"I thought we'd already established that wasn't my style. I didn't take you up on your invitation the night we met because I thought you'd had too much to drink. And I didn't know you were my grandmother's partner in crime back then."

Nora sucked her Bahama Mama through a straw. "It's not you I'm worried about."

"Are you saying you don't think you can control yourself around me, Eleanor?"

She frowned. "Eleanor. How could he not remember a child named Eleanor?"

"It's his loss, sweetheart."

"Thank you for saying that." She looked out to the ocean. "I don't understand how something could feel like it was missing when I had so much love in my life from William."

"I think it's probably normal to be curious, to want to know who you came from."

I didn't say it, but I was curious to know where she'd come from too. For some fucked-up reason, I wanted to meet the stepfather she spoke so highly of. That wasn't normal for me. Ever since my divorce, if I went out with a woman a few times and she mentioned *meeting her parents*, I ran for the hills. Yet I was the one thinking it now.

Nora shook her head. "I didn't tell him. William, I mean. He doesn't know I joined 23andMe and found my father—I mean, my sperm donor. I wouldn't want him to feel like he wasn't enough. Because he was. He was such a good dad."

"Then he doesn't have to know. But it sounds like he's the type of person who would understand, anyway."

She sighed. "Do you get to spend a lot of time with your daughter?"

"Her mother and I split custody. So Maddie stays with me three nights one week and four the next."

"Wow. So you do baths and dinner and all that domestic stuff?"

"I have a sitter who picks her up from school in the afternoon, and she also handles dinner prep most weeknights. But I cook when I have Maddie on the weekends."

Nora smiled. "Tell me about her. Does she take dance classes and wear a tutu? Have her father's attitude?"

"Maddie marches to the beat of her own drum. She's not into dance as much as earning Girl Scout badges."

"Oh, she's a Girl Scout?"

I shook my head. "Nope. She has no interest in joining Brownies or Girl Scouts, but she's obsessed with earning badges. About a year ago, she watched a movie where the little girl was a Girl Scout trying to earn a wilderness badge. The next week, she came home from school with a book of all the badges from the library. There are a hundred and thirty-five of those damn things, you know. My daughter is intent on earning every single one. Louise has even indulged her with a full set of all the badges. I'm not sure where she got them. I wouldn't put it past her to have mugged a scout leader to make Maddie happy. But I'd like to kill her for not removing the *bugling* badge. To earn it, you have to be able to play ten bugle calls. Taps is pretty painful when performed by a six-year-old."

Nora covered her mouth. "Oh my God. That's hysterical. So who decides if she's earned the badges if she's not actually in Scouts?"

'That would be me."

"How many has she earned so far?"

"I think we're up to seventeen. In the fall, we'll go camping so she can earn her wilderness badge. I bought blow-up mattresses, but I've been told we have to sleep in sleeping bags on the ground. I'm not looking forward to that part."

Nora's eyes warmed. "You're like William—a big, tough guy on the outside, but the inside is filled with mush."

"You wouldn't say that if you knew how I'd failed her on the invention badge."

"Why did you fail her?"

"She invented these inserts that go in your shoes to keep your feet warm."

Nora's forehead wrinkled. "You mean like socks?"

I deadpanned. "Exactly. *Socks.*"

We laughed, and I shook my head. "I guess I should be glad she eased up on her other hobby, the one she had before earning Girl Scout badges."

"What was the other hobby?"

"Searching real estate listings."

"Like, regular house listings?"

"Yep. She would spend hours looking through the listings with photos. Sometimes she'd find features we don't have at home and get upset when I wouldn't add them to our place."

"Like what?"

"Well, for one, she wanted me to add a dog-washing station."

"That could be useful at least."

"We don't have a dog."

Nora laughed. "Oh my God."

SOMETHING UNEXPECTED

"Tell me about it. Another time she asked me to add a urinal. Not sure what she was going to do with that."

"Does Maddie look like you?"

"You tell me..." I pulled up a selfie she'd taken last week and turned the phone screen to Nora.

"Oh my gosh." She took my phone from my hand. "Look at all that blond curly hair."

"She gets that from her mother."

"But she has your aquamarine eyes though. And your nice full lips. She's beautiful, Beck."

"Thanks. She keeps me on my toes."

"I bet." She handed me back my phone. "Maddie sounds pretty awesome. And for the record, her dad sounds pretty great, too." Nora held up her drink, which was three-quarters of the way gone, and made a toast. "To good dads."

I smiled. "And to the little girls who made us better men."

Nora finished off that drink and another. After that, she started to slur her words.

"What do you say we go back to the hotel?" I asked.

She leaned close. "You want to come back to my room?"

I groaned and stood. "Yes, I do. But no, I won't. I think you've had enough of asshole men for one day."

She held out her hand. "Help me up?"

I did, and when she stood, she fell forward and wrapped her arms around my neck. Her gorgeous tits pushed up against me. "How about if I just get you off?" she whispered. "Then you won't be taking advantage of me."

In a weaker moment, I might've accepted that logic. But Nora was pretty shitfaced. "I would like nothing more, but I'm going to have to take a rain check."

114

Her response was to lick a line from the bottom of my neck up to my ear. I groaned again. "Definitely gotta get you somewhere safe. Like behind a steel door."

Since I'd been drinking too, I asked the guy who ran the makeshift bar if it was alright to leave the rental car here until tomorrow morning, and if he could call a taxi. He promptly pulled a wooden sign that read *Be back in five minutes* from his backpack and asked us to follow him. Then he drove us to the hotel for eight bucks.

I kept one arm wrapped around Nora's waist as we walked through the lobby and rode the elevator up to her room. It took her three tries to swipe her room key, but she managed to open the door.

I waited in the doorway to make sure she'd be okay.

"Will you stay until I fall asleep?" she said. "I won't attack you, I promise."

Being in a room with not much more than a bed and this gorgeous woman wasn't a smart idea. But she wobbled trying to pull off one of her sandals, and I wasn't so sure I should leave her either. So I let the door close behind me.

Nora sat down on the bed and lifted one leg. "Will you take this one off for me?"

I swallowed, but kneeled down at the foot of the bed and unbuckled the sandal. She dug her fingers into my hair and started to massage my scalp. It felt good, and I couldn't help but think how I'd like her to yank on my hair as I buried my face between her legs. Finding myself leaning closer to that area, I quickly pulled off the shoe and stood.

"You think you'll be okay? I really need to go."

She pouted. "Why?"

"Because apparently I'm not as much of a gentleman as I like to think I am."

"Just let me get changed, and you can tuck me in and go."

Nora walked a crooked line to the bathroom and disappeared inside for a few minutes. She came out wearing only a V-neck LA Dodgers T-shirt, with a hem that barely covered her ass. And a blind man couldn't have missed that she'd taken off her bra.

I took a few steps back as she crossed the room and climbed into bed. She laid on her side with her hands tucked under her cheek and shut her eyes. "You can tuck me in now."

I shook my head and grumbled under my breath. Nevertheless, I walked to the bed, pulled up the covers, and kissed her forehead. "The Dodgers suck, by the way."

"They're the best team in baseball."

"That would be the Yankees, sweetheart."

A goofy smile spread across her face. "Wanna fight about it?"

"Not a chance." I chuckled. "Goodnight, Nora."

"Goodnight, Beck. I owe you one."

"I doubt you'll ever find me drunk enough that I need to be tucked in."

She smiled. "I didn't mean I owed you a tuck-in. I meant I owed you a blowjob."

By the time I got to the door, I could hear the soft purr of her snore. So Nora didn't hear the last thing I said.

"I plan to collect, sweetheart. Really soon."

CHAPTER 13

Beck

It's been too damn long.

The following week, I forced myself to go out, though I hadn't been in the mood at all. But one look at Chelsea Redmond in the two-piece dress she had on, her nipples piercing through the silky material of the top, and I was glad she'd been persistent.

She took the seat next to me at the bar after returning from the bathroom and leaned to whisper, "The way you were just watching me. It looked like you want to skip dinner." She gave me a sultry smile. "We can do that, if you'd like."

I'm definitely getting laid. Thank fuck.

Not that I'd doubted Chelsea would be up for it. We'd gone out a few times before, and every time the evening ended the same way—with me back at her place. But I had started to worry *I* wouldn't be up for it.

I hadn't been in the mood lately. Well, that's not entirely true. It was more like I hadn't been in the mood to have sex with anyone else. My right hand had been there for the task plenty of times in recent days—twice yesterday after Nora had posted videos on her blog of her riding a horse at the ranch she and my grandmother were visiting. *Up and down. Up and down.* Fuck, I couldn't think about that now or I'd wind up needing to use the men's room. Plus, it was a dick move to do that shit while I was out with Chelsea.

The hostess walked over, letting us know our table was ready. I was glad, because Chelsea hadn't been kidding about her offer.

"Are we staying?" she said.

I took her hand and yanked her from her seat, wrapping her in my arms. "Yeah, I'm gonna feed you first," I whispered in her ear. "You're going to need the energy later."

Chelsea rubbed her tits against me and preened. "I can't wait."

Once seated, we ordered a bottle of wine, and I listened to stories of all the famous people she'd met since the last time I saw her. Chelsea was a flight attendant on a private airline that catered to Hollywood types. I wasn't much into celebrity gossip, but I nodded along and tried not to let my mind wander too much. She was in the middle of some story about a musician who threw a hissy fit because they didn't have the right brand of sparkling water when my cell buzzed on the table.

It was face down, but I glanced over at it. Not too many people would text me on a Friday night at nine o'clock. My brother, Jake, maybe—though he'd more than likely be out partying by now. So I flipped my phone over. *Nora* flashed on the screen.

It's probably just another video or some pics of Gram. Nora was the absolute last person I should've opened a text from on a date. I'd been having enough trouble getting her out of my mind since I'd returned from the Bahamas.

I'm not going to open it.

Focus on your date—the ready, willing, and very *able woman sitting in front of you.*

I dragged my eyes back to Chelsea, to the creamy skin on her delicate neck, and all of the things I would be doing to it in a few hours. But then my cell buzzed again. And I couldn't stop myself from staring at Nora's name.

This time, instead of giving me a pass, Chelsea gestured to my phone. "Do you need to get that? Who's Nora?"

I didn't want her to feel bad, so I used the truth to my advantage. "Sorry. She's the woman traveling with my grandmother." I realized I'd never told Chelsea that my grandmother was sick, or even that she was the woman who'd raised me. We didn't have that type of relationship. So I added, "My grandmother has some health issues."

"Oh. I'm sorry. Why don't you get it then?"

Great. Now I had the woman I should be paying attention to urging me to check in with the one I shouldn't be focused on. I shook my head. "Sorry. I'll just be a minute."

I swiped my phone to find a few pictures—my grandmother in a cowboy hat on a horse, my grandmother swinging a lasso around her head while standing in a pen with a steer, some shots of her laughing and roasting marshmallows around a campfire—but it was the last picture that stopped me in my tracks. Nora sat on a wooden fence, wearing black fringe chaps and a matching cowboy hat. Her smile stretched ear to ear, and I couldn't stop staring. I was a little annoyed when Chelsea interrupted.

"What are the pictures of?" she asked.

"Just some pictures of them riding horses and stuff. They're at a ranch in Montana."

"I thought you said your grandmother was sick?"

I had said her health wasn't good, not that she was sick. But I also didn't feel like explaining or sharing what was going on. "Looks like she's feeling better."

Chelsea smiled. "Oh, that's great. Can I see?"

My brows drew together.

She gestured to the phone. "The pictures of your grandmother."

"Oh. Yeah. I guess so."

I didn't feel like sharing, yet I swiped back to the first picture and turned the phone so she could see. Chelsea plucked the phone from my hand and swiped through them all. She stopped at the last one, too.

"Who's this?"

"Nora. My grandmother's friend."

Chelsea looked up at me. "She's beautiful."

I shrugged, trying to cut off the conversation. Luckily, the waiter came by and took care of that for me. I slipped my phone from Chelsea's hand, and by the time we were done ordering dinner, my date seemed to have forgotten all about the photos. She went back to rambling on about another celebrity.

But I couldn't get the pictures out of my mind—not during dinner and not after, when Chelsea invited me back to her place.

I wanted to want to go home with her in the worst way. Lord knows I hadn't had sex in what felt like forever. But that ship had now sailed. It made me miserable to decline.

"I have an early morning, so I think I'm going to head home."

Chelsea looked as confused as my insides felt. "Really?" She pushed her bottom lip into a pout. "Come for an hour or two. It's only ten thirty."

"Another time, maybe?"

She shrugged. "Well, I guess it's a good sign that we went out even if you weren't looking to get laid. I was starting to think you were only interested in one thing."

Shit. Talk about reading the room wrong. Now she thought I was interested in more than just sex, when I wasn't even interested in that with her anymore. I'd have to cut things off entirely after tonight. But right now, I didn't feel like having that conversation. I just wanted to go home.

"I'll grab us a cab and have them drop you off first."

A half hour later, I tossed my keys on the kitchen counter. Bitsy greeted me with her usual growling and barking, then ran down the hall to Maddie's room, though my daughter wouldn't be back for a few more days.

I wasn't tired, so I headed to the cabinet and poured two fingers of whiskey. Kicking off my shoes, I put my feet up on the coffee table and grabbed the remote. Nothing caught my attention as I flicked around, so I turned the TV back off and picked up my laptop to check my calendar for tomorrow instead. But it opened to the last website I'd visited—Nora's blog.

Great. Just great.

She'd posted another video, too.

It's probably more of her riding. Because the hour I'd already spent watching the thirty-second recording of her going *up and down, up and down* wasn't enough. The woman was a menace. I needed to ignore the video, wipe my search history from my laptop's memory, and block her webpage.

Yeah, that's what I'll do.

I sucked back a mouthful of my drink, staring at the screen.

Oh, who the fuck am I kidding?

I'd left a sure thing to come home because a picture had distracted me. There wasn't a chance in hell that I was leaving this video unwatched. So I stopped fighting it and hit play.

"Howdy, y'all." Nora smiled at the camera. "How did that sound? Can I pull off a howdy? I kind of like it. It's friendlier than a New York chin lift and *what's up*, don't you think? Anywho... for those of you joining our vlog for the first time, welcome to *Live Like You're Dying*, episode eighteen—a docuseries of the extraordinary end of Louise Aster's life. If you'd like to know more about Louise's diagnosis and treatment decisions..." Nora pointed down, and some words popped up on the screen. "Just click over to *Live Like You're Dying*, episode one, which should be right there on the bottom of your screen. If you're already familiar with our series, you know that Louise is busy enjoying her life—living every day like it might be her last—and these last two days have been no different. This week, we're out in Montana at Sunny Acres Ranch, riding horses and corralling cattle, something we don't get to do too much of in New York City. We hope you'll find these new videos inspiring, and maybe you'll go out and live your days as if they could be your last. So without further ado—oh wait." She held up a finger. "Before I move on to the highlight reel, I wanted to show you what Louise and I picked up at the souvenir store today." Nora set the camera down and held open her jacket. She had on a pink T-shirt that read: *World's Okayest Horse Rider*.

She spoke to someone off camera and waved them over. "Hey. I want to show our followers your new T-shirt. Come here."

My grandmother walked over and opened her jacket, flashing a shit-eating grin. Her T-shirt was also pink, but this one read: *Save a horse. Ride a cowboy.*

I chuckled. *Figures.*

After that, there was about ten minutes of footage of Gram riding, corralling steer from atop a horse, shooting a bow and arrow at a target, and nailing a bullseye. Even I had to smile. It was pretty damn inspiring to watch, especially knowing her age and how cancer had ravaged her body.

After the videos were done, Nora came back on screen.

"I've received a ton of emails from people wanting to donate to a charity that supports end-of-life adventures." She pointed up this time, and words flashed above her head. "So I've added some links to amazing organizations for those of you who want to contribute. You can even donate in the name of a loved one." She waved at the camera. "That's it for today. Stop back soon for more adventures, and remember—live every day like it's your last!"

The screen froze on Nora's smiling face. I finished off my whiskey, enjoying the view. Once my shoulders relaxed a bit, I picked up my phone to text Nora back and see how Gram's cough was doing. I hadn't responded to her photos from earlier, so I started there.

Beck: Great pics. Thanks for sharing. How is Annie Oakley's cough?

A few seconds later my phone vibrated.

Nora: dhr's frrling netted

My brows drew together. I typed back.

Beck: They serve wine at chow time?

A minute went by, and then my phone rang. Nora. "Hello?"

"Hey. Sorry about that. My new cell is on the fritz. I'm outside, and it's pretty dark. For some reason, it illuminates when messages come in, but it won't light up for me to send a response. I was guessing where the keys were. Guess I didn't do so well?"

"Let's put it this way, I thought you were drunk."

Nora laughed, and I felt a warmth run through me. *Must be heartburn from that wine at dinner.*

"Her cough is about the same," Nora said. "No better, but also no worse. It's definitely not holding her back any. I'm having a hard time keeping up with her this week."

Music played in the background. It had been pretty loud when she first started talking, but it faded now. I thought maybe she'd walked outside at a bar or something.

"Where are you?"

"At a bonfire. The ranch we're staying at does one every night. It's pretty amazing. They make the biggest fire I've ever seen, and then some of the cowboys sit around and play music."

"Sounds like fun."

She laughed. "I bet you'd hate it. Though your daughter could definitely earn her wilderness badge out here."

In the background, I heard a man's voice. "There you are. I've been looking for you."

"Hang on a second, Beck, okay?"

"Yep."

The conversation became muffled, but I could still hear what they were saying.

"Is everything okay with Louise?" Nora asked.

"She's fine," the man said. "Was looking for you to see if you wanted to take a ride down to a pasture not too far from here. It's got some of the best stargazing in the state of Montana."

"Oh, that sounds nice. When are you all leaving?"

"Whenever you want. Was hoping it would just be me and you."

"Oh..."

"Sorry," the man said. "I didn't realize you were on the phone."

"I'll be off in a minute."

"No rush. Come find me, if you're up for it."

"Thanks."

My fists clenched. *Great.* I had the urge to beat the crap out of a cowboy.

Nora came back on the phone. "Sorry about that. Where were we?"

"You were telling me my grandmother's cough is about the same, but I'm wondering if you've been too busy to notice any change."

"What's that supposed to mean?"

"Nothing." I shook my head, hating myself. "I should go. Be careful."

"Fine. Have a wonderful evening, Beck." Nora's voice was laced with sarcasm.

Whatever. I swiped off and tossed my phone on the couch cushion next to me. Then I proceeded to pour more whiskey—this time, I filled the glass three-quarters full, rather than stopping at a reasonable amount.

I was still stewing after knocking back half, when my phone buzzed again.

Nora: I declined the cowboy's invitation. Figured I'd let you know since you sounded concerned for my safety...or something.

I wasn't sure what pissed me off more—the fact that I was so transparent to Nora, or that my jaw unclenched after hearing she wasn't riding off to some pasture with a cowboy. Of course, I would deny both. I texted back.

Beck: I wasn't jealous, if that's what you're insinuating.

Nora: Mmm-hmm...

Beck: I wasn't.

Nora: He wasn't my type anyway.

Beck: Why not?

I sucked back more of my drink, watching the dots jump around.

Nora: Well, today he asked me if I'd ever considered moving out west. The man is looking for a wife.

Beck: That's right. I forgot your type was no-strings-attached.

Nora: Preferably one whose custom-made slacks can't hide the third leg he's walking around with.

My lip twitched. Apparently all I needed was a little stroking of the ego to soothe the jealous beast within. I typed back.

Beck: I can be there in five hours.

Nora: LOL. Considering I haven't ventured back on Tinder since Married Guy turned me sour, I might take you up on it, if you keep offering.

I felt better and better by the minute.

Beck: Now you're talking...

Nora: How about you? Any dates lately?

Beck: I actually had one tonight.

I watched as the little dots jumped around, stopped, then started again.

Nora: What is it, about eleven thirty in New York now? A little early to be home from a date, isn't it?

Beck: Wasn't into it tonight.

Nora: Why not?

Beck: Just wasn't.

Nora: Hmmm...

Thirty seconds later, another text popped up.

Nora: What are you into tonight, Beck?

I was more excited at the thought of a little sexting with a woman two-thousand miles away than I'd been at the prospect of going home with my actual date for the evening.

Beck: Considering I'm home all alone and you declined my offer to hop on a flight, I could be into some pictures...

Nora: What type of pictures?

The liquor had definitely kicked in now. I didn't want to come off like a dirtbag and tell her to send me some skin shots—even if that's exactly what I wanted. Instead, I treaded lightly.

Beck: The bikini one with the dolphin was kind of nice.

Again the dots jumped around, then stopped for a few minutes before my phone vibrated again.

Nora: Goodnight, Beck.

I sighed. Guess I'd pushed things too far.

A half hour later, I was in the bathroom getting undressed when my phone buzzed again. It was Nora, and when I opened the text, a video popped up.

She was standing to the side with her camera pointed at the mirror, wearing the same pair of leather chaps with fringe down the sides that she'd been wearing earlier. She zoomed in on her bottom half and then turned until her ass was facing me.

Jesus.

Freaking.

Christ.

And I do mean her ass was facing me—because she had on only a thong under those assless chaps now. She bent, giving me an amazing close-up of two big round globes, and then looked back over her shoulder and winked right before the video stopped.

I pressed play twice more before I even realized another text had come in after.

Nora: Sweet dreams.

I shut my eyes, trying to calm down, but that only made things worse. A visual of my hand leaving a print on that beautiful ass had my eyes springing open and searching for the play button yet again. I watched the video one more time before swallowing and typing back.

Beck: There will be nothing sweet in my dreams tonight as I imagine all the things I would do to that ass if it were here.

CHAPTER 14

Beck

Round two.

A week later, I found myself on another date. This time it was with Claire Wren, a woman I'd gone out with three times before—on the same day for three of the last four years, our joint birthdays.

Claire was an IT security expert who owned her own firm. She'd done some work for me a few years back and somehow we'd figured out that we shared a birthday—not just the day, but the year, too. A few months later, I was out for drinks with my friends when she texted to wish me a happy birthday. She wound up coming to the bar where I was, and we ended the night by celebrating back at her place, just the two of us. Claire was driven—maybe the one person I knew who was busier than I was at the time—so it wasn't until the same day the next year that we got together again. After that, it became our thing. She texted on our birthday each year, and we got together for our once-a-year celebration. The only time we hadn't was the year I was out of the country. Tonight I'd almost declined and said I couldn't make it, because I wasn't in the mood, but I'd convinced myself to go in the end. Birthdays alone were just sad, as was sitting home drinking alone, which I'd done all too often lately.

Claire ordered us shots of Bailey's at the bar, and we held them up in a toast.

"A smart, handsome, successful person was born today." She smiled. "Unfortunately, it wasn't you. It was me. Who knows, maybe next year will be your year. Happy birthday, my birthday twin."

I laughed and clinked glasses, and we knocked back the shots.

"So...what's new the last three-hundred-and-sixty-four days?" I asked.

"Not much. Working nonstop. More money than free time." She raised a finger. "Oh, actually, there is something new. I was in a committed relationship for about six months."

"What happened there?"

She shrugged. "He accused me of being more in love with my work than him. So he gave me an ultimatum: cut back on work or it was over." Claire smiled. "Turned out he was right. I did love my work more." She lifted the toothpick from her martini and used her teeth to slip the olives off. "What about you? Any special woman in your life this year?"

I immediately thought of Nora. We hadn't spoken or texted since the night of my last date, the night she'd sent me the ass shot. My gut told me the next morning she'd decided she'd gone too far and reined things in again. Which was just as well. I needed to disconnect from her. Though stalking her vlog wasn't exactly making a clean break—but baby steps. I was getting there. Tonight would be a giant leap.

I shook my head and lifted my drink. "Nope. Just my daughter."

A half hour later, I was starting to enjoy myself. The food was good, and the company even better. Claire was smart and funny. There was never a lull in conversation. But then my phone rang, and Nora's name appeared on the screen. I watched it flash two or three times, fighting the urge to pick it up.

Claire looked from my cell to me and back again. Her brows dipped together. "Do you need to get that?"

Images of Nora flooded my brain—and not even the ass shot or the bikini picture, but ones of her laughing. I fucking hated that I'd let her infiltrate my date. So I blew out a deep breath and reached across the table, taking Claire's hand just as the buzzing finally stopped. "Nope. It's not important."

As if to call *bullshit*, my phone immediately started buzzing again. I tried to ignore it a second time, but each flash of her name had me growing more concerned. Nora didn't call often. Definitely not twice in a row.

I pulled my hand from Claire's. "I'm sorry. I'm just going to answer it quick."

"Of course. Take your time."

I swiped to answer. "What's up?"

"Beck—" I knew something was wrong in that one syllable.

I stood from my seat. "What's wrong?"

"It's Louise. She's in the hospital. They say she had a stroke."

"Where are you?"

"We're in Tennessee. Memorial Hospital in Gatlinburg."

"I'll be there as soon as I can."

I swiped my phone off, dug into my pocket, and tossed a few hundred-dollar bills on the table. "I'm sorry, Claire. I need to go."

"What happened?"

"My grandmother had a stroke."

I grabbed the first cab I could hail and told him to start driving to the airport. I didn't even know if there were any more flights out tonight, but I had to try. Using my phone on the way, I was able to grab a seat on a plane to Knoxville, but it was going to be tight to make. Fortunately, the line at security was light for once, and since I didn't have anything with me other than my wallet, I made it to the gate just as they were announcing final call.

Two hours later, I was in Tennessee and a waiting cab took me the forty-minute drive to Gatlinburg. Nora had given me updates, so when we pulled up at the hospital, I went straight to the ICU. Nora was waiting in the hallway. The look on her face stopped me in my tracks.

"Did she..."

Nora shook her head. "No. No. She's okay. Well, not okay. But stable at the moment. The nurses are getting her changed into a gown and stuff. They said it wouldn't take more than a few minutes, and they'd let me know when I could come back in."

I raked a hand through my hair. "What happened?"

"We were just swimming in the pool. One minute she was fine and laughing, and the next she started slurring her words and stringing together random things that don't go together. At first I thought maybe she'd had a few drinks and hadn't mentioned it. But then I noticed one side of her face drooping a little, so I called nine-one-one."

"It was definitely a stroke?"

Nora nodded. "They did scans. One of her tumors has grown larger and is pushing on her blood supply."

"What do they do? Take it out?"

Nora frowned. "She has an advanced medical directive and a living will. Surgery isn't an option. They put her on blood thinners, which seems to have restored the blood flow for now."

"For now? What about later?"

The doors to the ICU opened, and a nurse waved to Nora. "You can come back in."

"Thank you."

The woman glanced at me as I followed as well.

"This is Louise's grandson, Beck," Nora said. "He just flew in from New York."

"How nice. Two grandchildren by her side."

I looked at Nora, who gave me the wide-eyed, lips-pursed signal for *shut up.*

When we got to the glass-enclosed pod, the nurse motioned to a closed door. "You can go on in. The doctor will be by to speak with you shortly."

"Thank you."

My heart felt lodged in my throat as I stepped inside. Gram looked so tiny. So frail. I started to think *old, too,* but she'd kick my ass for that last part, so I didn't let myself go there.

"Did she lose weight?"

"I'm not sure. But we came straight from swimming, so her hair was wet and she has no makeup on. Plus, she's not one to lie down and rest, so it seems odd to see her so..." Nora shook her head, and her eyes welled up. "I don't know. I put the silver glitter headband on her because Louise isn't Louise without a little sparkle."

I walked around the bed and put my arm around Nora. "I'm sorry. That was a dumb question. And I'm positive she very much appreciates the headband."

Nora sniffled. "Do you think she can hear us?"

"I don't know. I guess we should ask the doctor."

We got our answer to that question a few minutes later when the ICU attending walked in. He gestured to the door. "Why don't we speak outside?"

Dr. Cornelius introduced himself and got right to the nitty gritty. "As you know, your grandmother suffered a stroke. There are two main types of strokes: an ischemic stroke, which is caused by the blood supply to the brain being cut off, normally from a blockage; and a hemorrhagic stroke, which is caused by bleeding in the brain. Louise suffered an ischemic stroke caused by a tumor that blocked her carotid artery. Ischemic has a much higher survival rate than hemorrhagic."

The doctor must've read the relief on my face. He held up a hand. "However, normally in these types of strokes, we can remove the obstruction and restore the blood flow to the brain. But your grandmother has made her wishes clear—she does not want any surgical procedures to extend her life. Luckily the blood thinners we've given her seemed to have worked."

"Can she stay on blood thinners long term?"

He nodded. "We're giving her medication through her stomach right now, but blood thinners can be taken in pill form with relatively few complications."

"Oh, that's great," Nora said.

But something in his tone told me not to breathe a sigh of relief too soon. "What about the tumor?" I asked.

Dr. Cornelius smiled sadly. "I called over to Sloan Kettering in New York to have her last scans sent so I could compare. It's an aggressive tumor. We can only make her blood so thin. Chances are it will continue to grow and cause another blockage."

"And then what?"

The doctor looked me in the eye. "She won't likely survive the next one, son."

I don't remember anything anyone said after that—not even the nice words I know Nora spoke as we sat by Gram's bedside for hours. At some point, the nurse who'd been checking on Gram all night came over to talk to us.

"Hi. They're going to kick you out soon, when the change of shift starts. The only time visitors aren't allowed is from five to eight AM. So you two should go home and get some rest. Your grandmother's body has been through a lot, and she's likely going to sleep for several hours more. I know you want to be with her, but the most important thing a caretaker can do is take care of themselves. Get some sleep. Eat a healthy breakfast. Then come back."

I glanced over at Nora, who looked exhausted. I didn't have just me to think about. So I nodded. "Can I make sure you have both our numbers in case anything changes?"

"Of course." The nurse walked over to a white board and picked up a marker. "You can write them right up here, so it's easy for whoever is on duty to call if they need you or if there's any change. I'll also make sure your numbers are in our computer system."

"Thank you."

Nora had come in the ambulance, so we called an Uber since neither of us had a car. The sun was coming up as we wound our way up the Smoky Mountains. I'd never given the name much thought, but the haze of thick, bluish fog below made it self-explanatory. Shades of purple and orange rose above through the peaks of mountains.

"Wow." I stared out. "It's beautiful."

"We got up to watch the sunrise the last two days." Nora swallowed. "I'm really glad we did that now."

It was hard to think there might be a sunrise in the future without my grandmother around to see it. My throat swelled with emotion as I realized that reality might arrive sooner rather than later. Nora and I stayed silent, each staring out our windows until we slowed at a plateau and a hotel came into sight.

"This is us," she said. "Louise and I always get two room keys and give each other one, for backup. So I have her key, if you want to stay in her room."

"I think I'll see if they have anything available. That way if she gets..." Realizing what I'd said, I stopped myself. "When. *When* she gets out, everything is how she left it."

Nora forced a smile and nodded.

The hotel turned out to be pretty empty, so they had plenty of rooms available. The clerk remembered Nora's name and set me up with a room right next door. We walked from the elevator with a gloomy feeling following us.

When we arrived at Nora's room, she stopped at the door. "What time do you want to go back to the hospital?"

"Why don't you get some sleep? I'll go back in a few hours by myself, and you can come when you wake up."

She shook her head. "No, I really want to go."

I looked at my watch. "How about ten? That'll give us about four hours."

"That's good." She looked me up and down. "I'd say I would lend you a shirt or something, but I don't think anything of mine would fit you."

I shrugged. "The lady at the desk said there was a toiletry kit in the room. That's all I need."

"Okay. Well, you know where I am if you think of anything."

I nodded. "Get some sleep."

The door to my room was almost shut when I heard Nora yell. "Wait! Beck!"

I stepped back into the hallway. "Yeah?"

Nora smiled sweetly. "I didn't say happy birthday. I suppose now it's happy belated birthday. Your grandmother told me, and I had planned to text you, but then things went awry."

"Thank you. I'll see you in a few hours."

When we were at the hospital, I'd thought I would be too wired to sleep, but one look at the big bed, and I let out a giant yawn—though I needed a quick shower before I could get in. So I peeled off the suit I'd been wearing since yesterday morning and laid the pieces over the back of the chair in the corner. I was in and out in less than five minutes and just needed to brush my teeth. But when I dug back into the complimentary toiletry bag, I realized there was no toothpaste, just a toothbrush. I debated saying *fuck it*, but I'd had too many cups of coffee to count, and it would drive me nuts.

Nora's room wasn't only next door, there was an adjoining door. So I put on the hotel robe and walked over to listen to see if I could tell whether she was still up. There was definitely movement, and I thought the TV might be on too. So I knocked lightly.

"Beck?" It sounded like she was standing right on the other side of the door. "Was that you knocking?"

"Yeah. Sorry. Could I borrow some toothpaste?"

"Oh, sure. Hang on."

The door opened, and she held out her hand with a tube of Crest, her eyes pointed to the floor. I went to take it, but it struck me as odd that she hadn't raised her head.

"Nora?"

After a moment, she looked up. Her face was covered in blotches, and her bottom lip quivered.

My heart had been hanging on by a thread, and seeing how upset she was snapped my last bit of control.

"Fuck," I grumbled and reached for her. "Come here."

She didn't even try to fight it. It was like a floodgate opened. Nora cried out, a horrible, gut-wrenching sob. Her hands fisted my robe, and she hid her face against my chest as her shoulders shook. I scooped her up and carried her into her room, taking a seat on the edge of the bed and cradling her on my lap as she cried.

"I'm not ready to lose her yet," she choked out.

The broken sound of her voice shredded me. I tasted salt in my throat, and I was grateful for the lump that formed, because it was the only thing that kept me from losing it right along with her.

I stroked her hair. "It's going to be okay."

She sobbed louder. "It's *not* going to be okay. The world is just going to keep on, and everything will be the same. And that is not okay."

I held her tighter. "That's not true. Everything won't be the same. You know why? Because she's not leaving the world the way she found it. Louise changed lives." My voice broke. "She made you and me better people."

I was trying to help, but what I said only made things worse. Nora cried harder. The sound came from a place deep within. I didn't have too much experience giving comfort, except to my daughter, so I tried what worked best for her and rocked back and forth.

It seemed to help. Eventually Nora's shoulders shook less, and her gasps for air became less frequent. After a while, she let out a big sigh. "Thank you."

"Nothing to thank me for, sweetheart." I kissed her forehead. "If anything, I should be thanking you. My grandmother is lucky to have someone who cares so much."

She wiped her cheeks. "I think I'm going to raid the mini bar for wine and take a warm bath."

I smiled. "That sounds like a plan."

Nora crawled from my lap and stood. "Thanks, Beck. Your grandmother is lucky to have you, too."

I nodded and got up. "I'll leave the door open a crack in case you want to talk when you get out of the bath."

"I think I'll be okay. But I appreciate that."

At least a half hour went by before I heard movement next door. The lamp in Nora's room was on, and a sliver of light streamed in from the door that separated our rooms. There was a distant click, and then that sliver went dark. So I settled back into bed, giving in to the heavy weight of my eyelids. I started to drift off, but then I heard a creak.

"Beck?"

I lifted to my elbows. The curtains were drawn, but there was still enough light to see Nora's silhouette. She was wearing the hotel robe, and her wet hair was slicked back like it had just been brushed.

"Are you okay?"

"No." She paused. "I want to forget."

I froze. Those were the words she'd used the first time we met, the night of her Tinder date. I was relatively sure I understood what she was saying, but I didn't want any doubt at all. "What are you asking me, Nora?"

Her response was to untie her robe and slip it from her shoulders. "Make me forget, Beck."

When I didn't say anything, she took a few steps closer. She was completely naked, and since I didn't have any clothes to change into, so was I.

"I only had one glass of wine," she said. "And yes, I'm emotional. But I'm not so emotional that I'm making a rash decision. I've thought about you every night since the first night we met. I've touched myself remembering the sound of your deep voice and imagining my nails scraping your beautiful tan skin."

Oh fuck.

She moved closer.

"Nora...you don't want this. You've told me that yourself, multiple times."

She smiled. "No, you're wrong. I lied. I've told you I didn't want you because I was trying to convince myself it was true. But I want you so badly, I couldn't even force myself to be with a man. God knows I tried with that cowboy on the last night in Montana."

All the hesitancy and uncertainty I felt was suddenly pushed to the side by a new emotion—jealousy. *A fucking cowboy.*

I pulled back the blanket. "Did you let him touch you?"

"No, but I almost did. I thought about sucking him off while I pretended it was you." She took another step so we were toe to toe. "I want you, Beck. I want you in my mouth."

I stood, my cock fully erect. He and I were ready to show her who those lips belonged to.

"Get on your knees. And there won't be any pretending going on..."

CHAPTER 15
Nora

Oh *God.*

Never in my life had I been so turned on. I sank to my knees on the carpet. This is exactly what I wanted. To not think. To be told what to do. To be desired the way I had heard in the grit of his voice.

Beck reached down and stroked my cheek. "Lick it."

My body came alive with tingles. I couldn't wait to please him. Opening my mouth wide, I fluttered my tongue along the underside until the crown bumped against the top of my palate. Then I wrapped my lips around his girth and sucked as I pulled him back out slowly.

Beck made a sound—a cross between agony and ecstasy. He reached around to the back of my head and fisted a wad of my hair.

"*Fuck.* That mouth. It's mine, and I'm going to take it. Open wider. I want to be deep in your throat, sweetheart."

I would've given him what he wanted, but it was sooo much better to have him take it. Flattening my tongue, I sucked him back in but stopped short of swallowing. Then

I took a deep breath, preparing for it to be my last for a while, and looked up.

"Fuck," Beck growled. He tightened his grip in my hair. "Open wider. You're going to take all of me."

I swallowed air through my nose and unhinged my jaw as wide as it could go. Beck thrust forward, filling my throat so snugly that I was sure I'd be raw after. Yet I gripped the back of his thighs, loving every second as he took over fucking my mouth. He stripped away every thought, every memory, every emotion I didn't want to think about, until there was nothing but need. *Raw. Carnal. Greedy need.*

Beck swelled in my mouth, growing impossibly thick and hard. I was certain all it would take to detonate my own orgasm was reaching down to touch my clit, but I wanted Beck to come more than I wanted relief. His thrusts grew harder, and I assumed I was about to get what I needed more than anything—but then Beck growled and pulled away. He reached down, gripped me under the arms, and tossed me through the air, perching me on the edge of the bed.

I tried to catch my breath. "Why did you stop?"

Beck dropped to his knees. "Because you can't scream my name when I'm filling your throat, and the first time you come, I want you screaming my name."

"Oh my God. Egomaniac much?"

Beck's grin was wicked. "Lean back and spread wide for me."

"What if I don't want you to do that?"

His answer was to push open my legs and lift my knees over his shoulders. "On your back, Nora," he said sternly.

I rolled my eyes, yet did what I was told. Beck wasted no time diving in. His tongue flickered over my already swollen bud, causing a spark that shot electricity through my body. He licked up and down my opening, nudging my knees wider as he buried his face in me. I tightened my grip on his hair and pulled him against me.

"Beck!"

"That's it. Come, baby. I want to drink every last drop of you."

He sank his face deeper, his nose pushing against my clit while his tongue speared in and out. It felt like heaven. I didn't think it could get any better, but then he slipped two fingers inside, and I lost it. "Oh God."

He pumped faster, in and out, sucking and swirling.

My body began to tremble, and my eyes rolled back in my head. "Beck. Don't stop!"

"Not a fucking chance, baby." His muffled words vibrated against my tender flesh, and my body started to pulsate on its own.

"Beck..." My back arched off of the bed as my orgasm bloomed.

Beck reached up and used one hand to hold me down. Then he sucked on my clit hard.

And it hit.

Oh God.

Oh God.

Did it ever hit.

I barreled down the rollercoaster in free fall. My orgasm tore its way through my body, and I moaned through every mind-blowing moment. I could no longer feel my legs. When my body started to come down, I got a little choked up. I'd never cried from an orgasm before, but this one was *that* good.

My breathing hadn't yet returned to normal when Beck climbed up my body. His eyes roamed my face. For some reason, I thought he was debating kissing me. I knew some people didn't like that after oral sex, and maybe I didn't usually either. But I didn't care at the moment.

"You can kiss me," I said. "If that's what you're thinking about."

Beck's eyes gleamed. "It wasn't. And I wasn't planning on asking permission. But thanks for letting me know."

I slapped his abs. "God, you're a jerk."

"A jerk whose named you just moaned, sweetheart."

I rolled my eyes. "Don't make me regret it."

His playful face grew serious. "I don't want you to regret us being together."

"I was teasing." I stroked his cheek. "I won't regret anything."

Beck nodded. I liked that he could show a vulnerable side so soon after being all alpha. He wasn't afraid of expressing emotion—a trait that was rare in a strong-willed male.

"While I wasn't going to ask permission to kiss you, I will ask permission to take you bare."

"That's what I was watching you debate? You want to have sex without a condom?"

"If it's okay with you. I've only been with one woman without, and I had a checkup recently and haven't been with anyone since."

"I had a full physical before we left for our trip, too." I paused. "Do you not have any condoms with you?"

"I do. In my wallet. I'll use one if you aren't comfortable."

There were definitely a lot of things to ponder about this conversation, but whether I trusted Beck wasn't one of them. "I'm on birth control. I'm okay without."

He smiled. "Thank you."

Beck lifted to his knees and scooped me up, moving me to the center of the mattress. There was nothing sexier than a confident man who knew who he was and what he wanted—especially one who didn't expect the same submissive behavior outside of the bedroom.

Beck climbed over me, weaving our fingers together before pulling my hands up and over my head. Then he kissed me gently, his tongue exploring my mouth in a way that felt intimate and sensual, very different than the kiss we'd shared that night in the bar. He looked into my eyes as he pushed inside. I was still so wet from his mouth and my orgasm, it made his thickness bearable.

"Fuck. You're so warm and tight." Beck eased in and out, each time going a little deeper. His eyes briefly closed once he was fully seated. "You're wrapped around me like a glove. It feels so damn good." He began to move with more intensity. Gliding in and out became rooting deeply, and his thrusts grew harder and faster. But he never took his gaze from mine. The way he looked into my eyes scared the crap out of me, yet it also made me feel safe. This was supposed to be just sex, a way to forget for a while, but it felt like so much more—something beautiful.

Everything else in the world faded away. It was just Beck and me, two people connecting deeply, the sound of our bodies slapping against each other engulfing us in our own private world. When I moaned, Beck smashed his lips against mine. Our kiss turned heated and wild. I yanked at his hair, and Beck's breaths turned to short, shallow spurts. We were both close, but my body couldn't wait.

"Oh God. Beck! I'm gonna…"

"Right there with you, sweetheart. Come around my cock."

His words pushed me over the edge. My body clamped down and began to pulse once again. I heard Beck's name being shouted, but I scarcely realized it was coming from me.

Beck lifted my leg, and the change in position caused him to rub against a spot that made me see stars. When I finally started to come down, he sank deep and stilled. I felt spasms inside of me but couldn't be sure whose body was doing it.

After, I waited for the moment he would collapse and roll off of me. But it didn't come. Instead, Beck kissed me softly, continuing to glide in and out languidly. He wiped my hair from my face and smiled.

"Did it work? Forget for a while?"

I flashed a goofy smile. "Who are you? What's your name again?"

He kissed my lips once more. "Good. I'm glad you had some peace."

A few minutes later, Beck got up to go to the bathroom. While he was gone, I scurried to get my robe. I was tying it closed when he walked back out with a towel in hand.

His brows dipped. "What are you doing?"

"I, uh..." I thumbed behind me, to the door that connected our rooms. "I'm going to go back to my room. Try to get some sleep."

He frowned. "Seriously? A hooker probably sticks around longer."

"Did you just call me a whore?"

He walked over to me and stood toe to toe. "No. But get back in bed." He gestured to the king-size mattress behind him. "That one, in case I'm not clear."

My hands flew to my hips. "That sounds like an order and not a request."

Beck sighed. "I'm tired. And you made my dick limp. Can we not argue? Because the only time I enjoy that is when it's foreplay, and I need ten minutes to recharge."

"*I* made your dick limp?"

Beck scooped me off my feet and into his arms. He walked back to his bed and unceremoniously plopped me in the middle with a bounce.

"What the hell?"

He climbed into bed next to me. "Shut up and go to sleep."

"Shut up?"

Hooking an arm around my waist, he hauled my ass back against him. "I gave you what you wanted without a hassle. Now let me have what I want."

"What I wanted was sex! Are you saying it was a chore?"

"I'm not saying anything, because my eyes are shut and I'm going to sleep. Now let me snuggle, and yell at me about it later."

Let.

Me.

Snuggle.

I blinked a few times. I wasn't sure what to make of that at all.

But...it did feel pretty good.

His body was warm, even through the robe I'd put on. And his arms made me feel like nothing bad could happen while I was in this spot.

Maybe I'd just stay for a little while.

I yawned.

Yeah. Just ten or fifteen minutes...

CHAPTER 16

Nora

"What are you doing?"

Beck sat on the chair next to the bed, staring at me. "Watching you sleep."

I pulled up the covers. "That's creepy, Cross."

His lip twitched. "How did you sleep?"

I thought about it. I felt pretty well rested. But *oh shit*—we needed to get back to the hospital. I pushed up to my elbows. "What time is it?"

"Nine."

My brows pinched. "In the morning?"

Beck looked amused. "Yes. Nine in the morning."

"On Saturday?"

"Yes, on Saturday."

"So I only slept what, two or three hours?"

He shrugged. "About that."

"But I feel so rested, like I slept a full night."

A cocky smile curved Beck's lips. "Must've been the snuggling."

I rolled my eyes, but I wondered if he was right. Though there were two problems with admitting that.

One, I'd be admitting Beck was right, and two, I'd be admitting I was wrong.

So I sat up and stretched. "Did you already shower?"

He nodded. "I did."

"Alright. I'll just take a quick one to wake up, but I won't wash my hair, so I can be ready in about twenty minutes."

"Take your time. I have a conference call in ten minutes that will probably run a half hour."

Back in my room, I went straight to the bathroom. I was horrified by what stared at me in the mirror.

"Oh my God," I mumbled. And here I was thinking he'd been admiring me while I slept. He was probably wondering who the lunatic in his bed was. I'd gone to his room with wet hair, so it had dried on its own, which meant it was sticking up all over the place now. A line of dried drool streaked from my mouth to my neck, and while I'd woken feeling rested, my puffy, red eyes told another story.

I groaned and twisted the hot water on in the shower. I'd need to be even quicker than usual so I could lay a cold rag over my swollen eyes for a few minutes. As soon as I hit the water, my brain woke up and fired off questions.

What the hell did you do—having sex with Beck?

What were you thinking?

Can't you control yourself?

You have a vibrator in your suitcase, for God's sake. Why didn't you use that?

All excellent questions, and I didn't have an answer for a single one of them.

But my stomach did a little somersault when I thought back to what had happened.

"On your knees."

"Lick it."

And when I'd told him not to stop...

"Not a fucking chance, baby."

Oh God. This was the last thing I needed to be thinking about right now. What I needed was coffee.

Lots of coffee.

I got out of the shower to get dressed, but a knock at my hotel-room door stopped me. Pulling on the hotel robe, I took a quick peek through the peephole to find an employee with a rolling cart. I hadn't ordered any room service.

I opened the door and smiled. "Hi. I think you have the wrong room. I didn't order anything."

The cart was set beautifully, with white linens, a bouquet of gorgeous hot pink flowers, a covered silver platter, orange juice, newspapers, and what smelled like a pot of delicious coffee. I was tempted to change my tune and bring that sucker inside.

The waiter lifted the padfolio from the table and opened it. "Are you Ms. Sutton?"

"Yes?"

"The order was placed by Mr. Cross in room three fifteen. He gave specific instructions not to deliver it to his room but yours."

"Oh." I stepped aside. "Well, then..."

The waiter rolled the cart into my room. I dug out some cash for a tip, but he waved a hand. "It's already been taken care of."

"Oh. Okay, thank you."

This was a really nice hotel, but I still couldn't get over how gorgeous everything was on the cart. The flowers had to have cost more than the meal. The setup was Instagram worthy.

"Would you like me to make your coffee?" the waiter asked.

"No, I'm good." I smiled. "I can handle that, even before caffeine."

He did a little bow. "Very well. Have a good day."

"You too."

He was halfway out my door when I stopped him. "Excuse me?"

He turned back. "Yes?"

I motioned to the breakfast cart. "Is this how all room service is delivered? With a big bouquet of flowers and all these newspapers?"

The waiter smiled. "No, ma'am. Just yours."

My brows dipped down. "Why just mine?"

"The gentleman who placed the order had the concierge get the flowers and papers. He specified pink only."

I nodded slowly. "Pink only?"

"Hot pink, actually."

"Really? Do you know when the order was placed?"

The waiter slipped the padfolio from his inside pocket. "Looks like it was placed at six forty-five. Probably took the concierge a while to find a florist open so early."

I had no idea what to make of that information, so I just nodded. "Okay. Thank you again."

Once I was alone, I checked out what was underneath the covered platter—eggs benedict and fresh fruit. I salivated. Then I got a whiff of the flowers and leaned down to get the full effect, still amazed at the trouble Beck had gone to. I heard talking next door, so it sounded like he was still on his call, but I figured the least I could do to show my appreciation was bring him some caffeine. I made two mugs, sipped one, and headed next door with his in hand.

Beck sat at the desk, his laptop open and voices chatting away, but his eyes raked down my body as I stepped inside. They took their time making their way back up, and

I silently reprimanded myself for not looking in the mirror before I'd come in.

Even the way he watched me deliver his coffee gave off a dominant vibe, the same way he'd been in bed. His eyes followed my every step, yet his head never moved. It made goosebumps break out on my arms.

I set the coffee to the side of his laptop, careful to keep out of the camera's view. The entire time, Beck remained cool and restrained—eyes following me, yet never displaying any expression on camera. So I couldn't help myself. It seemed like a silent challenge.

When I got back to the doorway, I untied the belt to my robe and turned back, opening it wide to flash my birthday suit underneath.

That did it.

Beck's control snapped. His eyes went wide, and a giant smile broke out on his face as he shook his head.

Satisfied that he wasn't always the one in control, I walked back to my room with a bit more swagger in my step.

⤳

"Oh my God. You're awake..."

Louise surprised us both when we walked into the ICU ward an hour later. She looked a thousand times better than when we'd left a few hours ago. Relief made me choked up, and I went to her bedside and hugged her. Beck did the same.

"Did you think I was going to miss Harry?"

Beck looked to me.

"We got Harry Styles tickets for next Friday night. Third row floor seats. He's playing in New York. We're going to fly home to see it."

"Harry Styles? Seriously? Isn't he for teenagers?"

I narrowed my eyes. "Harry Styles is for *everyone*."

Beck shrugged and looked at Louise. "How do you feel?"

"I feel like getting out of here, that's how I feel."

He glanced back to me. "Yep. She's feeling better."

A few minutes later, a group of doctors came in. One of them was the neurologist from yesterday, Dr. Cornelius.

"Good morning," he said.

"Morning."

He typed something into his iPad, smiled, and motioned to Louise. "How are you feeling, Ms. Aster?"

"Great. I'm ready to check out."

Dr. Cornelius turned to us. "Normally I like to ask the family if the patient seems like themself. It's actually an important part of my neurological exam. But something tells me the answer to that is yes."

Beck smirked. "Most definitely."

"That's a good sign. I came in to check on Ms. Aster about an hour ago when the nurses told me she was awake. We discussed what had transpired and spoke a little about her condition. But I'm not an oncologist, so I wanted to speak to her doctors in New York and consult with my colleagues here before we discussed a treatment plan."

Beck nodded. "Okay..."

"Ms. Aster has expressed that she's made the decision to enjoy the final phase of her life, rather than spend it getting chemo and radiation that will only extend her life so long, and at a cost of the quality of her days."

"I don't necessarily agree with that," Beck said. "But it's her choice."

Dr. Cornelius nodded. "When we're dealing with terminal illness, I normally accept the wishes of the patient without question. However, in my opinion, the tumor pushing on the carotid artery is likely to cause another stroke if left untreated—sooner rather than later."

"How soon?" Louise asked.

The doctor shook his head. "I can't tell you that. But I wouldn't be surprised if it was only a matter of days. Weeks at best. The blood thinners are only a very short-term Band-Aid."

"Is there anything noninvasive that can be done?" I asked.

Dr. Cornelius looked to Louise. "I spoke to your oncologist in New York, Dr. Ludlow. He believes a short regimen of radiation would be best. Taking into consideration your wishes not to undergo further treatment that would interfere with your quality of life, he recommends just two weeks of radiation, approximately ten sessions. The majority of tumors shrink during the first few weeks, while causing the least amount of side effects. We can't say definitively that it will work, or how long it might buy you until the tumor grows large enough to cause a problem again, but Dr. Ludlow believes it should shrink enough in ten sessions that it would be at least three to six months before it becomes an issue."

Louise sighed. "The radiation made me so tired last time, I couldn't get out of bed."

"Yes," Beck added. "But you were doing chemo at the same time. This would only be radiation, correct?"

"That's right." Dr. Cornelius nodded. "Your oncologist wouldn't be trying to cure the disease; he'd only be trying to make living through it more manageable, so you could have more time to live your life while you're feeling good."

"I don't know..." Louise said. She looked to me. "What do you think?"

I felt Beck's eyes on me, but tried to ignore the influence. "I think it's a decision you should consider carefully."

Louise shrugged. "I need to think about it."

"Of course." The doctor nodded. "But like I said, the blood thinners are only a temporary fix. So it's best not to take too long."

The doctors stayed another ten minutes, examining Louise's eyes and strength. She was able to grip the doctor's fingers with both hands, but one side was noticeably weaker than the other. When they were done, Dr. Cornelius asked if we had any questions.

"How long does she need to stay in the hospital here, barring any further episodes?" Beck asked. "You said it could be only a matter of days before another stroke, so I'd like to get her back to New York to start treatment."

Louise pursed her lips. "*If* I start treatment."

Beck ignored her. "How fast could we get her on a plane?"

"I'd like to monitor her today and try to get Ms. Aster up and around this afternoon. How about if we discuss that during evening rounds?"

"Okay. Great."

Louise pulled the covers off and started to swing her legs over the side of the bed.

"Whoa—hang on there," Dr. Cornelius said. "You need a nurse and someone from PT to get up. Probably a walker to start, too."

I winced at the word *walker*, knowing what was about to come. And it did.

"I don't need any damn walker. I can't help but get older, but I'm far from old, son. Just dying. I'll be fine on my own."

The doctor tried to hide his smile. "How about we compromise and have the nurse and PT help you without a walker?"

"Fine."

Beck shook his head as the medical team left Louise's room. "He's just looking out for you. It won't kill you to humor him and use the walker for a few minutes to make sure you're okay on your feet. You don't always have to be in charge."

"Oh really? When was the last time *you* let someone be in charge?"

I grinned. The more time I spent with these two, the more I realized how much they were alike.

Beck scowled at me. "What are you smiling at?"

My mouth split wider. "Who me? I'm not smiling."

He grumbled something under his breath. After that, a nurse came in, and Louise asked for coffee.

"Sorry." She shrugged. "Only decaf today."

"That's like showering while wearing a raincoat. Pointless."

Yep. Louise is just fine. At least for the time being.

A few hours went by, and then a guy in blue scrubs knocked on the door. He was probably only about twenty-five and really cute. He smiled. "I'm Evan from physical therapy. You ready to rock the road, Ms. Aster?"

"Sure am." Louise again lifted the covers off her legs.

Evan held his hands up. "Hang on one minute. We need to have two people, one on each side. I'm going to grab a nurse."

"I don't need two people."

"Oh, you definitely don't. I can see that. But it's a dumb hospital policy, and it'll keep me out of trouble." He winked at Beck and me on the way out. Young, but already knew how to manage people.

"He has her number," I whispered to Beck.

"Must have read the troublemaker note in her chart."

"I heard that!" Louise yelled.

After she finished walking the halls—proving not only that she didn't need a walker, but not the people beside her either—they took her down for a repeat scan to make sure things hadn't changed. Beck and I went to the cafeteria for some lunch, since they said she'd be about an hour. Our table had one sad-looking carnation in a dollar-store vase sitting in the middle. But it reminded me of the flowers on my tray at breakfast.

"Thank you for the room service this morning."

Beck gave a curt nod. "Of course."

"Oh...of course, huh? I get it now. The fancy breakfast is a go-to move after spending the night with a woman."

He narrowed his eyes. "What are you talking about?"

"Did I get the Beck Cross special? Is the order always the same? Eggs benedict, coffee, juice, fancy flowers, and a few newspapers... Do you order in when you're not at a hotel? Is it a standard order you have set up on an app and you just hit re-order? Oh, and do you always find out their favorite color beforehand to give it that personalized touch?"

Beck tilted his head. "What am I missing here?"

I pushed my salad around with my fork. "The flowers you sent this morning were gorgeous. And my favorite color."

"So?"

"I'm just saying, it's a smooth move. I bet the women melt the next morning."

"What women?"

"The ones you have breakfast delivered to with their favorite-color flowers."

Beck looked flummoxed. "Did you hit your head?"

I rolled my eyes. "Forget it. But thank you for the flowers anyway. They were beautiful."

"You're welcome. Just so you know, I sent you flowers because you came into my room wanting to forget life for a little while. I figured that meant you were feeling down, and you said hot pink helps your mood." He paused and caught my eyes. "It's not my go-to move, as you called it. It was only for you."

My belly did a little whoosh. Who knew Beck could be so sweet?

While I attempted not to let his answer affect me, he leaned in and lowered his voice. "I would have preferred to feed you my cock again this morning to improve your mood, but I thought you needed your sleep." He winked. "Eggs. Next best thing."

And...the real Beck is back.

Since the whoosh had dropped lower than my belly now, I thought it time for a change of subject.

"I don't think you should push Louise into getting the radiation."

He frowned. "Why not?"

"Because I think she's going to get there on her own. But if she doesn't, the last thing she needs is to feel guilty for possibly robbing you of more time with her."

Beck's face changed. It looked like I'd shot an arrow and made a direct hit to his heart. "That's how she feels?"

"She doesn't say it in so many words, but yes. It took a lot for her to come to the decision to put herself first. She's spent fifty years of her life raising a family—first your mom, and then you and your brother. I know she wouldn't change that for anything, but this is what she wants, Beck."

Tears filled his eyes. He nodded. "Okay."

He was quiet through the rest of lunch. And he stayed that way until Dr. Cornelius came back at four o'clock in the afternoon.

"I heard you're ready to run the NYC marathon," he said as he entered.

"Not quite." Louise smiled. "But I am ready for a Harry Styles concert."

Dr. Cornelius sat on the edge of her bed. He took Louise's hand. "So, have you given any thought to the treatment plan your doctor in New York suggested?"

She looked up at Beck. "I'll try it, but if I feel sick or it's making me too exhausted to live, I'm going to stop. I quit treatment to live out the end of my life, and that's what I intend to do—whether it's three days or three months."

Beck turned to Dr. Cornelius. "How soon can I get her on a plane to New York?"

"I'll discharge her into your care as soon as you can make arrangements." He pointed at Louise. "But you need to go directly to the hospital in New York and let them admit you for continued monitoring. Do not pass go and collect two-hundred dollars—go directly to the hospital from the airport. Then it's up to your oncologist to decide whether the radiation can be done inpatient or out."

"Fine," Louise said.

Beck took out his phone. "I'll take care of the arrangements and make sure she goes right to the hospital once we land."

Four-and-a-half hours later, we boarded a flight to New York. Beck had set up one of those motorized carts to take us from security to the gate. Louise was weak, and by the time we took off, she was already sound asleep next to him.

I sat across the aisle from them. I leaned over and whispered, "Thank you for buying my ticket home. You didn't have to." I smiled. "If I was paying, I'd be sitting back in the squishy seats instead of this comfy first class."

"No problem. And thank you for taking such good care of my grandmother while she was sick."

I nodded. "I'd do anything for Louise."

Beck looked back and forth between my eyes. "I know you would."

"I was thinking, when we get back, I'm sure you have to work, and you must have your daughter on certain days, so why don't we plan to take shifts keeping an eye on Louise? Whether she's in the hospital or not, I'd like to be there."

Beck smiled sadly. "That would be great. Thank you. You're a really good friend to her."

"It works both ways. She gives more than she gets."

He held my eyes again, but didn't respond.

"As long as we're having a moment of being nice to each other and saying thank you—which may not last with us—I want to say thank you for this morning. I needed that more than you could know."

"Anytime."

I looked down at his crotch and sighed. He seriously had the sexiest bulge in those dress pants. "As tempting as the prospect of another round or two might be, I think it was just a one-time thing. I hope you understand."

He grinned. "We'll see."

CHAPTER 17

Nora

"Oh, sorry. I didn't see you there." An adorable young guy flashed a dimpled smile and thumbed over his shoulder. "I think I might be in the wrong hospital room. But..." He shrugged and raised one of the Starbucks cups in his hands. "I brought you coffee."

I chuckled. "You brought me coffee, yet you're in the wrong room?"

"I brought it for my brother, but he won't appreciate it as much as I'll enjoy having coffee with you."

I wasn't sure if it was the unappreciative brother comment, or the happy-go-lucky, hot-guy attitude that tipped me off. "Oh my gosh. I bet you're Jake?"

His dimples deepened. "You've been looking for me all your life, too?"

I stood and extended my hand. "I'm a friend of your grandmother's. Nora Sutton."

"Oh shit." He put down both coffees and surprised me by engulfing me in a big hug. "The woman who wing jumps and doesn't jump at my brother's command. It's great to meet you, Nora. I've heard a lot about you."

I laughed. "If it's from Beck, I'm not sure that's a good thing."

He picked up his coffee again. "Seriously, have the other one if you want. I only brought it to butter him up because I screwed up something at work."

"Thanks. I think I will. The coffee here is godawful, and it'll taste better knowing I deprived Beck of it."

Jake's grin was infectious. The two brothers resembled each other, both gorgeous, yet somehow still very different. Beck was broad shouldered, angular, and impeccably dressed. He was buttoned up and commanding, while Jake was leaner, with slightly softer features, and it looked like he could use a haircut and shave. Yet I'd bet my last dollar that women ate up his look just as much. *Especially* those cavernous dimples.

He lifted his chin to the empty bed. "Where's Gram? She make a run for it already?"

"They took her down for radiation a little while ago. It usually only takes about a half hour, so she should be back soon."

"How's she feeling today?"

"She's not too happy that the doctor said she can't go to the Harry Styles concert tonight."

"I love Harry!"

I smiled. *Yeah, these brothers are sooo different.* "Anyway, it's funny you mention her making a run for it, because she's trying to get me to sneak her out for a few hours. I keep telling her I can't. We might want to put the nurses on alert when we leave though."

"Well, if you need a replacement date for the concert tonight..." Jake rocked back on his heels and slipped his hands into his pockets. "I can cancel my plans."

I was half tempted to take him up on the offer, just because I thought it might drive Beck nuts, but I'd already given the tickets to him to sell online for me. "Sorry. I think the tickets are sold already."

"Damn." He grinned. "Next time."

Jake slipped off his shoes and hopped up on Louise's bed. Spreading his long legs and making himself comfy, he locked his hands behind his head, elbows out.

"So...did you hear the story about why Gram's dog hates Beck?"

I smiled. "I don't think so. Although I have seen all the nip wounds on his fingers. The first time I met him, I think he was wearing four Band-Aids."

"Yep. Dog hates him. He likes to tell people it's because Gram talks to Bitsy and he doesn't. But that's not the reason at all."

"What's the real dirt?"

"Bitsy's gotta be eight now, but she was only about a year when Beck picked her up from grooming one time. Gram was away for the weekend, and she asked him to watch her. She'd dropped Bitsy off at the groomer, and Beck was supposed to pick her up."

"He forgot?"

"Oh no, he showed up. And he took a little dog home, too. It just wasn't Bitsy."

"Oh my God. Didn't he take the wrong baby carrier once and leave you at daycare?"

Jake's smile widened. "He did indeed. For a guy who doesn't miss a beat, he can be pretty inattentive at times."

"I'd say. How long did it take him to figure out he didn't have Bitsy?"

"He had the wrong dog in his apartment for two full days and never even noticed. And just in case you're thinking *Oh, all Pomeranians look alike, so that can be easy to do*, don't. Because the dog he brought home from the groomer was a *Yorkshire terrier*."

I laughed. "You're kidding me?"

"Nope. He had no clue that the dog our grandmother had owned for the last year wasn't the one he'd dognapped. I was only a teenager at the time, so I was still living with her. But he stopped by a few times a month."

"What about the Yorkie owner? Didn't they notice?"

"The other dog happened to have the same name and was there for boarding for the weekend, so the owners didn't notice until they arrived to pick up their dog. They tried to reach Louise after they figured out what must've happened, but she was on her way back home, and she doesn't answer while she's driving. So the other owner called the cops. Gram and Beck had to go down to the police station, because the Yorkie owner wanted to press charges for dognapping. It was the funniest shit I ever watched go down."

I couldn't stop laughing as I imagined Beck petting and feeding a dog all weekend without noticing it looked nothing like the one he was supposed to be watching. Jake cracked up right along with me. Which of course, made it the perfect time for Beck to walk in.

"Oh shit." Beck stopped short a few steps over the threshold. He shook his head. "This can't be good."

Jake pointed to Beck's fingers, and there were Band-Aids on three of them. That only made us laugh harder. Tears streamed down my cheeks. "What's up, dognapper?"

Beck looked up at the sky, shaking his head. "You're such a dick, Jake."

"You're lucky you got here so soon. I was about to tell her about the bananas last week."

"What happened with bananas?" I asked.

"He gets his groceries delivered. Maddie likes banan-as, so he ordered ten, but he didn't read that they were sold in bunches. He got seventy bananas. He brought them to work, and I ate six in one day." Jake rubbed his belly. "I don't advise it."

Beck put his hands on his hips. "It's only four thirty. Shouldn't you still *be* at work?"

"Nah." He grinned. "I only work six hours a day. Too much work causes stress, which causes wrinkles. I'm too pretty to shrivel this young."

Beck shook his head.

The nurse wheeled Louise in. Her eyes lit up when she saw all of us waiting for her. "Three of you at once? Is today the day I'm going to kick the bucket and no one told me?"

"That's not even funny, Gram," Beck said.

She waved him off. "Oh...lighten up, tight ass."

Both Beck and Jake kissed their grandmother, and Beck watched over the nurse as she helped Louise into bed. The man was protective, to say the least.

Louise settled herself in and looked at me. "So you finally met my Jake?"

"I did. He kept me amused while I was waiting for you to get back."

Her eyes sparkled. "He's single, you know."

As soon as she said it, her eyes shifted to Beck. It was clear she was looking to get a rise out of him. Beck kept quiet, not taking the bait, though the clench of his jaw spoke volumes.

"So, my little Jakey." Louise reached out to her grand-son. "You know you were always my favorite grandchild, right?"

"Of course." He grinned and lifted her hand to his lips for a kiss. "And you're my favorite girl."

"Good," Louise said. "How about you bust me out of here about nine tonight? There's a man with a boa I need to go see."

"You're not going to Harry Styles," Beck muttered. "I already sold the tickets."

Louise stuck her tongue out. "I know you only offered to help Nora sell them because you were afraid she'd change her mind and take me."

Beck shrugged. "Just trying to keep you healthy."

Over the next two hours, I was entertained by story after amusing story about Jake and Beck as kids. I'd once told Beck that I'd never felt deprived of anything growing up with just one parent, and watching these three interact told me I wasn't the only one who felt that way.

An announcement came overhead that visiting hours in the unit would be ending in fifteen minutes. I looked at my watch, surprised that it was already almost seven.

"Welp..." Jake slapped his hands on his thighs. "I better get going. I have a double header tonight."

"You hate baseball," Beck said.

Jake grinned. "Who said anything about baseball? I have two dates. One I'm meeting for drinks at eight, and the other I'm meeting at the club at midnight."

"And you were going to give all that up to go with me to Harry?" I teased.

Jake took my hand and cupped it to his cheek. "I'd give my right nut to take you anywhere, beautiful."

"Maybe you should go out with him," Beck grumbled. "If he has one less nut, he might not be able to procreate."

After Jake left, Beck and I said goodbye to Louise. "I'll be back in the morning," I told her.

"Or...you could park outside my window, and I'll jump down about nine o'clock. I'm only on the second floor. I think I can hack the jump. We can scalp tickets."

I kissed Louise's cheek. "Get some rest. You're doing great. I'm already plotting our next adventures."

Beck and I walked to the elevators.

"She's tolerating the radiation great so far," I said.

He nodded. "Her spirits are better than I expected, too. But I think a lot of that is because of you. You make her young again."

I smiled. "That's sweet. But I'm pretty sure you and your brother are what keep her spirit alive."

The elevator doors slid open, and Beck and I stepped in. "Did you eat yet?" he asked.

"No. I'll pick up something on the way home."

"Why don't we grab something together? My favorite Italian place is only a block from here. They make the best gnocchi in pesto sauce I've ever tasted."

I bit my bottom lip. That sounded much better than eating half-cold Chinese food straight from the carton in front of the TV, but... "I don't think that's a good idea."

Beck's brows drew together. "Why not?"

"I don't want to give you the wrong impression."

Beck frowned. "I was looking for dinner company, not to get laid."

The elevator opened on the ground floor. Beck gestured for me to walk into the lobby first. Then he opened the door to the street. "So? Are you coming or am I eating alone?"

"I suppose two friends having dinner is okay, right?"

"Of course." He put a hand on my back and guided me to walk to the right. "Besides, once was enough for me."

I stopped in place. "What did you just say?"

He grinned. "Oh, so only you can decide once was enough, and I shouldn't be insulted?"

"I didn't say once was enough; I said it wasn't a good idea. There's a difference."

"Oh, so once wasn't enough?"

I rolled my eyes. "Just shut up and feed me."

"Oh, I'll feed you alright..."

A few minutes later, we walked into Gustoso. The maître d', an older man with a thick head of silver hair, smiled when he saw Beck and rushed over to shake his hand.

"Ah...Beckham. How are you, my friend? It's been too long."

"I'm good, Enzo. How are you?"

The man patted the belly hanging over his pants. "Still fat, so still happy. People are only skinny when they're sad, right?"

Beck smiled. "You look good. How's Allesia?"

"Good. She's off tonight. It's her book club night. Though I think *book* is secretly American for *wine* because she comes home tipsy." Enzo looked to me. "But enough about my old bat of a wife. Tell me who this beautiful creature is."

"This is Nora. Nora, this is Enzo Aurucci. He owns the place."

Enzo held up a finger. "Part owner only now, eh?"

Beck smiled. "That's right."

"Give me a minute. I'll get the best table in the house set up."

"Thanks, Enzo."

I looked around the restaurant. Brick walls and ancient beams gave the small place a warm feeling. A big fireplace took up half of one wall, and the dim lighting cast a romantic glow over the cozy setting.

"I can see why this is your favorite. It's very romantic. Is it your go-to place to warm up your concubines? You must come here a lot if they remember your name."

"Enzo and his wife are clients," Beck explained. "They owned a few restaurants here in the city and wanted to partially retire, so I helped them sell to a big conglomerate. Now they go to Italy for two months in the winter and only work three days a week. I've only ever brought Jake and Gram here. It's Gram's favorite restaurant."

"Oh..."

"You like to think the worst of me, don't you? I ask you to dinner, it's because I want to get laid. I bring you to a place where I think the food is good, and you think they know me because I'm taking women out five nights a week. Maybe you were right... Once was enough."

Now I felt bad. I was just teasing, but I hadn't thought about how my comments sounded. "I'm sorry. I'm being a jerk."

Enzo came back and showed us to a table. It was a high-backed, curved booth seat that faced out to the restaurant, so we sat shoulder to shoulder and not across from each other. Enzo insisted we allow him to bring us his favorite dishes. Then he came back with a delicious bottle of wine and basket of warm bread.

I looked over at Beck. "Whenever I see couples sitting like this, next to each other and not across, it seems odd. I guess usually it's because there are two other seats and the couple chooses to sit together in one. But this still seems strange to me."

Beck motioned to the roaring fireplace to the right. "Probably so both people can enjoy the ambiance."

"Yeah, I guess so."

He picked up the breadbasket and held it out to me before taking a piece for himself. "So I spoke to the oncologist on the phone this morning. He said he's already seeing some shrinkage, even after only four treatments."

"I know. He came in to speak to Louise right before you and Jake arrived."

"He mentioned maybe extending—"

I put my hand on Beck's arm. "Do you think we could have dinner without talking about illness and treatment? Being in the hospital oncology ward all this week, seeing sick kids and stuff, I'm sort of in need of something more upbeat."

"Yeah." Beck nodded. "I get it. That's a good idea."

I tore off a piece of my bread and dipped it into the bowl of seasoned oil and vinegar. "Thanks. Happy topics only. So what should we talk about?"

Beck shrugged. "We can talk about how good I was in bed?"

I chuckled. I'd insulted him earlier, so maybe it was time for a compliment—one that was easy to offer because it was true. "Don't let it go to your head, but you *were* very good in bed."

Beck's lips curled into a gloating smile. "I know."

I rolled my eyes. "You could at least be gracious..."

"Nah. Not my style." He chuckled. "But I do have a serious question. If you had a good time, and there isn't anyone else in the picture, why are you so insistent it was a one-time deal?"

I sighed. "I'm moving across the country in a few months. Plus, I'm just not in that place in my life right now. I don't want to be tied down."

Beck lowered his voice, leaning to me with a purr. "How about being tied up?"

And just like that, my day went from hospital-induced melancholy to all the hair on my arms zinging to attention. "Be good..." I warned.

His eyes sparkled. "That's the opposite of what I feel like doing while I'm this close to you. By the way, your sundress is my favorite color. Baby blue. Did you wear it for me?"

"Beck..."

"Your mouth says we were a one-time thing, but your body says something very different." He looked down at my nipples, now protruding through the fabric of my dress, then back up at my parted lips. "Can I touch you?"

"Touch me where?"

He slipped a hand under the table and onto my thigh. I jumped, though it also caused a whoosh of lust to fill my belly. Beck's fingers dipped down to the inside of my thigh. "Just tell me to stop and I will."

The slightest contact with this man made me crazy. But was I really going to let him touch me in a public place?

Beck whispered in my ear. "Where's your sense of adventure? Close your eyes. No one can see. The tablecloth hangs low enough to cover you."

His fingers slipped beneath my sundress and glided a little farther up my thigh. His hand was still six inches from my apex, yet it felt like he was brushing along my center already. I felt him *everywhere*. My breathing grew as erratic as my heartbeat.

"This feels good, doesn't it?" Beck's voice sounded as strained as my willpower felt.

I swallowed and nodded.

Without warning, his hand moved up, fingers gently trailing up and down my panties. "You're already wet for me."

I couldn't believe I was doing this in a restaurant. I'd never even had sex near a window before.

"Open your legs a little," Beck whispered into my neck. His hot breath sent goosebumps racing over my skin.

When I didn't immediately comply, he pushed his thumb down on my clit over my panties. "Let me make you feel good, make you forget."

I was breathless. "Anywhere but here would be preferable."

"Then you should have answered my texts this week. Trust me, I'd have chosen somewhere I could hear you call my name when you come, but this is what you've given me. So open your legs, sweetheart."

I knew I would probably hate myself tomorrow, but I wanted it too badly. I let my knees fall shamelessly open beneath the table. I still stared straight ahead, but I saw Beck's mouth curve to a smile in my peripheral vision.

The air crackled between us as he fingered the edge of my panties, then slipped underneath. He traced a line through my center, dipping inside and making my body quiver.

I hadn't stopped staring into the restaurant, yet it took Beck's fingers stilling for me to notice something was wrong.

"Enzo is coming with a plate," he said.

"Oh my God. Move your hand."

"Just stay still."

Enzo smiled as he arrived at our table. "My favorite eggplant parmigiana. Sliced thin, like it should be. With my famous homemade ricotta between the layers."

"That looks incredible," Beck said. "Thanks, Enzo."

To my horror, Beck decided that was the right moment to push one of his fingers inside me. My head snapped to look at him, and he smiled—a calm, cool, and fully-in-control mask in place. "Doesn't it look great, Nora?"

As soon as he said it, he pushed a second finger inside. And pumped in and out.

I swallowed and nodded, unable to speak.

"Bon appetit," Enzo said. If he had any inkling what was going on under the table, it certainly didn't show. "I'll be back with more in a little while."

"Thanks, Enzo," Beck said.

The restaurant owner was barely out of earshot when I laid into the man next to me. "I can't believe you just did that."

His response was to plunge his fingers deeper. As crazy as it was, I think I got off on the fact that we could've just gotten caught. It felt like the adrenaline high of jumping out of an airplane, only better. And Beck wasn't pulling the parachute strings just yet. His eyes darkened as he continued to pump his fingers. It didn't take long before I felt my impending orgasm barreling down.

"Beck..."

He growled in my ear. "Kiss me. No one will interrupt us, and it'll stifle the sound when you come."

The man's fingers were inside of me in the middle of a restaurant, and *kissing him* was what I was second-guessing?

Beck read the hesitation on my face. "Oh, for fuck's sake. Give me your mouth."

I leaned forward a fraction of an inch, and Beck smashed his lips against mine. As soon as we were connected, he crooked the fingers inside me and his thumb reached for my clit, pressing a small circle. Orgasm jolted through me. Afraid of the sound I might make, even muffled by our mouths, I sank my teeth into Beck's bottom lip.

He groaned, and it traveled through me like an after-shock.

A few minutes later, I was still panting. Beck cupped the back of my neck and kept me close. "You good?"

I nodded.

He swiped his tongue along his bottom lip and brought it back into his mouth. "You drew blood."

"Sorry."

"No, you're not."

That made me smile. "Maybe you're right."

We laughed. And then, it went with the craziness of the last ten minutes that we just started eating after that. I was suddenly starving.

I pointed to the eggplant parm on my plate. "Maybe it's post-orgasmic high, but this is the best thing I've eaten in...maybe ever."

"It's delicious. But I can think of one other thing I've eaten recently that was better." He winked.

Enzo brought three more dishes after that, each one better than the last. By the end, as much as I wanted to, I couldn't eat another bite of the pasta on my plate. I sat back with my hand on my belly.

"I'm stuffed. I'm glad I'm wearing this dress and not jeans."

"I'm glad you're wearing that dress too, but it has nothing to do with being full."

I chuckled. "I still can't get over I did that. Too bad we didn't drive here. I'm feeling adventurous now. I've never given a blowjob in a car."

"So not having a car is the only hinderance, not your one-time-only rule?"

I bit down on my bottom lip. "I think we already broke that rule."

A little while later, Enzo wheeled over a cart full of desserts. I'd said I was too full, but he insisted I at least taste the tiramisu. Beck had a piece of cheesecake *and* a cannoli. I shook my head watching him finish the last of it.

"I don't know where you put it."

He wiggled his eyebrows. "I know where I'd like to put it."

I laughed. "I meant all the food you ate. Each of your servings was twice the size of mine, and you still had room for two desserts. Do you eat like that all the time?"

"Only if the food's good. If it's not, I have just enough to fill me up." He smiled. "I guess the same can be said for *other* things. If I like it enough, I want to devour it." Beck reached out and tangled a lock of my hair around his finger. "You ready to get going? I actually have something to do at ten, but I'll drop you on the way."

"Oh. Okay." The little horns of jealousy wanted to poke out. Did he have a date? I didn't want to send mixed signals, so I buried my urge to pepper him with questions. "Sure. And you don't have to drop me at home. I can grab an Uber or the subway."

Beck peeled a bunch of hundreds from his billfold and tucked them into the padfolio. "Oh no, I'm *definitely* dropping you off."

I thought there was something odd in his tone, but he stood and held his hand out to help me from the booth, so it was quickly forgotten. At least until we walked outside.

A super-stretch limousine was parked at the curb, and a uniformed driver leaned against it. He stood as Beck walked over.

"Mr. Cross?"

"Yes."

The man went to open the back door, but Beck shook his head. "I got it. Thank you."

I looked at Beck. "This is for you?"

"It's for us."

"It's a little excessive, isn't it? An Uber would have worked."

His eyes sparkled. "Maybe. But an Uber doesn't have a privacy panel. You said you were feeling adventurous, and this, technically, is a car."

My eyes widened, and my jaw dropped open. "Are you saying you ordered this so I could..."

Beck tapped my chin. "Just like that. Nice and wide." He opened the back door and motioned for me to get in.

"Are you really this crazy?"

He winked. "I prefer to be called adventurous. Now get in."

CHAPTER 18
Beck

"**G**igi!" Maddie raced to Gram's hospital bed and climbed up. She had on her usual Saturday outfit of shorts and a T-shirt, with her green Girl Scout sash across her body displaying her seventeen badges.

"Easy, baby. Gigi is feeling better, but you need to be careful."

Gram also looked a heck of a lot better. It helped that she was sitting up in bed, already dressed in street clothes, with a full face of makeup on.

Gram frowned. "Don't listen to Captain No-fun. What's shakin', pip squeak?"

Maddie pointed to her great grandmother's eyes. "I like your eyeshadow. It's sparkly."

"Everything is better when it sparkles. If I could eat glitter for breakfast and shine all day, I would."

Maddie flashed her tiny teeth. "I want to sparkle, too."

"You do? Well, grab me that makeup bag on the end table, and we'll fix you right up."

Watching my grandmother with my daughter reminded me so much of my mom and me—not that she'd made up my face with glitter, but she'd had a way of passing on experiences without making me feel like I was a little kid.

"Daddy said you're coming to stay with us," Maddie said.

That had been a bone of contention over the last few days since Gram and the doctors had started talking about discharge. She had been in the hospital for two weeks, so it wasn't surprising that she wanted to go home to her own place. But the doctors had said she shouldn't be alone right after discharge, since she might become weak and light-headed. I waited for the argument to come again today. Shockingly, it didn't.

"That's right, my love." She tapped her finger on Maddie's nose. "I'm looking forward to it."

Gram's smile seemed to glitter as much as her eye-shadow. And the fact that she'd come around to the idea of staying with me without another fight made me think I should be scared. But maybe she was starting to feel the weakness the doctors had warned about. Either way, I thought it was best not to look a gift horse in the mouth. So I took a seat at the foot of the bed and watched as Gram colored my six-year-old's eyelids with purple sparkly shit.

A nurse walked in as they were finishing up. "Hey, Ms. Aster." She looked at Maddie and smiled. "Oh, hello. Who do we have here? I love your eyeshadow."

My daughter beamed. "I'm Maddie. I'm six years old, and this is my Gigi."

"My goodness, look at all those badges. Are they all yours?"

Maddie nodded. "I'm going to earn them all."

The nurse smiled. "Well, if you're as determined as your great grandmother, I have no doubt that you will." The nurse spoke to Gram. "I'm just finishing up with your discharge paperwork. Give me about fifteen minutes, and I'll come in and take out your port. Then we can go over your medication and discharge instructions so you can bust out of here."

"Thanks, Lena."

As she walked out, Nora walked in.

I hadn't seen her since our infamous limousine ride home, though I'd replayed it a million times since then. I'd also broken down and called her twice, but each time my call went to voicemail. I didn't leave a message, since her messages to me had been loud and clear since the start.

"Hey." Nora smiled. "How you doing, Beck?"

She had on another sundress, and my mind immediately went to what I'd done to her under the table, how I'd had to kiss her to stifle the moan as she came all over my hand. That sound was better than porn.

Nora walked over to Maddie and Gram with a smile. "You must be Maddie."

Maddie nodded and pointed to her eyes. "Gigi did my makeup."

"I see that. It's very pretty."

"Do you work for my dad?"

Nora shook her head. "No, I don't. I'm actually a friend of your great grandmother's."

"What made you ask that, Maddie?" I said.

She shrugged. "Because the only time I ever see you with girls is at work."

It's funny to get a kid's perspective. Maddie was right that I didn't bring women I went out with around her. I didn't want to introduce her to anyone unless that person was sticking around for a while. And there hadn't been any of those since my divorce.

Maddie looked at Nora. "Do you have a boyfriend?"

"Maddie," I scolded. "It's not nice to ask people that type of stuff."

"How come?"

"You know how I told you some questions are private?"

"Like the lady I asked if she was having a baby?"

"Oh boy." Nora chuckled.

I nodded. "Yeah, she was probably sixty and definitely wasn't." I spoke to my daughter. "Yes, questions like that— we went over this. You don't ask questions about age, babies, girlfriends and boyfriends, money, or God to strangers."

Nora smiled at Maddie. "You should listen to your dad. But also, no, I don't have a boyfriend."

"My friend Lizzie says pretty girls always have boyfriends."

Nora and I looked at each other. "Can I take this one?" she asked.

I held my hands out. "Please do."

"Pretty girls definitely don't always have boyfriends. And if a boy likes a girl *only* because she's pretty, he's probably not someone who should be her boyfriend."

Maddie nodded. "You're pretty."

"Thank you. So are you."

"What is that?" My daughter pointed to the Mason jar in Nora's hand.

She set it down on the rolling food tray. "This is a gratitude jar. This one belongs to your great grandmother, but I have one, too."

"What's in it?"

"Well, those are good memories. When good things happen, we write them down and put them in the jar. That way, when we're having a bad day, we can read them, and it reminds us how much good we have in our life."

"Daddy, I want to make a gratitude jar!"

"I think yours would be overflowing," I said. "Because someone I know is pretty spoiled and doesn't have many bad days."

The nurse came back to take Gram's vitals and remove her port. I figured we should give her some privacy. "Maddie, there's a vending machine down the hall. You want to check it out?"

Her eyes grew wide, and she jumped from the bed. "Chocolate!"

I looked to Nora. "You want something?"

She shook her head. "I'll take the walk with you guys anyway."

The visitors' room was empty. Maddie ran over to the machine and licked her lips while perusing the selections.

"Her mother doesn't allow her to have much sugar. Carrie's been obsessive about her weight since Maddie was born and counts every carb, even Maddie's."

"Oh, that's not good."

"Don't get me wrong, sugar isn't great for you. But I don't want my daughter to start obsessing about her weight and have an eating disorder. I'm more of the belief that moderation is the key to diet."

"Me too. As you can tell from the five pounds of pasta I ate last week at dinner."

I looked her up and down. "Whatever you're doing. It's working."

"Thanks again for dinner, by the way."

"You're welcome." I winked. "Thank you for the ride home."

She blushed.

I debated saying more, but who knew when I might see her again with Gram being discharged. So I had to go for it. "I called you a couple of times last week..."

She smiled resignedly. "I know."

"You know because you saw my name come up in your missed calls, or because you watched it flash on the screen until it went to voicemail?"

Her face answered my question. I nodded. "Got it."

Nora shook her head. "I'm sorry. It's just... You're hard to say no to. So it's easier to avoid the question."

"Maybe that means you shouldn't say no."

Maddie ran over, jumping up and down. "Daddy, can I have Skittles?"

"I'll get them, but you can only eat some now. You save the rest for after lunch."

"Okay, Daddy."

I turned to Nora. "You want something?"

Her eyes dropped to my lips for a millisecond. "No, I'm good."

I shelled out two fifty for a seventy-five-cent bag of candy, and then my cell phone rang. I handed it to my daughter. "Mom's calling."

Maddie answered her daily call from my ex, while Nora and I stepped outside the waiting room. "My grandmother mentioned that you came every day this week and cheered her up. She puts on a brave face, but I could see she's been down. So thank you for visiting often and lifting her mood."

Nora shrugged. "I didn't have to do any lifting. We just talked about our adventures and wound up laughing for an hour or two every day."

"Well, thank you anyway."

She smiled. "You're welcome."

Our eyes caught. I could lose myself in that beautiful shade of green. I used to want her when we argued, but now I wanted her when she was sweet and vulnerable too.

182

If I was being honest, I wanted her pretty much all the time these days. Luckily, Maddie popped out of the waiting room and stopped me from saying something I'd probably regret. The three of us went back to Gram's room. She finished signing all the discharge paperwork, and Nora and I went over her new medication list, even though Gram said we didn't need to.

I picked up Maddie's backpack. "Alright, you ready to get out of here and take Gram to our house?"

Nora's brow furrowed. "Your house? I thought Louise was going home. She asked me to keep her company so she wouldn't be alone."

I looked to my grandmother, who was sporting a sly smile. "Oh. I must've forgotten to mention that I decided to stay at Beck's house for a few days. Would you come keep me company there, dear?"

I smelled bullshit. "You forgot, huh?"

Gram didn't even try to cover her indulgent smile. "Must be all the meds." She waved her hand around her head. "Brain fog."

Brain fog, my ass.

Nora smiled politely. "I'll come visit you one day this week. Maybe when Beck is at work?"

"That would be lovely. But could you also come today? I could use some company."

Now I was offended. "What am I, chopped liver?"

Gram shook her head. What was I getting mad about anyway? I couldn't get Nora to answer my calls. Gram was getting her inside my apartment.

But Nora looked hesitant. "I don't know..."

"You should come. I picked up stuff to grill for lunch, but I was hungry when I went to the store this morning, so I have enough to feed twelve, not three."

The nurse helped Gram into a wheelchair. "I insist," Gram said. "Plus, I want to talk about some new ideas I have for our trip. What do you think about the German Autobahn?"

Oh Jesus. We weren't even out of the hospital yet, and she was already thinking of more daredevil shit she could do.

Nora's eyes sparkled. "I've always wanted to go to Oktoberfest in Bavaria."

My grandmother clapped her hands. "We'll do both."

"I hope the Autobahn comes before the beer-drinking marathon," I grumbled.

"What do you say?" Gram said. "Spend the afternoon with me?"

Nora looked between me and Gram. She was definitely not gung-ho, yet she smiled. "Sure."

∾

"This is absolutely incredible." Nora walked out onto the terrace and looked around. "Is it even legal to barbecue out here in New York City?"

I smiled. "Not in most places. You have to be ten feet away from the building and any overhang. It was my only requirement when I was looking for a place to buy."

"Big barbecuer?"

"I like to grill. When I was a kid, my parents took me out to Montauk every summer. The place we stayed at had charcoal grills, and my dad would sit outside for hours looking at the ocean and cooking ribs. I don't know if it was the salt air or the smoke, but those things were the best meal I ate all year. After my parents were gone, I mentioned to Gram how much I loved barbecuing. For Christ-

184

mas one year, I think I was about thirteen, she got me a smokeless electric grill. It wasn't the same, but it got me into grilling. I would plug it in by the kitchen window so the breeze would come in—even in the winter—and grill all different dinners for us." I shrugged. "I find it really peaceful, and food is so good cooked on a charcoal grill."

"That's a really nice memory."

Today I had sausage, ribs, and chicken on the grill. I pointed to the biggest sausage. "I earmarked this one for you. I know how much you enjoy a big, hot sausage."

Nora rolled her eyes with a chuckle. "You know, I'm on to you. You show a glimpse of a sweet guy and quickly cover it up with something dirty, so I won't think you're a big softie."

I raised a brow. "I thought I'd already shown you there was nothing soft on me."

"See? There you go again." She wagged her finger at me. "But I see you, Beck Cross. You're not the guy you want everyone to think you are."

"Oh yeah? Then who am I?"

"Someone who goes to the Harry Styles concert and livestreams it for his grandmother because she's too sick to go. I can't believe you did that after our limousine ride home."

My shoulders slumped. "She told you about that?"

"Why didn't *you* tell me you were doing that? I would have gone with you."

"I only had one ticket. I really did sell them to someone, a woman at my office. They were for her seventeen-year-old daughter and a friend, but the friend got sick, so her daughter went alone to meet up with her other friends and sneak over to sit in their section. Plus, I wasn't sure I'd make it more than five minutes at that concert, or that

Gram would be awake when I called. She's a night owl, but her sleeping schedule has been off at the hospital. So I called a nurse to see if she was still up. When they said she was, I figured I'd stop in at the concert and livestream the end for her."

"You went to Harry Styles all by yourself..."

I nodded. "And I think that'll be my last Harry concert. I was sandwiched between a gazillion screaming teenage girls wearing boas and too much perfume."

Nora smiled. "That must've been some sight. I can picture it now. You, with your arms folded across your chest like you're security, standing in a sea of teenyboppers. You must've looked as out of place as a fly on a wedding cake."

I squinted. "A fly on a wedding cake?"

"Yeah. Who wouldn't stare at a big fat fly sitting on a pristine white cake?"

I chuckled and flipped over the rack of ribs. "If you say so."

"Anyway...Louise couldn't stop talking about her private livestream the next day when I went to see her. Apparently a few of the nurses watched it with her. They were young and pretty, too. If your not-so-sly grandmother weren't so busy trying to push us together, she might've fixed you up with one of them. They were swooning over the sweet grandson who would do something so thoughtful."

My eyes met Nora's. "I didn't have anything to do with it, but I'm glad Gram got you here."

Nora's face went soft, but she quickly caught herself and scowled. "Stop saying nice things. It'll give me a rash."

Maddie came skipping out of the house. "Nora, do you want to see the badge I'm working on? It's called digital leadership. I'm making a website to earn it!"

"You are? I actually have a website, too. It's more of a vlog."

"What's a vlog?"

"It's a video blog. And you know who the star is?"

"Who?"

Nora bent down, putting her hands on her knees. "*Your* great grandmother."

Maddie giggled. "Gigi can't make a website. She told me the only web she knows about is the one growing over her hooha." My daughter looked at me. "I almost forgot. Daddy, what's a hooha? I asked Gigi, but she said to ask you because you couldn't wait to tell me."

I groaned, and Nora looked exceedingly amused. But she stood and held out her hand. "How about I show you my website and then you can show me yours?"

Maddie beamed. "Okay!"

I watched the two of them walk back into the house hand in hand. I must've had a little indigestion again, because I found myself rubbing at an ache just below my breastbone.

Don't even go there, Cross.

She wants a relationship even less than you do.

Plus, she was a pain in my ass. We bickered all the time. Though shutting her up by sticking something in her mouth was one of my favorite pastimes.

I stole one last glance at Nora and Maddie, now sitting together on the couch, and forced myself to turn away.

A half hour later, we were all sitting at the dining room table eating lunch. I'd cooked way too much food, but at least everyone seemed hungry.

"Daddy, Gigi is friends with a woman named Mad Dog!" Her eyes were filled with delight.

"I know."

"She wrote on her wall."

I looked at Nora for a translation.

"My blog," she explained. "There's an area where people can leave notes and comments next to each video. Louise has become somewhat of a celebrity."

"What are you talking about?"

"Well, when I first started the site, right before our trip, I had one regular visitor and commentor—my dad, William. But the video I did in the hospital the other day got almost two-thousand comments."

"You're kidding me."

She shook her head. "Nope. I know what we've been doing has never quite sat right with you, but Louise has touched a lot of people."

"Where did all the people commenting come from?"

Nora shrugged. "We've met a lot of people during our travels. Once we tell them Louise's story and that we're documenting it to inspire others living with terminal illness, people start following the vlog and telling their friends. Like when we were at the ranch in Montana, we met a blacksmith. We watched him put shoes on a few of the older horses. Turns out his wife works at a residential retirement community. When we told him about the trip we were taking, he told his wife, and the next day he brought her to the ranch. She'd shown some of our videos to the residents where she worked, and a few who had started to be homebodies reached out to their families to go out more, make plans to do things they'd been putting off. I think a hundred new people followed us that day alone. People hear about Louise—or better yet, meet her—and they can't help but be inspired."

"Wow."

"You should check out my recent vlog posts, read some of the comments. People from all over are rooting for her with each activity. Louise and I have even talked about starting a foundation because so many people have offered to sponsor our trip or just send money via Venmo."

I searched Nora's face. "How about you show me the comments after dinner?"

Her genuine smile was beautiful. I rubbed my breastbone again. I should've taken a Prilosec or something.

After we finished eating, Nora and Maddie insisted on cleaning up since I'd done all the cooking. Nora set me up with her laptop in the living room, giving me a quick tour of her website before leaving me at the page with all the videos. Of course, I pretended I hadn't already stalked her videos—especially the ones of her in the bikini. But in truth, I hadn't checked it in a few weeks. I hadn't realized she'd continued posting once Gram was admitted to the hospital.

I scrolled down to the bottom and watched the first video done in the hospital. Gram's face came on the screen. I recognized the background as the ICU ward in Gatlinburg. She must've recorded it when I'd stepped out to do a Zoom call once or twice, because the rest of the time Nora and I had been together.

My grandmother looked frail and weak, night-and-day different from the way she looked today. She talked about what had happened to her—giving details of the tumor location and the stroke she'd suffered. The last part got me choked up.

"Listen, I've had fun. Lived a good life. Loved hard. Helped raise two boys I couldn't be prouder of. So if this is my last video, don't worry, I'll never be dead—not even when my heart stops pumping. Because you never truly die when you live in the souls of the people you leave behind."

I swallowed the lump in my throat and read through the thousands of comments—people from her night in jail, people from the ranch she'd visited in Montana, her sky-diving instructor, people who were sick themselves. There were quite a few posts from people outside the country.

It might've been the first time I truly understood what they were doing, why Nora was so taken with Gram and had basically put her life on hold to travel with a woman forty-nine years her senior. My grandmother defined life. And to many who went about their day-to-day existences forgetting to actually live—maybe myself included—she was an inspiration.

Nora walked over, drying her hands on a dishtowel. "Louise is going to lie down. Today was a busy day for her, being sprung and all."

I started to get up. "Alright, I'll help her."

Nora shook her head. "I got it. Enjoy the videos."

I nodded. But the last video had hit me hard, and I shut the laptop. Even scrolling back to lift my mood by watching a bikini video didn't appeal to me. Instead, I thought I'd have another beer. On my way to the kitchen, someone knocked at my door.

When I opened it, I found a woman who lived in the building with her daughter. She and Maddie were the same age and had become good friends. They often got together on the days I had Maddie.

"Hi," the woman said.

"Hello."

She looked around me. "Is Maddie ready?"

My brows drew together. "Ready for...?"

"Oh, I'm sorry. I assumed you knew. Maddie called Arianna and asked if she could come over for a playdate. The call came from your cell, so I thought you were okay with it. She said her great grandmother just got home from the hospital, and the apartment needed to be quiet."

My daughter ran down the hall with her backpack on.

"Maddie, you called Arianna's mom and asked if you could come over without telling me?"

"Gigi told me to. She said she needed to rest."

Considering my daughter could quietly play by herself for hours, and my grandmother knew it, I smelled something fishy.

Arianna's mom interrupted my ruminations. "We're happy to have her. Arianna and I are going to the library for story time and then to the park for a little while."

Maddie clasped her hands together in the prayer position. "Please, Daddy, can I go? I love the li-berry."

I ruffled her hair. "It's li-brary, and how can I say no when you're more excited about the library than the park?"

Maddie jumped up and down. "Thanks, Daddy!"

"I'll have her back by say..." Arianna's mom looked at her watch. "Is six okay? That way we have time to stop for ice cream, too."

I smiled. "That's great. Thank you very much."

As soon as I shut the door, Nora came walking down the hall. She looked left and right. "Where's Maddie?"

"She just went on a playdate, which my grandmother apparently arranged."

Nora shook her head. "I'm guessing that's why I was just kicked out of her room, yet she asked me to stay until she woke up—in case she needs help going to the ladies' room."

I squinted. "Does she seem like she needs help going to the bathroom?"

Nora laughed. "Definitely not. She's at it again."

"I feel like we're all just marionettes, living in Louise's puppet theatre."

"And I fall for it every time." She sighed. "I should go."

"No. Stay, please."

"You just said she doesn't need my help."

I was quiet for a minute, debating whether I should be honest. Nora was skittish when it came to me, almost like an abused dog adopted by a new family. She would let me near her when she felt like it, but God forbid I advance first. Yet I went with the truth.

"She doesn't need help. But I want you to stay anyway."

"Beck…"

"Can't we be friends?"

"The last time we had an innocent few hours together, it ended with you getting me off in public, and me returning the favor on the ride home."

I grinned. "It's a fucking *great* friendship, isn't it?"

Nora chuckled. "I thought we'd already decided we weren't friends. I believe your exact words were '*we don't like each other enough.*'"

"I changed my mind."

She made a skeptical face. "I'm going to call bullshit."

I started to feel a little panicky, like she wasn't going to stay no matter what I said. So I was forced to pull out the big guns.

"One drink. Watching the videos and seeing all the comments strangers posted on your wall got to me. I don't feel like being alone. Besides, I want to talk to you about something."

Nora looked back and forth between my eyes like she was gauging my sincerity. Then she nodded. "Okay. But not one piece of clothing comes off."

I could think of a thousand ways to please this woman while not technically removing an article of clothing. But I kept that to myself. Instead, I treated her like any other friend who'd come over. "How about we have cigars and whiskey out on the balcony?"

Nora's face lit up. "I've never tried a cigar."

It wasn't my first choice of items for her to wrap her lips around, but it would have to do...*for now.*

CHAPTER 19

Nora

I blew out six smoke rings in a row. "Did you see that?"

Beck's eyes were locked on my lips. He groaned. "You're fucking killing me, woman."

"Maybe if you thought about something *other* than sex, you might be able to see that I have some true cigar-smoking talent."

"You got talents alright..."

I laughed and looked around. "Your apartment is amazing. This balcony is bigger than my entire place."

"Do you have a different layout than Gram has? Her place isn't that small."

"Oh. Yeah, she has a two bedroom, and I have a studio."

He nodded.

"I bet the sunset is incredible from up here."

"It is. You should stay and watch it."

The whiskey had loosened my shoulders, and I was enjoying the breeze. I felt more relaxed than I had in days.

I puffed on my cigar again and blew out more smoke rings. "Maybe I will."

"Sunrise is even better. You should stay for both."

I chuckled. "Smooth, Cross. Smooth."

"I try."

Beck drew a puff on his cigar, and my eyes lasered in on the way his lips wrapped around the end. I forced myself to look away before he could notice.

"So is that why you're leaving New York?" he asked. "Because it costs a small fortune to rent a three-hundred-square-foot place?"

"No. Actually the tiny space doesn't bother me. I just want to be closer to my dad."

"You said you're leaving when your lease is up? When is that?"

"The end of the summer."

We enjoyed a few minutes of quiet. It was rare that I felt comfortable in silence. It was nice.

"So what did you want to talk to me about?" I asked eventually.

"Hmmm?"

"When you asked me to stay, you said you wanted to discuss something with me."

"Oh." He looked down at my near-empty whiskey glass. "You want another one?"

"Uh-oh. You're trying to get me liquored up before you start a conversation. That doesn't sound good."

"Not trying to get you liquored up. Just trying to be a good host."

I was skeptical, but curious. "What's on your mind?" I tilted my head back and took a big, long drag on the cigar, blowing out smoke rings again.

"I was hoping for a better lead-in to this discussion. But since it doesn't look like I'm getting one, I'll just toss it out there."

Now I was intrigued. "Okay..."

"I really need to fuck you again."

I was forming my fourth smoke ring and sucked in instead of blowing out. I immediately started to choke. Cigar smoke was *not* meant to be inhaled.

Beck leaned over and put his hand on my back. "Are you okay? You want some water?"

I shook my head. After a minute, my throat still burned, and my eyes were filled with tears, but I was able to squeak out a few words. "Why would you say that?"

He looked confused. "Because it's true?"

I shook my head. "First of all, there's a nicer way to ask a girl to sleep with you, and second of all, how about a little notice when you're going to say something like that?"

"I told you I was hoping for a better lead-in. You forced me to tell you."

"Oh, so now it's my fault that you're a pig and say inappropriate things?"

Beck's eyes zeroed in on my mouth, and he leaned closer. "Fuck. Yeah, let's argue."

I nudged him to sit back into his chair, putting a little space between us. "We've had this discussion. I told you, it's not the right time for me to have a relationship."

"It's not for me either."

"So you don't want to date me, you only want to... what, fuck me?"

He shrugged. "Exactly."

"Beck..."

"Hear me out. I have some bullet points for this. I knew it wouldn't be a simple discussion."

"You have bullet points?"

"Yep. It's what you do at two in the morning when you can't sleep because you can't stop thinking about the sound a woman makes when she comes on your hand in a restaurant." Beck picked up his phone from the table and scrolled. "Okay, number one: Neither of us wants a relationship. Number two: You're moving across the country at the end of the summer. There's a pretty definitive lifespan to this arrangement I'm proposing. Number three: I'm attracted to you. Very attracted. And I think you feel the same. Number four: We've test driven the car, so we already know it's a nice ride. No disappointments. Number five..." Beck paused and held my eyes. "I really want you. I haven't had a good night's sleep since the restaurant—too busy thinking about that little mewl sound you make when you come."

He set his phone back on the table. I leaned forward and checked his screen. He really did have a numbered list. Though it looked like there were more things listed than five. "What else is on that list?"

"Nothing."

I held out my hand. "Let me see then?"

Beck held my eyes for a few heartbeats. Then I did a quick grab and took it.

"Number six: Best head ever." I raised my eyes to his. "You seem to have forgotten a few."

"You just told me I was a pig, so I was trying to accommodate your request to be polite."

I chuckled and kept reading. "Number seven: Phenomenal tits. Need her to ride me so I can watch them go up and down."

I lowered the phone. "You are seriously a thirteen-year-old boy."

After the last two, I probably should've stopped reading. But I didn't. And it was the last one that got me.

Number eight: *She makes me forget.*

I sighed and sucked in my bottom lip as I thought it over. I hadn't been able to stop thinking about him since the night in the restaurant either. Hell, maybe since that first kiss we'd shared in the middle of an argument. "I can't get attached to you…"

"We'll keep it to sex. No romantic walks on the beach."

Why was I considering this? Bottom line, each day was getting harder and harder. And when I was with Beck, whether we were having sex or just hanging out, there was no room to remember the rest of my life—he knew how to make me forget. "I need to think about it."

"Okay…"

"But if we decide to do this, I don't think I want Louise to know. I feel like we'd be getting her hopes up."

"I don't often discuss sex with my grandmother anyway."

I shook my head with a smile. "I can't believe I'm even considering this."

Beck leaned forward and put his hand on my knee. His thumb caressed the inside of my leg and sent shockwaves through my body. "How about a do-over of the restaurant?" His hand inched up higher. "You know, to help you decide."

I slapped a hand over his, stopping his ascent. "I think I'd like to decide this one on my own."

He pouted. "Shame."

"In fact, I should get going. I told Louise I'd do some travel planning. I'm not sure if she mentioned it to you yet, but she's planning on getting back on the road on the fifteenth, the day after her doctor's appointment, as long as he gives her the green light."

Beck frowned. "I know she's doing well, but I don't think she's strong enough yet. That's only a little more than a week away."

"I agree. So I suggested we start slow and maybe hit one of her bucket-list items that isn't so adventurous."

"What's that? Climbing the Sears Tower?"

"No. Going to visit Charles Tote."

"Who's Charles Tote?"

"Her first love."

"She married my grandfather at twenty-two."

"So?"

"You're saying she was in love with someone else before that?"

"Yep."

"And after sixty years, forty of which she was married to my grandfather, she's still thinking about this guy enough to need to visit him as part of her bucket list?"

I shrugged. "I think she has a lot of guilt surrounding him."

"Why does she have guilt?"

"Well, they met when they were thirteen and were apparently totally smitten right from the start. But it was the fifties, and things were a lot different back then. You had to court a girl, and he had to get her parents' permission. The two of them had planned to start dating at sixteen, but a week before Charles's birthday, he contracted polio. The vaccine was new and not yet widely available."

"Shit."

"Yeah. Apparently it left him in a wheelchair, paralyzed from the waist down. Louise didn't care, but her father forbade her from dating a man he didn't think could provide for her. She snuck out to visit him, but like Louise's father, Charles didn't think it was a good idea for them to be together anymore. Louise was crushed and told him she was going to wait for him to change his mind. They stayed close, good friends, but a year later, he told her he'd met someone else at physical therapy and had fallen in love. It broke her heart."

"And she wants to go see this guy?"

"She found out years later, after she met your grandfather, that Charles hadn't met anyone at physical therapy. He just knew she would never leave him unless he did something, so he made up the relationship. In hindsight, Louise said she sort of suspected that might be the case, though she allowed herself to accept it and put the blame for their demise on him. And part of her had been relieved when their relationship came to an end after she'd realized how much work it would be to take care of him."

"Damn. That's heavy."

"Yeah. Your grandfather was the love of her life, so it all worked out in the end. But she and Charles reconnected on Facebook a dozen years ago. He eventually married and had a nice life, but they'd like to see each other again. His wife passed almost as long ago as your grandfather. He's in a retirement community, and it's pretty hard for him to get around much now, so she'd like to go visit."

Beck shook his head. "I can't believe I never heard that story."

"I don't think it's something she's thought about on a daily basis. But when you start to ponder your own mortality, it dredges up a lot of things from the past."

He stared at me for a long time. "I'm glad she has you. And I'm glad I do, too—for reasons other than you give great head." He winked. "I needed a reminder of how little time she likely has left. I know this sounds ridiculous, but I don't think I accepted it until recently."

"It doesn't sound ridiculous. We all accept things in our own time."

"Where does Charles live?"

"Utah. We had talked about hitting Bryce Canyon, too. That was something from my list. But we'll see how she feels."

Beck nodded.

I put out my cigar in the ashtray. "I'm going to go. I'm sorry for wasting this."

"I'm not. I'll light it up later when I'm thinking about you and put my mouth right where yours was."

I smiled. "Pig."

"Give some thought to what we talked about. I'd rather have my mouth on the real thing."

CHAPTER 20
Beck

"**P**lease tell me you're reading a joke right now." My brother Jake strolled into my office and found me with my nose buried in my cell. "Because you're smiling like a schoolgirl with a crush."

"What do you want, Jake? I have a lot of work to do."

As usual, he ignored me and planted himself in one of the guest chairs. He used his chin to point to my phone. "Who are you texting?"

"None of your business."

He grinned. "It's that Nora woman, isn't it? She's hot, dude. Nice figure."

I clenched my teeth. It annoyed me that my brother had even been looking.

He pointed to my jaw. "Oh yeah. You got it bad. It's definitely her you're texting. What's the deal with her anyway? Is she single?"

"Yes." I pulled my chair up to my desk and put my phone down. "Now, what did you come in here for?"

"I sent you over the new prospectus to review. The old one was outdated and didn't include some of our key investors. Plus, it was boring and had too many words on the page."

"It's a document that informs people about the company. Of course it has a lot of words. It's informational."

"Yes, but you need fewer words on the page and more bulleted information. People in my generation have the attention spans of a gnat. We like our information bite-sized. Our brains are wired by TikTok and Snapchat. All your boring information will be there. But it will be snappier and easier to digest. And we also need more pretty pictures." He grinned. "Come to think of it, I should've put myself on one of the pages."

I shook my head. "Whatever. I'll look at it this afternoon."

Jake kicked his feet up on my desk and locked his hands behind his head. "So getting back to this Nora chickadee. Why haven't you made a move yet if she's single?"

I frowned.

Jake's eyes widened, along with his smile. "Holy shit. She shot you down, didn't she?"

"She didn't *shoot me down*, if you must know. We've... spent some time together."

"You mean you've hooked up?"

I rolled my eyes. "Yes, Jake."

"But you like her. I can tell. I saw the way you looked at her at the hospital, and every time you talk about her, you have this goofy smile."

"It helps when you like the people you hook up with..."

Jake shook his head. "No. This is more than that. You *like her*, like her. So why is it only a hookup? Why don't you ask her out and see where it goes?"

The only thing Jake liked better than looking in the mirror was gossip. He wasn't going to let this go. I sighed. "She doesn't want a relationship, which is fine with me. I'm too busy for one. So we're keeping it simple." I didn't add that Nora hadn't even committed to an ongoing physical relationship yet. It had been three days since our conversation at my place. We'd texted about Louise, but neither of us had raised the subject. I didn't want to come off as desperate, even if that's how I felt waiting for her to make her decision.

"Oh shit. So you're doing what you hate when women do the same to you."

I squinted. "What are you talking about?"

"You're upfront with women that you don't want a relationship. They agree to a casual arrangement, and then after hooking up a few times, they want more. They bait-and-switch you."

I wasn't doing that. *Was I?* Would I take more if Nora was offering it? Yes. But that didn't mean I wasn't capable of hookup only. Hell, I was the king of hookup only.

"That's not what I'm doing."

Jake shook his head. "No strings attached doesn't work when one of you has feelings."

"I like her, but she also drives me damn nuts at times. I don't have *feelings*."

"Sure, Mr. I-Make-Goo-Goo-Eyes-When-I-Text-Her. But whatever. It's your string to choke on."

"Is there anything else we need to discuss, or is Dear Abby hour over? I have shit to do."

"Who's Abby?"

"Jesus Christ," I grumbled and pointed to the door. "Get the hell out of my office."

Jake left. But his words irked me all morning. I'd definitely complained to him more than once about a woman I'd started something casual with who all of a sudden wasn't happy with our arrangement. I remembered having this conversation only a few months ago about a woman named Piper I'd been seeing. When I'd told her I wasn't interested in more and reminded her that she'd said the same, she'd gotten upset and said she'd been hoping I would change my mind. Was that what I was doing with Nora?

Let's face it, I did like her. And for the first time in longer than I could remember, I would've liked more—to get to know her, have dinner, wake up next to her, maybe see where things went. Something about being with her just felt right.

My phone buzzed from my desk, and I was grateful for the interruption. I'd never admit it, but Jake was right. I was acting like a schoolgirl with a crush. I needed to pull up my panties and get my ass back to work. Maybe it was best that Nora seemed to have forgotten about the arrangement I'd proposed.

I didn't need the headache.

But then I turned my phone over and read the incoming text.

Nora: I've thought about your...arrangement.

My heart started to pump. It pissed me off. Yet I was already typing back.

Beck: And...

Nora: As you so eloquently put it, I'd like to fuck you, too. So I'm in.

I salivated like a starved dog served a sizzling steak.

Beck: When can I see you?

Nora: Is see you code for get naked?

Beck: It's code for how wide can you spread your legs? I can't wait to eat your pussy.

The dots started to bounce around, then stopped. It was a solid thirty seconds before they started moving again.

Nora: Sugarcoating isn't your thing, huh?

I was typing that I'd coat her with sugar if she wanted, when a second text arrived.

Nora: But yeah, I can't wait for you to do that too...

I cleared what I'd typed, too impatient to waste time.

Beck: What are you doing right now? I can come to you.

Nora: LOL. Slow down, cowboy. I'm currently at the nail salon with Louise. I was thinking more like tomorrow night.

Even the mention of my grandmother didn't dull my hunger.

Beck: How about tonight?

Nora: Anxious much?

Beck: YOU. HAVE. NO. IDEA.

Nora: I just snort-laughed out loud and scared the woman getting her nails done next to me.

I pictured it—her big pouty smile and how gorgeous she looked with a little gleam in her eye, laughing at the screen.

Beck: So tonight?

Nora: Fine, Mr. Impatient. But I have a few things to do. So it will have to be later.

Beck: Whatever you want. Tell me where and when, and I'll be there.

Nora: I'd actually prefer to come to you.

Maddie was with her mom for the next three days. My grandmother was doing well and had gone back to her place with Bitsy this morning. So I didn't even have the little barking shit to interrupt giving Nora my full attention.

Beck: Works for me. What time?

Nora: I can probably get there about ten.

Beck: Can't wait. See you then.

Nora: Oh, and Beck, we need to talk first. I think we need to set some ground rules for this thing.

Beck: Fine. But it's going to be hard to talk with my cock in your mouth. So maybe we talk second.

Nora: Pig.

Beck: We'll see who's the one squealing when I get my hands on you.

She sent back a pig emoji, and that was the end of it.

I guess I was going to be stopping at the pharmacy on the way home tonight to pick up a bottle of aspirin. Because whether it proved to be a giant headache or not, there was no fucking way I wasn't doing this.

The doorman rang to let me know I had a guest, and I suddenly got palm-sweaty nervous. It had been a long-ass time since a woman made me feel this way. And I wasn't sure I liked it. Since it was late, and Nora had probably eaten dinner by now, I'd had my assistant order a charcuterie board. She'd asked if it was for a date or the guys coming over, since I occasionally played cards with my buddies, and she'd ordered a spread for those nights. I normally loved that my assistant took the initiative. When she'd ordered for our last card night, I'd come home to a delivery of not only food, but a selection of cigars and whiskies that had been paired together, as well as a half-dozen combination wooden cigar tray-coasters, so the guys could set their drinks and their cigar down while holding their cards. But now, as I looked over at the dining room table, I thought it might be too much. Gwen had sent not only the charcuterie board, but also chilled wine, a flower arrangement, and a few candles.

My heart thumped faster as I heard the elevator slide open from the hall. But when I opened the door and got a look at her, it almost knocked the wind out of me.

It's a hookup, Cross. Not a date.

Luckily, I was a master at not showing my nerves.

Nora looked incredible—way more dressed up than I'd expected. She had on a Kelly green, silky-looking slip dress with high heels that wrapped up her ankles. Her thick, blond, normally straight hair was done up in loose curls, and she had more makeup on than I'd ever seen her wear. I couldn't stop staring at her scarlet red lips. Maybe this was a date after all...

"Down, boy," she said. "I'm not dressed like this to come over. I had a hot date before this."

My exuberance came to a screeching halt. *She had a freaking date before coming over?*

Nora took one look at my face and chuckled. She stood toe to toe with me and patted my chest. "The date was my father, Mr. Cool."

"I thought your father lived in California?"

"He does. But he came to visit for a few days. We went to see an opera at the Met at seven. That's why I'm dressed up and couldn't come until this late."

My shoulders loosened. "Oh."

She smirked. "You should've seen your face. It looked like you wanted to kick someone's ass."

"And you find that amusing?"

She tapped her nails against my chest. "I do."

I wrapped a hand around the back of her neck, gave it a gentle squeeze, and pulled her against me. "You're going to pay for that, Sutton. Now give me that pain-in-my-ass mouth."

I planted my lips over hers, and she eagerly opened for me. The stress of my day dissolved almost instantly. Her tits pushed up against me, and she made that little moan sound that drove me nuts. They say things that take away anxiety and stress are often addicting—like Xanax and alcohol. I understood that now.

Nora wrenched her mouth from mine. "Are you going to maul me in the doorway or invite me in?"

I took her bottom lip between my teeth and gave it a good, firm tug. "Doorway works for me."

She giggled and pushed at my chest. "Let's go inside, caveman."

I begrudgingly opened the door and let her walk in. Though I was thanked for my gentlemanly behavior by a phenomenal view of her ass in that dress.

I wonder if she'd let me in the rear door.

I cleared my throat and pushed that thought to the back of my mind—for now. Nora set her clutch down on the dining room table, which screamed romance with the wine chilling in a bucket, flowers, and candles.

"What's all this?" she asked.

"I wasn't sure if you'd eaten dinner. So I went with something you could pick at."

"That was thoughtful." She turned back to the table for a minute. "And the flowers and wine?"

I shoved my hands in my pockets. "My assistant did that."

Nora smiled. "Is that a bashful look? It's kind of cute, though not one I thought you had in your arsenal of expressions."

"Wiseass. After I set it all up, I realized it was a bit much for...you know, for our purposes."

"You mean for a hookup night?"

"Yeah."

"Well, at least you have a good assistant."

"I do. Would you like a glass of wine from my romantic setup?"

Nora smiled. "Sure."

I grabbed the bottle from the ice bucket and went into the kitchen to uncork it.

Nora took a seat on a chair on the opposite side of the island. "So, I think we should probably talk about ground rules before we go any further."

I slid a glass of wine over to her and poured mine. "Shoot. I like rules."

"You do?"

"Of course. It's not any fun to break them when you don't know what they are."

"Beck..."

"Relax. I'm joking." I sipped my wine and shrugged. "I'm ready. Lay what you got on me."

"Okay, well, I think these types of arrangements are often ruined because people keep pushing the boundaries further and further, and one of the two people looks back and realizes their hookup has inched into relationship territory. So the point of making some ground rules is to keep us firmly in the hookup zone."

"Alright. So what are these rules?"

"First, I think unless we're with Louise, we should keep our time together limited to sex."

"So you walk in, I strip you naked, and you hightail it out of here when we're done?"

She laughed. "Maybe not that dramatic, but more along the lines of we shouldn't watch movies together beforehand or spend the night after."

I didn't love that, but I also understood why she would make the rule. It might have been where I'd gone wrong with my previous supposedly no-strings-attached relationships.

"Okay. What else?"

"No dates. No restaurants or movies or whatever."

"Alright."

"No chit-chatting on the phone or exchanging texts, unless it's Louise-related or we're setting up a time to meet."

That sucked. Her texts had become the highlight of my day.

"Fine."

"I think we should also try to limit the affection. No hand holding or flower sending. No sweet gestures at all."

"Hang on, is letting your head loose long enough that you can take a breath while I'm fucking your face considered sweet? In my book, there's a fine line between considerate and sweet."

"Now who's the wiseass?"

"Are we done?"

"One last thing. I think normally these types of situations aren't monogamous. They're more like *don't ask, don't tell.* But we've already had sex without a condom, so unless you want to go back to using one, I think we should forego sex with anyone else. Dating others is fine, of course."

The thought of her fucking anyone, or even dating another man, made me irate, so that was the easiest rule to accept.

I nodded. "Deal."

She sipped her wine, then set it down and ran her finger along the rim of the glass. She looked up under thick lashes. "That's it. So...we could get started whenever you're ready."

I held her gaze while I chugged the rest of my wine and walked around to the island. I lifted her from her chair, tossed her over one shoulder, and stalked to my bedroom. I'd briefly considered fucking her on the counter, but the thought of her spread eagle in my bed was too good to resist. She giggled, and the sound shot straight to my heart.

In my bedroom, I set her down on her feet near the edge of my bed, then walked to a chair ten feet away and planted myself there.

"What are you doing?" She laughed.

"Undress for me."

The smile on her face morphed into something very different. She *liked* when I took control in the bedroom.

Nora reached back and unzipped her dress slowly. The sound of each tooth coming apart made me want to rip the fabric to shreds. I had to grip the arms of the chair in order to stay put while she slipped the thin straps from her shoulders and let the silky material puddle on the ground. Standing only in heels that wrapped up her legs and a black lace strapless bra and matching panties, she couldn't have been any sexier. But then she lifted her chin, defying whatever discomfort was probably seeping in at being on display, and my half-mast cock hardened to full salute.

"You're gorgeous." My voice came out strained, with some tremble to it. "Turn around. I want to see the back."

She made a slow pivot. Damn, I wanted to be that piece of string tucked inside the crack of her fantastic ass.

I licked my lips, which had gone dry. "Sit on the edge of the bed."

I could almost come from watching this woman take my commands. This was a gift she was giving me.

Nora perched herself on the edge of the mattress, legs together.

I rubbed my bottom lip with my thumb. "I'd like to add a rule to your list."

"What's that?"

"No touching yourself unless we're together. I don't want you satisfying your own urges. I want you calling me. Often."

She swallowed and nodded.

"Thank you. Now spread your legs."

Her eyes flared and darkened, but she did as told.

"Wider."

She used her hands to push her knees until they couldn't go any farther.

"Now touch yourself. Rub your clit. Over your panties."

Her eyes jumped to meet mine. It looked like she might push back, but instead she held my gaze as she moved one hand over her panties and began to massage small circles around her clit. After a few seconds, her eyes drifted closed. Her lips parted, and I watched as her chest rose higher and faster.

Fuck.

My.

Life.

How in the world was I not supposed to fall in love with this woman? She was the entire package, with a great big sexually open bow on top.

I rubbed my cock through my pants as I watched. Nora's back arched and her head fell back. When her circles grew faster and she started to moan, I knew it wasn't going to be long. So I went to her. Dropping to my knees between her thighs, I yanked her panties down her legs and dove in with an open-mouthed hunger like she was my first meal in months. I lapped and sucked, speared my tongue into her sweet hole, and drank every bit of her juices.

Nora threaded her fingers into my hair, nails digging into my scalp. "Beck..."

I reached up and held her down, burying my entire face in her. I could've drowned in here and died a happy man. I ate her through her orgasm, through the writhing and shaking, until long after she fell back and collapsed on the bed. I wasn't letting one drop of her sweetness go to waste on the sheets.

When I was done, I wiped my mouth with the back of my hand and unleashed my straining cock. I knew how warm and wet she was, and I couldn't wait to dip inside and find my nirvana.

As I climbed over her, Nora's eyes fluttered open. A sated and silly grin spread across her beautiful face. "Hi," she said.

My lip twitched. "Hi."

"You're *really* good at that."

"Why thank you."

"I'm not sure how much of a participant I'm going to be right now." She moved her head to look at her right arm, which was spread out across the bed. "My limbs feel like jelly."

"It's okay. I'll pick up the slack."

She grinned. "Thanks. I owe you one."

"Which I will happily collect on in the near future."

I reached down and fisted my cock, lining it up with her opening, and pushed in. Even with only my crown inside, I was glad she'd already come, because this was going to be embarrassingly fast. I'd forgotten how tight she was.

My eyes squeezed closed as I pushed farther inside, her soft walls clenching around my cock. The way it felt, I thought tonight might shoot to the top of my best sexual experiences list, and I wasn't even fully seated and hadn't come yet. That was saying something.

I pushed in deeper, stretching her inch by painstaking inch, until my balls were resting against her ass. Nora looked up at me, eyes glazed over, lips parted in a pant, and I decided I was staying here. Not moving. Maybe forever.

But then Nora arched up, bringing her lips to meet mine, and I got lost in her kiss. At the risk of sounding like a giant pussy, everything else faded away. And I got my second wind. My hips started working, sliding in and out. She was so wet. So slippery, fucking phenomenal. But I needed her to come again first. It didn't matter that she'd just orgasmed five minutes ago, and my load was ready to shoot out like a cannon. I needed to satisfy her, needed to please her.

So I grabbed one of her knees, lifting it to hit inside her at a new angle. The look on her face went from happily sated to *oh shit, here we go again*. On the right path, I slipped a hand between us and massaged her clit as I glided in and out. Nora's muscles began to pulsate—she squeezed so tight around me that I could feel her twitching, milking my cock.

She moaned as her orgasm hit, saying my name over and over.

And...

There it was.

Nirvana.

Heaven.

I was going to have to set up the sound recording on my phone so I could replay that throughout my day. Especially if I wasn't allowed to talk to her.

Oddly, I'd never gotten off on a woman screaming my name during sex. But something about Nora doing it was almost better than my release itself. It made me feel warm and soft inside, yet like the king of the jungle at the same damn time.

Once she went slack again, I ramped up my speed and took my own release, filling her with what felt like an endless stream of cum. After, my body jerked and spasmed deep inside her. Reality began to seep back in, and I looked up to make sure Nora was okay. Again I found her with a giant, goofy smile.

I smiled back. "Hi."

Her smile widened. "Hi back."

I chuckled and pulled out, even though I had no desire to move. "One minute. I'll grab you a towel."

I came back with a damp cloth and a dry one. Nora hadn't moved a muscle. Since she was the one who'd let me make the mess, I figured the least I could do was clean it up. But when I looked between her legs, I saw my cum dripping out.

"Oh fuck," I groaned. "That's the hottest thing I've ever seen in my life."

Nora leaned up on her elbows, but I stopped her. "No, don't move. I want to watch it come out naturally."

She blushed. "Oh my God. That's totally weird, and I should probably feel self-conscious. But the way you're looking at me is so sexy, I don't even care."

My dick hadn't fully softened yet, and I started to harden as I watched. I couldn't take my eyes away as my

VI KEELAND

arousal dripped from her pussy and seeped along the crevice that led to her ass. When it got close to her hole, I reached with one finger and spread it around. Nora's eyes widened as I massaged my cum in and prodded her puckered opening.

"Is this off limits?" I asked.

She bit down on her pouty bottom lip. "I've never done it. Not fully anyway. My ex and I, we... He went for it once, but it hurt too much."

"That doesn't sound like a no..." I dipped my wet finger in, just the tip. Nora gasped, but relaxed as I started to push in and out gently. "Does that hurt?"

She shook her head.

"Not tonight. There's no rush. We'll take our time. Maybe just a little massage once in a while, to get you ready for it." I pushed in a little farther, not even to my knuckle. She clenched around me...but relaxed again after a minute. "You have to learn to trust me. Know that I'll go easy and take care of you."

She nodded. "Okay."

I gave it another minute, gently gliding in and out. Her body relaxed enough that I could've pushed farther, but I didn't want to take things too fast. So I slipped my finger out and cleaned her up properly. When I was done, I went into the bathroom. Nora was standing with her dress halfway back on when I came out.

"What are you doing?"

"Getting dressed..."

"You've only been here a half hour."

She smiled halfheartedly. "I know. But this is just sex, so..."

"Seriously? You're going to run out the door like this? Should I toss some cash at you, too?"

Nora narrowed her eyes. "Don't be a dick, Beck. This was our arrangement."

Yes, we'd agreed to sex only, but it still felt wrong. Though I stopped myself from bitching, afraid I might scare her away on day one.

"Fine," I grunted. "Let me at least drive you home."

She zipped the back of her dress. "I'll just grab an Uber."

I raked a hand through my hair. It was the first time in my life that I'd felt used. I didn't like it very much. I took a deep breath. "When can I see you again?"

"Soon."

"How about more of a definitive answer?"

"My dad is only in town for a few days, so I'll be with him." She ran her fingers through her hair like a comb. "We have a lot of plans. Museums, a play, a French restaurant with a seven-course tasting menu... We're even having lunch with Louise one day. I'm excited for them to meet."

Great. My grandmother gets to share a meal with Nora, but I don't.

She walked over and pushed up on her toes, kissing my lips. "You're pouting."

"No, I'm not." *I totally am.*

"I'll call you, okay?"

Not even a minute later, she was out the door. I leaned my forehead against it and listened for the sound of the elevator coming and going.

This no-strings-attached shit isn't going to be as easy as I thought.

CHAPTER 21

Beck

?"

Nora squinted at me. "Why do I think you're guessing wrong just so I'll keep doing this?"

Because you're a smart lady.

Her tracing a word on my back had become a new game we played. Well, it was *her* version of a game I'd started a week ago when I held her down and spelled out DELICIOUS with licks of my tongue on her pussy. She'd tried to return the favor by licking a word on my cock, but I could never get past the first letter without shoving my dick down her throat. So she'd started spelling words on my back with her nail. It felt great, but that wasn't why I pretended not to be able to identify the letters. It was because I knew after we were finished, she'd run out the damn door. I had to take whatever I could get with Nora.

"I'm too competitive to let you win. Do it again."

It didn't look like she believed me, yet she traced the letter M on my back a third time.

"O?" I said.

She slapped my back and laughed. "Now I know you're full of shit. There's no way you could mistake an M for an O."

I hooked an arm around her waist and rolled us so she was on top. Nora yelped, but there was a smile on her face. I wiped a lock of hair from her cheek. "I want to see you tomorrow."

"I'll be in Utah."

"You know what I meant." It was after midnight, so technically she and Gram were leaving tomorrow. But I wanted to see her again before she left. "Tonight then."

"I have to pack. We have an early flight and have to be at the airport at five AM."

"Packing takes an hour or less. I want to take you out."

Nora tried to wiggle away from me. "I have too much to do."

"I'll send Gwen over to pack for you."

"Gwen? Your assistant?"

I nodded. "She can run whatever errands you need, too. We can go to that French place you went to with your dad that you liked so much."

"Beck..."

I knew that tone. Knew the face, too. It was what I got anytime I tried to push the rules an inch or two—have her spend the night at my place instead of rushing out before my dick was even fully flaccid, meet me for a lunch that involved food and not just a quickie, exchange texts for no reason.

"One dinner. You're leaving tomorrow for two weeks. When you get back, there's not that much time before you move to California."

Fuck...there went that heartburn again. I needed to get to the doctor for a checkup. It had been hitting pretty frequently lately.

Nora nibbled on her bottom lip. For the first time, it seemed like she was actually considering breaking her dumb rules. "I did love that restaurant. Though you'll never be able to get a reservation. I had to make the one I got almost three months in advance."

"If I can get us a table, will you go?"

"Is the owner a client or something and you already know you can get us in?"

"Nope. No idea who the owner is."

"Fine. But I'm only saying yes because you're never going to be able to get a table."

I'd *buy* the fucking restaurant if I had to. I smiled. "I'll pick you up at eight."

"You didn't even try to get the reservation yet."

"It won't be a problem."

Nora rolled her eyes. "So cocky."

"Confident, not cocky."

"Whatever. You'll be eating those words when you can't get a table. I'm telling you, it's impossible to get in. And our dinner deal is only for that restaurant. No Chez Coucou, no dinner sharing."

I grinned. "The only thing I'll be eating later is a seven-course meal and *you* for dessert."

⌒

"I just spoke to John Morlin." Gwen shook her head. "No luck. He doesn't have a connection at Chez Coucou to get you a table, either."

"Jesus Christ. Try Alan Fortunato. He owns a shitload of clubs. He has to have connections."

"I actually did. And I tried Trey Peterson, too. He can get you a table at La Mer. It's Michelin starred. One of the owners is a silent partner in one of his clubs."

I raked a hand through my hair and looked at the time in the corner of my computer. It was already almost four. "La Mer won't work. Go through all of our old clients. See if there's someone I'm not thinking of with a connection."

Gwen shrugged. "Okay. Do you want me to make the reservation at La Mer, just in case?"

I frowned. "No. It needs to be Chez Coucou."

"Who's going to Chez Coucou?" My brother Jake walked into my office as my assistant was walking out.

I shook my head. "No one. I'm busy. What's up?"

As per usual, my brother planted his ass in one of my guest chairs. He leaned back, lifting the front two legs off the floor. "Do you know you tell me you're busy every time I come into your office?"

"That's because I'm always busy."

"You're going to give yourself a heart attack if you don't learn how to relax. I just joined a new meditation class. You should come."

That reminded me, I needed to make a cardiologist appointment for my heartburn. "I don't need meditation. What I need is for you to tell me why you walked in here so I can get back to work. I relax by getting shit done, not closing my eyes while some hippy hits a gong."

"Did you know Gram was going to see some old boy-friend of hers?"

I sighed. He wasn't getting out of my office. "Yes, I did."

"Nora said he lives near Bryce Canyon. I skied Utah and saw it from the plane once. Looked gorgeous."

My eyes narrowed. "When did you talk to Nora?"

"At lunch."

"You went to lunch with Nora? With Gram and Nora, you mean?"

Jake grinned and pointed. "I really want to say it was just Nora. But I think you might jump over the desk and beat the crap out of me, so I won't fuck with you. Yes, I had lunch with Gram and Nora today."

Am I the only person Nora won't eat with in the damn family?

"You really like her, huh?" Jake said.

"I didn't say that."

"You didn't have to. I can see it on your face."

My phone buzzed on the desk. It was a client I'd called earlier this morning to see if he could get me into Chez Coucou. His assistant had said he was overseas. I swiped to answer. "Hey, Robert. Thanks for calling me back."

"No problem. I'm just about to board a flight, so I don't have long."

"It's not that important. But since I have you, any chance you have a connection at Chez Coucou? I'm trying to get a reservation, but the place is locked down like damn Fort Knox."

"I don't. But have you tried Alan Fortunato?"

"Yeah, no luck."

"Sorry, man."

"Alright. I appreciate you calling back from the road."

"If you wind up getting into that place, let me know if it's worth the hype."

"I will."

I tossed my phone on my desk and sighed.

Jake still hadn't left. "Why do you need to get into Chez Coucou tonight?"

"None of your business."

Jake shrugged. "Alright. But I can probably get you in."

My eyes narrowed. "How?"

"I went to college with the manager, Brett Sumner." He tapped his fist to his chest. "Phi Sigma Kappa brothers. He'll do anything for me."

"Why the hell didn't you say so? Didn't you hear me talking to Gwen about it when you walked in?" I pointed to the cell perpetually in Jake's hand. "Call and see if I can get a table for eight thirty."

"For how many people?"

"Two."

"What's the name of the other person you'll be dining with?"

"Just put the reservation under my name."

Jake grinned. "I'm going to need to know the name of the other person if you want me to make the call."

"What the fuck for?"

"Because you seem pretty desperate to get this reservation. You turn away clients these days, so I know you're not desperate to impress one. I'm guessing it's a woman. And I'm curious to know who's under your skin."

I jabbed my finger in the direction of his cell. "Just make the fucking call."

His grin widened. "Not without telling me who you're trying to impress."

"I'm not trying to impress anyone. I just... I need the reservation. Can you do that for me?"

"It's Nora, isn't it?"

I didn't have time for my brother's shit. "Yes, it's Nora. Now make the fucking call."

"She told me at lunch that she might be going there for dinner with a friend."

"*So why the hell did you make me tell you who it was?*"

His smile spread to a full-blown grin. "I just wanted to hear you admit it."

"Make the damn call."

Jake picked up the phone and swiped around for a few seconds before bringing his cell to his ear. "Hey, Brett. What's up, man?"

I listened to one side of a dumbass conversation for a few minutes before he finally got around to asking about my reservation.

"Listen, my big bro is trying to impress a woman. He needs a resy at your place tonight at eight thirty. Think you can make that happen for me?"

I was waaaayyy too anxious waiting to hear.

Jake grinned. "You're the best, man. I owe you one." He listened and then chuckled. "You got it. I'll make that happen soon."

My brother swiped his phone off and flashed a smug smile. "Done-zito."

"Thank you."

"So I take it you two are keeping whatever is going on between you on the downlow? Since Nora didn't mention her *friend* was you, and you were trying to keep your dinner date's name top secret. Things have progressed from casual, I take it?"

I didn't answer, not verbally anyway.

Jake read my face. "Oh. Sorry. That sucks."

My brother was the last person I usually talked to about women. But in a moment of weakness, I let my guard down. "Yeah, it does."

"She's moving at the end of the summer, right?"

"Yeah."

"Some people can make long distance work."

"It's a little more than that."

Jake nodded. He finally set all four of the chair legs on the floor. "I'll let you get back to work."

I stopped him at the door. "Hey, Jake?"

He turned.

"Thanks for getting the reservation."

"No problem. Have a good time."

I nodded. "Hey. What did you come into my office for anyway?"

He flashed his boyish smile. "To rub your nose in the fact that I had lunch with Nora. I know how bad you have it for her—knew it even before you did."

CHAPTER 22

Nora

"I still can't believe you got us a table."

Beck winked, and another chunk of the frost guarding my heart melted off. It was a good thing I was leaving in the morning, because this was nice—a gentleman: opening the door, pulling out my chair, telling me I looked beautiful. Don't get me wrong, I also liked the other side of Beck—the one who wasn't a gentleman: opening my zipper rather than the door, pulling my hair rather than my chair, telling me to touch myself rather than how beautiful I looked. But I hadn't been on a date in a long time, and it felt nice to be treated special outside the bedroom.

"So, I feel like we've spent a lot of time together the last few weeks." I sipped my wine and watched Beck over the rim. He was always attentive, but tonight there was something different in the way he watched me, something even more intense than usual, if that were possible. "What will you do to occupy yourself while I'm gone?"

"First off, we haven't actually spent that much time together."

"We've seen each other five out of seven nights for the last two weeks."

"Yes, but only for an hour each time. Add that time up, and it's less than a day of work I put in at the office."

"Oh. Well, think of all the normal-length dates you can have when I'm gone." Even as I said it, my stomach roiled sour.

Beck's wine was halfway to his lips when his hand froze. "I wasn't planning on dating." His forehead creased. "Are you?"

The truth was, I had no desire to date. For the last few years, dating had been a means to an end. I liked sex occasionally. So I made small talk during drinks or listened to some stockbroker tell me how much money he made during an overpriced dinner. But I didn't miss the dating part. Then again, none of the men I'd dated were anything like Beck.

I shrugged, trying to come off casual. "No, but...you know, whatever happens, happens. I don't want you to feel like tonight—us going out together—changes anything."

Beck pursed his lips. "How could I do that, when you've reminded me five-hundred times that I'm nothing but a fuck to you?"

"That's what we agreed to."

"Yes, I know. But I'm not a dog who humps anything with legs. I think I can make it the two weeks you're gone."

"You don't have to get so pissy. I just wanted to put it out there that I wouldn't be upset if you...you know."

Beck's eyes roamed my face like he was looking for something. Then he squinted. "You wouldn't be upset if I... what, Nora? Say it, if it doesn't bother you."

I rolled my eyes. "I think we both know what I'm talking about. I don't need to be crass and say it."

Beck leaned forward. "But I want you to. It wouldn't bother you if I, what, fucked another woman? Maybe buried my face between her legs, like I do you? That wouldn't bother you, right?"

My jaw tightened. "That's fine."

"Really? Maybe I can take a date here. Bring her home. Feed her my cock for dessert."

I gripped my wine glass. "Do whatever you want."

"Riiight." He nodded. "Sure. Because you don't care what I do. It's all just, you know, casual."

I shrugged and looked away. The air between us crackled. I felt Beck's angry eyes on me, but I couldn't turn my head. Not yet anyway.

Eventually, he broke the silent tension. "Nora, look at me."

My eyes slanted back to meet his. Long seconds ticked by while he held my gaze. After a minute, he shook his head. "Fuck it. I'm a lot of things, but I'm not a liar. So I'm going to go out on a limb and be honest here—maybe for the first time since you kissed me that night in the bar." He leaned closer. "I don't want you fucking anyone else. Or sucking anyone's cock. And the thought of another man touching you..." He looked away for a few seconds before meeting my eyes again. "It makes me feel violent, Nora. And I'm not a violent man. So you sit there and pretend you give no fucks about what I do while you're gone. But I'm going to be real. Because while it might violate your rules to give a shit, I'd rather you be pissed off at me for being honest than happy when I lie to you."

I opened my mouth and closed it, unsure what to say.

Beck tossed his napkin on the table and stood. "I'm going to the men's room. Finish your wine, and when I come back, we can go back to pretending."

Before I could say anything, he stalked away from the table. He was gone for almost ten full minutes. I started to think maybe he'd left me here. But then he returned. His angry face had softened, and I felt like a fool.

Beck pulled in his chair as he spoke. "I'm sorry. I shouldn't have overstepped."

I held up a hand. "No, I'm the one who's sorry. You're right. It would bother me if you were with another woman."

"The funny thing is, I'm usually sitting where you are in these things—feeling like I got bait-and-switched in the deal I made."

I shook my head. "I'm not going to be with anyone while I'm away. And I don't want you to be with anyone either."

"Thank you." His smile brightened. "We should formalize this new agreement somehow. How about I finger you under the table?"

When he winked again, I felt it in the pit of my belly. After that, we somehow returned to normal. We ate seven bite-sized courses without a lull in our conversation. I told Beck all about my upcoming trip to Utah with Louise, lunch with his happy-go-lucky brother, and how I'd approved the final edits to my latest coffee table book that afternoon. He told me stories about some deals he was working on. After he paid the check, he stood and held his hand out to help me up. Once I was on my feet, he yanked me close, right at the table.

"Was tonight so bad? Did it kill you to share a meal with me?"

"No." I smiled. "I actually had a really good time."

"Good." He crushed his lips to mine in the same possessive manner he did when we were in private. It made my knees a little weak.

Outside, Beck lifted his arm to call a cab. "How about we go back to your place so you aren't traveling home late, since your flight is so early."

"Umm... It's a mess."

He cupped my cheek. "When you're underneath me, the place could burn down and I probably wouldn't notice."

"Another time, maybe?"

Beck gave me a look. "When I try to pick you up, you don't let me do that either. I'm starting to think you're hiding something. Are you sure you're not married?"

Crap. I forced a smile and wrapped my arms around his neck. "Definitely not married. I just...not my place tonight, okay?"

He looked skeptical, yet nodded. "How about when you get back?"

Not wanting to ruin the evening by saying no now, I decided to deal with that hurdle when we came to it. "Sure. Sounds like a plan."

CHAPTER 23

Beck

Five days later, I'd watched the same Bryce Canyon video on Nora's blog for the fourth time and checked my phone for the tenth time today.

Still no response from her. We'd texted every day since she left, but she'd gone radio silent yesterday morning. At first my messages showed as delivered, although not read, but now they weren't even showing as delivered anymore. Maybe her phone broke. I figured I was due to check in with Gram directly anyway, so after I tucked Maddie into bed, I poured myself a glass of whiskey and settled into the couch.

Gram answered on the third ring.

"Hey. How's my favorite girl?"

"Oh, just busy, busy, busy." I couldn't put my finger on it, but something in her voice sounded off.

"Busy, huh? What have you been up to the last two days?"

"Just a little bit of this and a little bit of that."

My grandmother was not shy. She also didn't talk on the phone for more than five seconds without sarcasm or a zinger being tossed across the line. "You feeling okay?"

"Oh yeah. Great. Never better."

Silence again.

"How about Nora? All okay with her? I sent her a few messages, but she hasn't responded."

"She's just...feeling a little under the weather."

I sprang upright. "She's sick?"

"Probably just too much wine last night."

My shoulders slumped. *Great. Now I'm picturing her at the bar waiting for some Tinder douche.*

Gram went quiet again. Though this time, it allowed me to pick up the background noise on her end. It sounded like some sort of an announcement, like maybe at the airport.

"Where are you?"

"Just in my hotel room."

"In your room? What was that announcement?"

"Oh, it must be the television."

Why did I feel like she was full of shit?

"I gotta get going, honey," Gram said.

"What's the rush if you're just sitting around in your room?"

"I need my beauty sleep."

I couldn't shake the feeling something was going on. But I knew my grandmother. If I pushed, she'd hang up on me.

"Will you do me a favor?"

"What's that?"

"Text me tomorrow morning and let me know that you and Nora are both feeling okay."

"Don't worry about us. We're fine, dear."

"Will you do it for me, please?"

She sighed. "Of course. Goodnight, Beck."

After I hung up, I finished off the whiskey in my glass and poured a second. I felt restless and hoped it would help me relax. But it didn't.

I tossed and turned all night and checked my phone a dozen times the next day. Gram never sent the text like she was supposed to. By dinner time, I'd lost my patience, so I shot a text to Nora first.

Beck: Hey. Gram said you weren't feeling well yesterday. Just checking in to see if things are better today?

I stared at my screen, waiting for the message to change from Sent to Delivered. But it never did. *What the fuck?* How sick can someone be from too much wine that they can't even charge their phone for two days? Rather than play any more games, I scrolled to Gram's contact and hit Call. It rang twice and went to voicemail, which meant my grandmother had sent me there, because if she was just not near her phone it would've rang a few more times. And if her phone was off, it would have gone directly to voicemail.

I growled at the phone before tossing it on the counter. Unfortunately, I hadn't noticed my daughter coming down the hall.

"What's the matter, Daddy?"

"Nothing, sweetheart."

She made a face that looked exactly like the one her mother made when she was calling bullshit. It made me smile. I lifted Maddie off the floor and flipped her upside down.

She giggled. "Daddy, what are you doing?"

"Trying to turn your frown to a smile." I shook her a few times, as if gravity could make the corners of her lips turn the opposite direction. And it worked, because my daughter was smiling when I set her on her feet.

"What do you want to eat for dinner?" I asked. We always ordered in on Saturday nights.

She jumped up and down. "Sushi and an açai bowl."

I chuckled. When I was little, McDonald's was a treat. These kids were something else.

"You want the same thing you ordered last time?"

"Yes, please."

I tapped the tip of her nose with my pointer. "You got it."

"Daddy, can you load the pictures I took today to your laptop? I want to pick out some to send to Nora."

My daughter was now working on her photography badge. Today, we'd walked all over the city so she could take pictures of graffiti, like Nora's project.

"Sure. But I'll show you how to do it. I already earned my Girl Scout photography badge."

Maddie giggled. "Daddy, you were never a Girl Scout."

"How do you know?"

"Because you're a boy!"

I smiled. "Go get your camera, kiddo. I'll teach you how to upload them, and then you can go through the photos after dinner, before your mom picks you up."

"Okay, Daddy!" She skipped down the hall.

After I placed our dinner order, I tried Gram again. The same thing happened: two rings and then voicemail. So I sent a text.

Beck: How are you and Nora feeling today?

Almost two hours went by before my phone chimed with an incoming text. Maddie and I were already done eating, and she was in her room packing her things to go to her mom's.

Gram: We're good.

I frowned at my phone yet again.

Beck: Then why do you keep sending me to voicemail? And why is Nora's phone off?

I watched as the dots started to jump around, then stopped for a few minutes. Then finally started again.

Gram: You shouldn't come. But I know you never listen to me.

What the fuck?

Beck: Are you telling me to fly out there? What's going on?

Gram: I'm not telling you anything. But I know how you can be.

Something was off.

Beck: Where is Nora right now?

There was another long lull before a response.

Gram: She's resting.

Still resting from a hangover? For two days?

Screw this. I hit Call instead of texting back again. It rang once and went to voicemail. Her phone had clearly been in her hand two seconds ago. I started to type a what-the-fuck-is-going-on text, when another message came in from Gram.

Gram: I can't talk right now.

Beck: WHY NOT? WHAT IS GOING ON?

Gram: I'll see you tomorrow, if you come.

I had no idea what the hell was happening, but I was about to find out since the next thing I did was book the first flight to Utah I could get.

⌒

"Do you have any cars available?" I stood at the rental counter at Cedar City Regional Airport in Utah.

"You don't have a reservation?" the guy on the other side asked.

"No."

"Let me check." He clicked on his keyboard for a minute before looking up again. "I only have SUVs available."

"That's perfect."

"Okay. And when will you be returning it?"

I had no damn idea. "Can I book it until tomorrow and call and extend if necessary?"

"Sure."

I had my grandmother's typed itinerary, so I knew where she was staying. But on the plane I remembered she'd also given me access to her location with the Find My app. So once I got in the rental, I set the GPS to her exact location, rather than looking up the hotel's address. It was eighty-two miles to wherever she was, but the roads were wide open, so it was only a little over an hour before the navigation directed me to exit the highway. A few miles down a busy road, it had me make a left...into Cannon Memorial Hospital's parking lot.

What the fuck?

My heart started to race. My grandmother was in the hospital? Why the hell wouldn't she tell me? The GPS flashed that I'd arrived at my destination, but I had no idea where the hell to go from here. So I parked near the main entrance and walked to the information desk.

"Hi. I'm visiting a patient, but I'm not sure of her room number."

An older woman wearing a pink blazer with *Volunteer* emblazoned on the front smiled. "What's the name?"

"Louise Aster."

She typed into the computer. "I don't see anyone with

the name Aster. It's after eleven, though. Could she have been discharged already today?"

I opened the Find My app on my phone and refreshed. My grandmother was definitely here somewhere. Perhaps she was being wheeled down from the floor she was on at this very moment. I shrugged and pointed to the door I'd just entered. "Maybe. Is this where she would come out if she was being discharged right now?"

The woman nodded. "Usually, yes."

I looked around the lobby. There was no sign of my grandmother. "Alright. Thanks." I started to walk away, but then... "Actually, what about Nora Sutton—Eleanor Sutton?"

The woman typed into her computer again. "Ms. Sutton is in ICU bed four."

It felt like a punch in the gut. "Can you tell me how to get there?"

She pointed toward a bank of elevators. "Take the east elevators to the third floor and make a right. You can't miss it."

"Thanks."

I could feel my heart beating in my throat as I rode the elevator up. It was less than thirty seconds, yet my gut was tied in a knot by the time I stepped off. I turned right and strode quickly toward a set of double doors marked Intensive Care.

The unit was a big, open room, with a nursing station in the middle and glass-partitioned rooms lining the perimeter. I walked over to the first person I saw in scrubs. He was on the phone, but that didn't stop me.

"Nora Sutton. Bed four?"

The guy pointed and went back to his conversation. I did a double take as I walked in the direction he'd motioned. Holy shit. Was that even Nora? I took a few more steps to be sure. Nora didn't look anything like Nora. She was pale and seemed so tiny, and there were a million wires and monitors hooked up to her. A nurse was adjusting one as I walked in.

She smiled politely. "Hello."

I couldn't take my eyes from Nora to give the nurse the courtesy of looking at her when I spoke. "Is she okay?"

"Ms. Sutton is doing as well as can be expected in her condition."

"Her condition? What's her condition?"

The nurse looked me up and down, and her friendly smile turned cautious. "I'm sorry. Who are you? How are you related to Ms. Sutton?"

A red sign on the wall over Nora's head caught my attention. *DNR. Do not resuscitate? Why the hell would that be there?*

I raised my voice. "What happened to Nora?"

"Sir, I'm going to have to ask you to step outside."

A familiar voice came from behind me. "Bea, this is my grandson. He's with me."

I turned to find my grandmother holding a cup of coffee. Her face was solemn, and dark circles hollowed the skin beneath her eyes. It looked like she hadn't slept in a while.

"Gram, what the hell is going on? What happened to Nora?"

My grandmother and the nurse exchanged glances before Gram pointed over her shoulder. "Why don't we go sit in the waiting room and talk for a few minutes?"

I stared at Nora's still body for a long time before finally following my grandmother out of the ICU and to an empty room at the end of the hall.

Gram sat on an orange plastic chair and patted the seat next to her. But I was too wired to sit. I raked a hand through my hair. "What the hell is going on, Gram? Is Nora okay? Are you okay?"

She smiled sadly. "I'm fine, sweetheart."

"Did you have an accident or something?"

She shook her head. "No, no accident. Nora isn't well, Beck. It isn't my place to tell you. She didn't want anyone to know about her condition. But since you're here... I suppose you'll find out anyway."

"Condition? What condition?"

"Nora has cardiac rhabdomyosarcoma—malignant recurring tumors that infiltrate her heart."

"Has? She told me she'd *had* a tumor, but it was removed and she was cured. I saw the scar on her chest."

"She's had quite a few surgeries. Her condition is recurring, just like her mother's was. But the current tumors are inoperable." Gram frowned. "She's been doing really well, but two days ago, she suffered a heart attack."

My eyes bulged. "A heart attack?"

Gram nodded. "She's holding her own. But they have her in a medically induced coma now. They'll probably keep her that way for a few more days." Gram held out her hand. Since my head was now spinning, I took it and sat.

"Why didn't she tell me?"

"Probably because she wanted her privacy. I know you think you're hiding it, but I can see something has grown between you two. She lights up when she's texting lately, and there's a brightness in her eyes that hadn't been there before. But I know it wasn't something she'd planned on. Nora didn't want to get close to anyone new, only to hurt them when..."

I swallowed. "When what? Are you saying she's dying?"

My grandmother squeezed my hand. "Nora doesn't live in my building, son. We met at a Living at the End of Your Life group meeting."

I couldn't breathe. The insipid brown walls closed in on me. I pulled at the collar of my shirt, though it wasn't tight around my neck. "I need air."

The color drained from my grandmother's face. "I'll go get a nurse."

"No. I just need air." I stood. "I'll be back."

My grandmother got to her feet. "I'll go with you."

"No." I shook my head. "I need a few minutes."

She hesitated but nodded. "I'll wait here for you."

I don't remember getting in the elevator or making my way through the halls, but suddenly I found myself outside. Bent over with my hands on my knees, I gulped air in big mouthfuls, like I'd been deprived of it for hours.

My head spun to the point that I thought the yogurt I'd eaten on the plane might come up. I must've looked as bad as I felt, because a woman in scrubs walked over.

"Sir, are you okay? Do you need medical attention?"

I managed to shake my head. "I'm fine. Just needed some air."

"Are you sure?"

I wasn't, and it didn't seem like she was going to walk away easily, so I forced myself to stand. I nodded again. "I'm okay. Just got some bad news."

"I'm sorry. There's a chapel at the end of the hall on the first floor, if that might help."

"Thank you."

After she went back inside, I decided to take a walk. I didn't want anyone else stopping to ask if I was okay.

Luckily, there was a path that led around the building, because I wasn't in the right state of mind to figure out where I was going on my own.

As I walked, so many things clicked into place.

Nora would never let me come to her apartment. It made sense now, since she hadn't really met my grandmother because they lived in the same building.

Nora didn't want a relationship. She was a giver, not a taker. She'd never get involved with anyone new because she didn't want to hurt them when...

I swallowed.

The scar on her chest.

Her wanting to meet her biological father for the first time in her life.

Her friendship with my grandmother never did add up. Nora had said some of the things they were doing were her ideas, too. It wasn't just my grandmother's bucket list. It was Nora's also.

There were so many signs that I couldn't believe I hadn't put two and two together. How the hell did I not see that there was more to their bond than just friendship?

Once all the answers fell into place, an entirely new crop of questions began to fill my head.

How long does she have?

Is there no treatment available?

Has she seen every expert possible?

Has she been to Mass General? What about London and Berlin? I'd recently read an article that said their cardiac care was leading the future.

Can I get a medicopter to take us all the way back to New York? Or do I need a plane?

The pace of my walk around the hospital picked up as I got my second wind. Not knowing details, I realized the time I was taking right now could be time Nora needed. So I jogged back toward the entrance. After a few seconds, the jog turned into a full sprint. I ran through the front door, ignoring the security guard telling me to slow down, and down the hall to the elevator bank. Pushing the button three times didn't help, so I found the nearest stairs and took them two at a time, rushing up.

My grandmother was waiting outside the little room we'd talked in. I stopped and pointed to the ICU doors.

"How many experts has she seen? Who's her primary doctor at home? We need to get her transferred back to New York ASAP. This little rinky-dink hospital can't give her what she needs and—"

My grandmother pushed her finger to my lips, quieting me.

"What she *needs* is peace. It doesn't matter where she is. The doctors here have been very accommodating and are making her comfortable."

"Comfortable? No. She needs experts."

"Beck..."

"Don't Beck me. She's not even thirty. She's young and healthy. There's got to be something they can do for her."

Gram frowned. "She's had three open-heart surgeries in ten years, and just as many rounds of chemo. The tumors returned with a vengeance, and they're in a place that they can't be resected."

"Who said? Someone has to be able to fix it."

"Not everything in life is fixable, sweetheart. And Nora has made her wishes very clear. She doesn't want any more treatments. She wants to go out on her terms."

It felt like someone had cracked open my ribs and pulled *my* heart out. I shook my head and yanked my cell phone from my pocket. "I need to make some calls. Find someone she hasn't seen before, someone who can help her."

"The only thing you need to do is *be there* for her. Support her decisions."

"No." I was already Googling the head of cardiac surgery at Mass General. "I can't sit by and let two people I love die because they think it's time to quit!"

My grandmother's face went soft. For a moment I wasn't sure why.

She lifted her hand and covered her heart. "You weren't supposed to fall in love with her, Beck."

I froze. Was I in love with her?

Oh fuck.

CHAPTER 24

Beck

Hours later, I wanted to pull my hair out. I'd found two doctors who'd agreed to look at Nora's chart, but no one would help me here in Utah.

Not the nurse.

Not the doctor.

Not the asshole administrator who threatened to have security escort me off the premises if I didn't stop harassing the staff.

Worst of all, my grandmother wouldn't even help me.

I felt helpless. Useless. Powerless.

Somehow I'd wandered into the chapel a half hour ago. I was sitting in the back row, staring at a statue of Jesus on the cross hanging above the altar when a man interrupted my thoughts.

"Is that seat next to you taken?" he asked.

I was the only one in the damn chapel. There were six or eight empty pews and two sides of the aisle. I turned, annoyed. "Take a damn seat somewh..." I trailed off when I saw the collar. "Shit. Sorry, Father." I shook my head. "And sorry for saying shit."

He smiled. "It's fine. But can I sit next to you?"

I wasn't in the mood to talk, particularly to someone I had to think before speaking to. Yet I moved down so he wouldn't have to climb over me.

He sat with a sigh and extended a hand. "Father Kelly. Kelly's my first name, not my last."

I shook. "How you doing, Father?"

"My knees hurt, I need a hip replacement, and my secretary still uses a typewriter even though there's a perfectly good computer sitting right on her desk." He smiled. "But from the looks of it, I think I'm better than you right now."

I smiled halfheartedly, but said nothing, still hoping he'd take the hint.

He didn't.

"Did you lose someone?" he asked.

I shook my head.

"Someone sick?"

I nodded.

We were both quiet for a long time. I had been raised Catholic but wasn't practicing now. The last time I'd been to church, other than a wedding, was for my mother's funeral. I was pretty sure that had been Gram's last time, too. The small chapel here in the hospital was peaceful, but as I sat next to the priest, I found myself growing more and more annoyed. I shifted in my seat to face him.

"How do you reconcile God's work and young people dying?"

"I don't. Faith can't explain or justify everything. But it can provide comfort, if you let it."

"How?"

"Well, your faith provides assurance that your loved ones will be okay. Happy even, after they're gone."

"How can they be happy if they won't be with the people they care about?"

He smiled. "We'll all be reunited someday. If you can accept that, truly rely on your faith, it can help you heal after the loss of a loved one."

"I've always felt that people who rely too heavily on a belief in the afterlife do it because they aren't very good at coping with their real one."

Rather than be insulted, the priest's smile widened. "And I've always suspected that many who don't believe in the afterlife are afraid to because they're worried they might go the other way." He pointed two thumbs down.

I chuckled. "You have a good point."

"Tell me about your loved one who's in the hospital."

I stared up at the altar. "She's beautiful and pigheaded. Smart. Creative. A bit of a daredevil. She doesn't judge people and makes friends with some pretty out-there types. She's a good person, very protective of the people she cares about."

"She sounds wonderful."

I sighed and raked a hand through my hair. "She is. And I stupidly didn't realize how great she was until it was too late."

"She's still with us, though?"

I nodded.

"Then it's not too late. Perhaps you're here now to provide comfort in her time of need. It can be scary for people to walk alone in their final days. Perhaps you can help her during this time, which will in turn bring you comfort someday when you reflect back."

"I'm not sure how I can do that."

"Focus on her needs. Whether that's holding a hand when she's scared, or going to see her favorite movie that you really don't like. Try not to burden her with your fears. And most of all, make sure she knows how you feel about her."

I swallowed. Those were all the things Nora had been doing for my grandmother—focusing on her needs, showing her she wasn't scared. Jesus Christ, and all I did was give her a hard time for doing it. I'd totally screwed up. I'd let my own selfishness stand in the way of supporting my grand-mother's decisions. I hadn't put her first, like Nora did.

My eyes welled up. Father Kelly put a hand on my shoulder. "It's never too late to be the man you need to be."

"It's almost midnight," I said to my grandmother. We'd sat in chairs on opposite sides of Nora's bed ever since I came back from the chapel this afternoon. "Why don't you get some sleep?"

She sat up like she was preparing to argue, so I nipped that in the bud.

"It's her turn to need you. And you won't be any use to her if you're in the bed next to hers because you're run down and not taking care of yourself."

Gram frowned but nodded.

"I'll drop you off and come back. They said they weren't going to extubate and try to wake her until after morning rounds. So not much is likely to change until then."

"What about you?"

"I can sleep anywhere. And I'm not the one who's sick."

"Okay." Gram took Nora's hand and closed her eyes for a moment. I was pretty sure the woman who hadn't been to church in twenty years just said a little prayer. It seemed the two of us were more religious today than we'd been in a long time. Gram lifted her purse onto her shoulder, but then stopped. "Hang on a second."

She set her purse on the foot of the bed and rummaged through, coming up with something wrapped in newspaper and handing it to me. "This is her gratitude jar. Just in case she wakes up before I get back and needs a reminder."

These two amazing women were carrying around glass containers filled with memories to hang on to when there was nothing left to grab. It was hard to fight my tears.

When I got back from dropping Gram at the hotel, it was almost one in the morning. The night nurse was fiddling with the machines as I walked in.

"Any change?" I asked.

She smiled politely. "No. But no news is good news in these types of situations. Tomorrow will be a big day for her, when they take her off the meds and allow her to wake up."

I nodded.

After the nurse took some vitals, she rolled her mobile laptop desk and chair to the next patient's fishbowl room. I went back to doing what I'd been doing most of the day—when I wasn't talking to my grandmother or staring at Nora—researching cardiac rhabdomyosarcoma. I'd learned a lot about the rare cancer, including that it was sometimes hereditary. Nora's mother had died from the disease in her early thirties. I'd also read that the five-year survival rate was only eleven percent, and Nora had been diagnosed more than ten years ago—she'd already beat the odds. But three open-heart surgeries had left her heart weak, and the tumors that came back this time were inoperable.

A few more hours passed, and my eyes grew blurry from reading on my phone, so I set it down on the food tray. The gratitude jar sitting nearby caught my eye and made me smile. I picked it up and held it.

The nurse from earlier stopped back in and changed Nora's IV bag. She gestured to the Mason jar in my hands.

"What's that?"

I smiled sadly. "Just some things Nora wants to remember."

The nurse nodded like she understood. Maybe she did, working here and being surrounded by critically ill people day in and day out. She finished hanging the fluids on the pole and looked over at me. "She can't respond, but I think she can hear you."

My brows furrowed.

She pointed her eyes to the jar once again. "It might bring her comfort."

After she walked out, I thought back to what Father Kelly had said. *"Perhaps you're here to provide comfort in her time of need."*

Twisting off the top felt intrusive, like I might be invading Nora's private thoughts. But when I slipped out the first piece of folded up paper, I got over that feeling real quick.

June 1st—I'm thankful I was able to get two Harry Styles tickets today.

I chuckled and took Nora's hand. I read it aloud for her before digging in for another one.

June 20th—Sunrise over the Smoky Mountains
June 9th—The smell of fresh gardenias

June 17ᵗʰ—The ability to Google the answers to anything. BTW, Google was right, and Tequila Tuesdays has the best tacos in Virginia.

I smiled.

June 9ᵗʰ—I'm thankful for William Sutton, the best father a girl could ever wish for.

A lump formed in my throat when I realized she'd written about her dad on the date we'd gone to meet her biological father in the Bahamas.

I pulled gratitude notes out and read them for almost half an hour. A few simple ones punched me in the gut—like the one that said puddles and rainboots. And some made me laugh—like the one she wrote on Thanksgiving last year that said she was glad she wasn't a turkey. But one stopped me in my tracks.

May 22ⁿᵈ—I'm thankful for the chance to have met a man who reminded me what love is.

May 22ⁿᵈ was the day we'd met.

CHAPTER 25
Beck

"How many hours has it been now?"

Gram patted my hand. "Let's not keep track. The doctor said it can take up to a full day for some people to wake up after they stop the medication."

I looked over at Nora. She hadn't stirred since they removed the breathing tube and turned off the sedation meds. That had been around eight this morning, and it was already dark outside. Gram was trying to be positive, but I could see the concern in her eyes as the hours dragged on, too. She also hadn't eaten anything since she'd come back around ten.

"You need to eat something," I said.

"I don't have an appetite."

Neither did I, but if I was going to force Gram to take care of herself, I had to do the same. "How about some soup? I saw a Panera a few blocks down."

Gram nodded. "Okay."

"Chicken noodle?"

"Sure."

"I'll be back as soon as I can."

What should've been a fifteen-minute errand wound up taking nearly an hour because the hospital's garage meter wasn't working, and a line of cars had formed behind the wooden blockade that only went up once a ticket was paid. Then the inside of the Panera was closed due to renovations, and I had to wait on a long drive-thru line. To top it off, when I got back to the hospital, there was no parking anywhere since they'd closed the garage due to the broken meter.

I was still grumbling about it all when I walked back into Nora's room, but my bitching came to a halt when I saw a set of beautiful green eyes.

"You're awake."

Gram smiled. "She woke up a few minutes after you left."

Nora's voice was groggy. "Why are you here?"

I leaned down and kissed her forehead. "Because you are."

She sighed. "Beck..."

Gram looked between us and stood. "I need to use the ladies' room."

I set the bag of soup down and took the seat next to Nora. "How are you feeling?"

"Tired."

I smirked. "Well, you shouldn't be. You slept for three damn days."

"I guess I don't have to worry about you treating me differently just because I'm sick..."

I winked. "Never."

Nora studied me a moment. "How much do you know?"

"Enough that I can now spell rhabdomyosarcoma after typing it into Google so many times." I wiped a lock of hair from her face. "Why didn't you tell me?"

"At first it was because I wanted to feel normal, to have a one-night stand who looked at me like a woman, and not a sick woman."

"And then later? Once we became more than a one-night stand?"

She swallowed. "I didn't want to hurt you. I thought we'd end before you figured it out. You were supposed to get tired of me, like you did all the others since your divorce."

I frowned. "But you aren't like anyone else, so your plan was flawed from the start."

Tears welled in Nora's eyes. "I'm sorry."

"What are you sorry for?"

"I shouldn't have gotten involved. Then it would've been easier when..." She looked away.

I swallowed. "Nora?"

Her eyes came back to mine. I cupped her cheeks in my hands to make sure she heard me loud and clear. "I would rather fall for you and get hurt than to never have gotten involved."

The tears she'd been fighting streamed down her face. I wiped them with my thumbs and moved closer, so we were almost nose to nose.

"And just so we're clear," I said, "I have fallen for you."

More tears rolled down her cheeks, but rather than waste time clearing them, I worked on changing her mood. I pressed my lips to hers until I felt the tension leave her body.

When I pulled back, she smiled. "You said I was out for three days, which means I haven't brushed my teeth in that long."

"I give zero fucks, sweetheart. Don't brush your teeth. Don't shave. Don't shower. I'm still going to want you." I took her hand, sliding it off the bed and guiding it to cup my growing hard-on. Nora's eyes widened. But that sparkle she always had was back. "No fucks, baby."

"Your grandmother could walk in any second."

"My grandmother won't be back for a while. She didn't have to use the bathroom. I know her. She's giving us time alone." I wiggled my brows. "I could climb under those covers with you for a quickie."

"Don't you dare," she said, smiling.

Father Kelly had said maybe my purpose was to provide Nora comfort, but I knew in that moment that it wasn't. My job was to make her face look like it did right now until the end, no matter when that time came.

Unfortunately, we were interrupted by a nurse who wanted to take her vitals. Then Gram came back, and a few minutes later, the cardiologist joined us.

"Welcome back." He smiled and extended a hand to Nora. "I'm Dr. Wallace. I've been visiting you a few times a day, but you weren't a very good host. Didn't say much."

Nora smiled. "Nice to meet you, Dr. Wallace."

He did a quick exam and typed into his iPad. "Your vitals are strong. Looking at the numbers, I wouldn't guess you were someone who suffered a massive heart attack just a few days ago. Then again, most people with that type of cardiac incident have thirty years on you."

Nora sat up in bed. "When can I leave?"

"Boy. I just met you, and you already can't wait to get away." He smiled. "I'd like to keep you for observation at least for another day or two. We'll get you up and walking in the next twelve hours, if you're ready, and then see how fast your strength comes back. While we assess, we can talk about your treatment options."

"Oh…" Nora shook her head. "I don't want any treatment."

Dr. Wallace nodded. "Ms. Aster gave us your advanced directive when you came in, and I spoke to your doctors in New York to get a better sense of your history. But you should know that your heart attack and being hospitalized moves up your status on the transplant list."

"She's a candidate for a transplant?" I said.

The doctor looked between Nora and me. "I'm sorry. This is a conversation we should have in private. I only meant to suggest that we should discuss things when you're feeling up to it."

Nora forced a smile. "I am feeling kind of tired."

My gut said she was full of shit and just wanted to end this conversation, but it worked.

Dr. Wallace nodded again. "Of course. I'm going to put in an order for an echocardiogram and an EKG, as well as some new bloodwork. It'll give us a better idea where we are anyway. I'll stop back in the morning to see if you're up for talking."

After a murmur of thank yous and goodbyes around the room, it was just the three of us again. The silence grew loud. I couldn't take it.

I threw my hands in the air. "Can someone please explain to me why you quit fighting when there are still options left? Because I'm apparently the only one in this room who doesn't belong to the club."

Gram squinted at me. "Don't raise your voice. I don't care if you're over thirty and I'm dying. I'll whip your ass."

I blew out two cheeks full of hot air and shook my head. "I need a minute. I'm going to take a walk."

"Hey."

My eyes opened to find Nora staring at me. I must've nodded off while she was sleeping. I sat up and wiped my cheek.

Nora smiled. "On the other side."

Shit. I rubbed the other cheek, but the smirk on Nora's face told me I was wasting my time. "There isn't any drool, is there?"

"Nope."

I chuckled. "What time is it?"

Nora's eyes lifted to the clock on the wall opposite her bed. I'm not sure if I'd even noticed it there before now. "Almost three AM."

I looked around. The ICU rooms were all glass pods, but Nora's curtain was partially drawn now. It was the first time I didn't feel like we were sitting in a fishbowl.

"Much cozier," I said.

"The nurse told me my boyfriend was handsome and then drew the privacy panels."

"Oh yeah?" I stretched and stood. "I'll have to bring her flowers. Move over. You're hogging the bed."

Nora smiled and scooched to one side. The shitty hospital bed was probably a single or a twin, so my right shoulder hung off the edge. But it was the best spot I'd sat in for days. I nudged Nora to sit up a little and wrapped my arm around her, nuzzling her to me. "Come here."

She rested her head on my chest and looked up at me. "Thank you for coming," she whispered.

"Of course."

She smiled sadly. "I think I'm going to push up my moving date to California."

"To when?"

"As soon as I feel up to it."

A sense of panic washed over me. "Why leave? All your doctors are in New York."

"I just think it's best."

"Best for who? Me or you?"

She looked away. "Me."

I wasn't sure I believed her, but it wasn't the time to argue. I sighed. "Can I ask you some questions about your health? I mean, I feel like I'm almost qualified to operate on my own after all the reading I've done the last few days. But I'd like to understand it from your point of view."

Nora nodded. "I told you my mother died when I was little. She had cardiac rhabdomyosarcoma. Some people just get one tumor once, but others like us get lots of them, and they come back. Most cases are actually not heredi-tary, but some people have genetic factors like we do."

"When were you diagnosed?"

"The day after my prom. I was having a lot of trou-ble breathing. It sort of felt like someone was sitting on my chest, but I'd been drinking prom night so I didn't say anything for a few days. I thought it was the world's worst hangover. A few days later, I was so exhausted, I couldn't even walk. My dad, William, took me to the ER, and they admitted me. I was diagnosed the next morning. I had chemotherapy and radiation, and I went into remission a few months later. The majority of patients with localized rhabdomyosarcoma can be cured. But mine came back two years later. And the tumor brought friends. That was the first time I had surgery—open-heart at twenty. The tumors had to be resected, cut out. After that, I was good for three years, I think. Then another surgery. And then a year later, it was back again. I've had three open-hearts in the last ten years, and three rounds of chemo and radiation."

"Jesus."

"The last time it came back was only six months after the last surgery, and the tumors are non-resectable. My surgeons described them as ivy wrapping around a trellis, except the trellis is my heart. They've just infiltrated in a way that makes them inoperable."

"Dr. Wallace mentioned a transplant. Moving up on the list?"

Nora sighed. "I'm type-O blood, which has the longest wait time for a donor. Type AB has an average of less than a month. Type O is well over a year. Even with a higher status on the list, it's not likely it would ever happen. Plus, the average survival rate in people with my type of damage is only sixteen months after a transplant."

"You keep saying average, but are there people who live full lives? Who are healthy into their seventies and eighties?"

Nora cupped my cheek. "I've come to terms with my fate. I want to enjoy the time I have left. I'm sorry this is going to be hard on you. But I'm not sorry I met you, Beck."

My voice broke as I looked into her eyes. "Nora, I'm in love with you. I can't lose you."

"Oh, Beck. You weren't supposed to do that."

I shook my head. "I couldn't stop it. Wasn't an option. Falling for you was a necessity."

CHAPTER 26

Nora

"I'm fine. I got it." I swatted Beck's hand away as I pushed myself from the wheelchair outside the front doors of the lobby four days later. I felt weak, but never so ready to get out of the hospital. I'd spent way too much time in them over the last decade. I closed my eyes and took a deep breath. *Fresh air.* Something I'd taken for granted for the better part of my life.

Beck stood dutifully by my side as I walked over to the waiting car. He opened the door and watched me like a hawk as I folded into the passenger seat. Once I was sitting, he pulled the seatbelt shoulder strap out and started to buckle me in.

"Can you possibly pretend I didn't have a heart attack? You're treating me like a five-year-old. I can do that myself."

Beck smirked. "You know they don't take away your women's-lib card for allowing a man to help, especially when that man *wants* to take care of you because he's in love with you."

And there it was again—*in love with me*. It was like the cork had come out of the bottle, and now it didn't fit anymore. I hadn't told Beck I loved him back, but he'd said it at least a half-dozen times over the last few days.

I stuck my tongue out. Beck eyed it and groaned. "I miss that mouth. It's going to be a long four to six weeks."

Beck clicked my seatbelt into place, and I grabbed his shirt as he went to stand. "The doctor said no sex for four to six weeks, but there are other things besides sex..."

"Nice try. I stepped out and asked the doctor to define sex. It includes any activity that gets your heart rate up too high. With us, that probably means no arguing too, since that tends to be our foreplay."

I pouted.

Beck chuckled but shut my door and jogged around to the driver's side. The hotel was only a twenty-minute drive. A few days ago, I'd asked Louise to check me out of my room and put my suitcase in hers. There was no point in paying for a hotel when I was in the hospital. I'd asked Beck to see if a new room was available for me before picking me up. He'd said there was. But when we arrived at the hotel, Beck walked toward the elevator bank, when I needed to go to the front desk.

"I have to check in and get my bag from Louise."

"No, you don't. Your bag's already in my room. I upgraded us to a suite. And we're having lunch with Gram."

I stopped walking. "I don't think that's a good idea, Beck."

"Well, you better warm up to it quick, because I'm not taking no for an answer."

"Beck..."

He rested his hands on my shoulders. "I'm done with your rules. I get that you were trying to protect me. You didn't want me to get too close so I wouldn't get hurt. But that's over now. It doesn't matter if we're in separate rooms or if you're in my bed. I'm with you, and I'm not going anywhere."

"But..."

Beck cut me off by pressing his lips to mine. It took less than two seconds before I melted into him. We stood in the middle of the lobby like that for a long time. When our kiss finally broke, I was missing that hospital wheelchair because I felt dizzy. As if he sensed it, Beck kept a tight grip on me.

"One room," he said firmly. "I want you next to me. And if you're thinking it's because I want to watch you, make sure you're okay, then you're giving me too much credit. I want you naked next to me, your body pressed against mine, even if I can't have you yet."

With a declaration like that, how could I say no? So I took a deep breath and nodded.

"Good. Then let's go upstairs. Because my grandmother expects us to join her for lunch, and I want you all to myself for a while before that."

Beck said he'd upgraded to a suite, but he hadn't mentioned it was the Presidential Suite. Our room was the entire top floor of the hotel. It had floor-to-ceiling views of the mountain range, a grand piano, a dining room table that could seat at least a dozen, and an internal elevator to get to the second-floor master bedroom.

"Holy crap." I walked over to the windows. "I don't think I want to know what this room costs."

Beck came up behind me. He pushed my hair to one side and kissed my shoulder. "It doesn't matter. You're worth it."

I turned and wrapped my arms around his neck. "Thank you. And I don't mean for dropping everything and coming to the hospital, or for splurging for this insane room. I mean for being you and somehow always sensing when to push and when to pull back."

Beck trailed his hands up and down my spine. "Come on. Let's get you upstairs and into bed for an hour or two before lunch. The doctor said you need rest."

I lifted a brow. "Rest isn't what normally happens when we're in a bed together."

"Trust me." He groaned. "It's not going to be easy."

But even getting dressed and leaving the hospital to come to this posh room had drained me. Beck wrapped his arms around me and held me so tight, it felt like I didn't have a care in the world. Or maybe I did, but he would hold them while I took a break from everything. I drifted off to dreamland almost immediately. When I awoke, Beck wasn't next to me anymore. I heard him talking somewhere off in the distance and pushed up onto my elbows to listen.

"Alright, great. And reach out to Phillip Matthews. He's the CEO of Sloan Kettering. His daughter owns a medical supply company. Her father was one of the investors. I helped her gobble up her two biggest competitors a few years back. Her father is a good guy. He was appreciative of all the work we did and told me if I ever needed anything not to hesitate to call. I need to cash that chip in now. See if you can set me up with a call, and I'll take it from there."

It was quiet for a moment, then...

"I'm still working on when I can get her back. I'll keep in touch. And nice work getting a consult with that doctor from the UK. I look forward to speaking with him tomorrow."

I closed my eyes. I should've known Beck wouldn't give up easily. He was too determined a person to accept that he couldn't find a way to fix me. I'd lulled myself into believing he accepted that I didn't want any more treatment, because then I wouldn't have to go back to pushing him away. But he never would accept it. I laid back and stared up at the ceiling.

I'd thought letting go of my hopes and dreams for a future was the hardest thing I'd ever had to do. But letting go of Beck might be harder. Tears prickled my eyes, and my chest felt heavy.

Beck came back to the bedroom ten minutes later. He had no shirt on, and it was painful to think I wouldn't be able to run my fingers along the peaks and valleys of his eight-pack anymore.

He smiled. "You're awake. How you feeling, sleepy-head?"

I stretched my arms over my head, pretending I hadn't overheard his conversation. "Good. Where were you?"

"Had some work calls to take care of."

I forced a smile. "Oh. Alright. What time is lunch with Louise?"

"I told her I'd text her when you were ready."

"Okay." I pushed the covers off. "I'm going to take a shower."

"Want company?"

I shook my head. "Not today."

The smile slipped from Beck's face, but he took it in stride. "Leave the door open a little so I can hear if you need anything, okay?"

"Thanks."

I started mourning Beck's loss in the shower, before I'd even formulated a plan to lose him. A profound feeling of emptiness struck as the hot water sluiced over my body. Tears clogged my throat, but I refused to let them pass, to let myself cry. I'd cried a river and then some. But more importantly, Beck had learned how to read me well. And I didn't want to explain puffy eyes and a red face. So I somehow held it in.

Though Beck was more observant than ever. For a man who could take the wrong baby home from daycare and keep the wrong dog in his apartment for two days, he wasn't missing a thing now.

"You okay?" he asked when I finally emerged from the bathroom almost an hour later. I'd dried my hair, but didn't have the energy to put on makeup.

"Fine. Just tired. My battery drains much faster than normal, even after a good charge."

"Well, that's to be expected. Your body needs time to heal. I told Louise we'd meet her downstairs at the hotel restaurant at one. But we can order something up to the room for the three of us if you don't feel up to leaving—or even cancel altogether."

"Actually...would you mind if I had lunch with Louise alone?"

Beck's face fell.

"I'm sorry. I don't mean to upset you. But I want to check in on her, and she'll be more open with me without you there. She wants to protect you."

Beck pursed his lips. "Of course. Whatever you want."

"I'll bring you back something for lunch."

He shook his head. "It's fine. I'll order something from room service. I have work to do anyway."

I pressed my lips to his. "Thank you for understanding. I won't be too long."

Downstairs at the hotel restaurant, Louise was already waiting. She smiled wide and stood as I walked toward the table.

"Finally, I can get a real hug. All those damn wires and monitors got in the way."

I embraced my friend. At this point, neither of us knew when a hug could be the last, and I wanted to make it a good one.

Louise's eyes were damp when we finally let go.

"Well, we did it again, lady," I said. "Defied the odds."

She nodded. "Can't keep a good bitch down."

I chuckled as we sat.

Louise lifted the cloth napkin from the table and laid it across her lap. "I thought Beck was joining us?"

"He wanted to. But I asked him if we could have lunch alone."

"Getting on your nerves already? He was always a bossy boy."

I smiled. His bossy side was one of the things I liked about him. "I wanted to check in on you. When you were in the hospital, it hit home for me. When we're out doing our shenanigans, it's easy to pretend we're not living on borrowed time. But when you see your friend in the hospital, hooked up to all kinds of machines, it makes us face our future in a really alarming way."

"I know what you mean. It wasn't easy seeing such a vibrant young woman with her whole life ahead of her lying there and knowing how sick she is..." Louise shook her head. "It was far more difficult than I'd imagined. If anything, the experience gave me a better understanding of how my grandson feels. Because I'm not so certain that if I wasn't going through the same thing as you, at the same time, that I wouldn't think you should fight for more time.

It just doesn't seem fair that this is all you get. Even I got almost eighty years."

I reached across the table and squeezed her hand. "That's why we need to make the best of our time left. I should feel up to going to see Charles by tomorrow."

"I don't need to see Charles right now. I already told him we could Zoom in a few days when I get back to New York. Even *I* think you need more rest than a day."

"No, I can go..."

"It's already canceled. My heart isn't in it anymore anyway."

"I'm sorry." I looked into her eyes. "My time is coming, Louise. The heart attack was a warning. I'm going to go back home to California sooner than planned, to be with William for the end. It's the only thing he's asked, to let him take care of me when it's time." I swallowed. "It's almost time."

"Oh, sweetheart..." Louise got up from her chair and hugged me again. We were both crying when she sat back down. "This sucks," she declared.

The way she said it made me laugh. I wiped tears from my cheeks. "You are the only person in the world who could make me laugh while I'm telling you I don't think I have long to live."

"I consider it an honor to be that person for you, Eleanor."

The waiter came over to take our order, and the interruption brought some much-needed levity. We had barely looked at the menu, so I ordered a salad, mostly out of habit.

Louise stopped me. "Do you actually like that rabbit food better than baby back ribs or baked macaroni and cheese?"

I shrugged. "No. But I try to keep balanced and have a healthy meal for lunch and whatever I want for dinner."

"I'd say right about now, you should stop worrying about eating healthy and enjoy every meal."

I looked at the waiter. "Can you change my order to the baked mac and cheese?"

He smiled. "Of course."

I held up the menu for him to take. "Actually...can I also have the baby back ribs?"

"Thatta girl," Louise said.

My eyes were definitely bigger than my stomach, and I couldn't finish either entrée. But they were both delicious, much better than a bed of lettuce. When the waiter brought the bill, I decided to confide in Louise about where things were going with Beck and me.

"Louise, I really care about your grandson."

"I'm pretty certain he feels the same. It's been a long time since that man has opened his heart to anyone."

I sighed. "That's the problem. I never meant for us to happen, for him to get hurt."

"Love can't be planned."

"No, it certainly can't. And in another life, I would be over the moon. My attraction to Beck was there from the moment we met, but I've fallen for the man he is underneath all that pomp and arrogance. Beck is nothing like I expected when I first met him. I let my guard down because I thought he was safe—a man I'd never go for."

Louise smiled. "Some men are wolves in sheep's clothing. My grandson is a sheep dressed up as a wolf."

"That's a very good analogy."

"I know my grandson well. He doesn't let many people in, but when he does, he loves hard. He gives his heart and soul and everything he has."

I frowned. "That's exactly why I need to back away now. I don't know how long I have, but every day is just going to make it harder in the end. He shouldn't have to go through watching the two of us die."

"I appreciate you worrying about him. But my guess is that it's too late for saving his eventual broken heart."

"Maybe. But some time and space between us will help."

Louise nodded. "I'll support whatever you do or say."

"Thank you. Once I'm in California, it will be easier. But I think I need to end things with him when we get back to New York."

"Don't you worry. You have my word that I'll watch out for him when that happens," Louise said.

I smiled sadly. "And you have my word that I'll watch out for him." I looked up. "Forever."

CHAPTER 27

Beck

I hated to involve my grandmother. But after four days in New York, things between Nora and me had changed. So I had no choice but to call and dig around.

"Hey. How are you feeling?"

"If I had a tail, I'd be wagging it."

I smiled. "Any plans for today?"

"Sip and paint. Can't wait."

"What's that?"

"It's a painting class where you drink wine. My friend Lucille and I are going. She found a place where the subject is a nude male model. Wine, naked men who aren't wrinkly prunes, and my friend—not sure it gets too much better than that."

There was my opening. "Lucille? How come Nora isn't going with you? That sounds right up her alley, too."

"She had other plans."

"What plans?" As soon as the words tumbled from my mouth, I knew I'd made a mistake. Gram would zip her lips tighter than a clam when she caught on that I was poking around for information and not just making conversation.

"That's a question for Nora, not me."

I raked a hand through my hair. "It's hard to ask someone a question when they don't return your calls."

"She's probably busy."

"Doing what?"

"Beck..."

"Fine," I grumbled. "Have a good time with your naked man."

"Oh, I will. I definitely will."

After I hung up, my brother walked into my office. I hadn't yet filled him in on everything that had gone down in Utah, about Nora's health.

"So get this..." As usual, he parked himself in my guest chair, reclining into it like he was at home on a La-Z-Boy. "This woman called me at one in the morning a few nights ago, bawling me out."

"What did you do?"

"Nothing. It was a wrong number. But we wound up talking for four hours."

I shook my head. "There's something wrong with you."

"What? She cursed at me in Italian. It was sexy as hell." My brother squinted. His eyes roamed my face. "Did you lose weight? Your eyes look kind of sunken into your head."

"Thanks."

"No, really. You don't look so hot." He thumbed over his shoulder toward the door. "Are you sick? Because I don't want to catch it and miss my date with my crank caller tomorrow night."

I sighed. "No, I'm not the one sick."

Jake frowned. "Gram isn't doing well? I talked to her last night, and she sounded great."

"No, she's fine."

"I'm lost. Then who's sick?"

I really needed someone to talk to other than my grandmother. Jake was younger and not the most mature person in the world, but I had no idea how to navigate things with Nora, and I could use an outsider's opinion. I motioned to my office door. "Shut that, will you?"

"You mean with me on the other side of it?"

That made me smile. "No, believe it or not, I actually mean with you on *this* side."

"Oh shit." He stood. "Big bro's got a secret to share with me. Don't think that's happened since you swore me to secrecy after I got bit by the neighbor's dog—with the secret being that I was now half dog and half human."

I shook my head. "You pissed holding up one leg for a month and started sniffing shit. You're so gullible."

Jake shut the door and returned to his seat. This time he sat tall, maybe even gave me his full attention. "What's up?" he said. "What's going on?"

There wasn't a good place to start, so I jumped right in. "Nora didn't meet Gram because they live in the same building. They met at a Living at the End of Your Life meeting. It's a support group. They're both members."

His brows knitted, and a few seconds later his eyes flared wide. "Nora's dying?"

For the next twenty minutes, I told Jake the whole story—about her surgeries, diagnosis, and the heart attack she'd had out in Utah.

"Damn. And there's nothing they can do? She's so young."

"I've had consults with six doctors, world-class experts in their field. They all say her only shot is a heart transplant. But the wait is long, and the survival rate post-op is short for someone with her illness. When I made the appointment, I'd hoped Nora would be the one talking to the doctors, but she's like Gram. She's made the decision to enjoy the time she has left and not have any more surgeries or treatments."

"Man..." Jake shook his head. "I'm really sorry. I knew you liked her a lot, and she and Gram seem really tight."

I looked my brother in the eyes. "We've been seeing each other. I'm in love with her."

"Oh fuck."

We sat quietly for a few minutes. Jake needed time to let it all sink in, and I needed time to suck back my emotions.

"Anyway," I said. "She's blowing me off now. When we got back from Utah, she started pulling away. She thinks she doesn't have much time, and she doesn't want to hurt me. I've been giving her space because I'm afraid if I don't, she'll cut me off completely. But I don't know how to handle things. I mean, if she's right and she doesn't..." I paused and swallowed. "If she doesn't have much time, I want to spend what's left with her."

"So why the hell are you sitting here?"

"I just told you. I'm afraid if I push, she'll close the door on me completely."

"When was the last time you saw her?"

"Four days ago, when the car dropped her off at home. I tried to get her to come home with me. She's still weak. But she wanted to go to her place. I called her the next morning, and she told me she was busy catching up on work. The next day it was a different excuse. The last two days she hasn't even returned my calls." I yanked at my hair from the root. "I'm going out of my fucking mind."

"It sounds like she's already closed the door. So what do you have to lose by pushing?"

He had a point. I nodded.

"You know what I think?"

"What?"

"You're way smarter than me. You know the only answer here is to push. But you're afraid that if you do, and she still doesn't budge, it will be the end. Sitting here miserable, you don't have to face that possibility. You can pretend it's not over."

Fuck. He was right. Of course I knew what I needed to do. I was just too chicken because I was afraid she'd confirm my worst fear—that it was over.

My brother watched my face and then smiled big. "You just figured out I'm right, didn't you?"

"Shut up."

He chuckled. "I'll take that as a yes."

My brother leaned forward. His face grew solemn. "I'm sorry, man. I was happy to see you actually interested in someone. If there's anything at all I can do, just name it. I'll step up with Gram more so you have time with Nora. You're the golden grandchild and all, but I'm more entertaining anyway."

"Thanks, Jake."

On his way out, Jake stopped at the door. "Between Gram and Nora, it's not going to be an easy road coming up."

I nodded. "I know. But those two are worth every rough day coming, and then some."

⌒

I stood outside Nora's brownstone, looking at the names under the buzzers. Thankfully, Google knew where she lived, because I certainly hadn't. The West Village brownstone seemed more fitting for her than my grandmother's high rise.

Shaking my hands out, I took a few calming breaths. I'd always hated *the drop-in* and couldn't remember ever doing it to someone in my adult years. But I'd called Nora twice more after my talk with my brother, and she'd left me no choice. I wasn't even sure if she was home. Worse, I wasn't confident that if she was, she'd let me in.

Nevertheless, I pressed the bell for 2D. A flood of adrenaline pumped through my veins as I waited.

"Hello?"

I let out a relieved sigh. "It's Beck."

"Oh. Ummm... Okay." A buzzer noise sounded, and the outside door unlocked. Nora waited on the second floor with her apartment door half open.

I smiled.

She didn't.

"I'm sorry," I said. "I hate when people drop in, too. But you haven't been returning my calls."

Nora sighed. "I've been busy."

She didn't move from the doorway when I got to the top of the stairs.

"Can I come in?"

She hesitated, but eventually nodded.

I only made it two steps into her apartment before I froze. Her kitchen was littered with cardboard boxes. "What's all this?"

She looked down. "I'm packing. I pushed up my moving date."

"To when?"

Nora wouldn't look at me, so I knew the answer was going to stab me in the heart.

"Monday."

"Monday? As in three days from now?"

She nodded.

It felt like I couldn't breathe. "Were you even going to tell me?"

"Of course I was."

"When?"

Nora kept looking down.

I was so angry and hurt, it was difficult to rein it in. I cupped her cheeks, forcing her head up until our eyes met. "When, Nora? When were you going to tell me? After you were gone? Were you going to send me a fucking postcard?"

Her eyes filled with tears. "I don't know. I hadn't figured it out yet."

"Why? Why are you leaving so soon?"

"That was always the plan. You knew that from the beginning."

"But why leave early?"

"Because it's time." Tears rolled down her face, leaving streaks. "I promised my dad I'd come at the end."

"But it doesn't have to be the end, Nora. I spoke to doctors, and you have a chance. At least go on the list."

Nora stepped back. My hands fell from her cheeks.

"You should go, Beck."

"No."

"*Please*, Beck. It's hard enough to do this."

I fell to my knees in front of her. Tears rained down my face. "*Please*, Nora." My voice cracked. "Just go on the list. If you don't want to do it for yourself, do it for me. Do it for Louise. Do it for William."

She shook her head. "Please go."

"Nora, *please*. I will get the best doctors, the best surgeon. Is it legal to buy a heart anywhere? I don't even care. I'll buy you one on the black market if I have to. Just don't quit on me. I'll do anything you want," I pleaded. "*Please, sweetheart.*"

She broke down in a sob. It killed me to cause her pain, but I didn't know any other way to get through. Though I also couldn't stand two feet away and watch her break down. So I wrapped her in my arms. She struggled for a few seconds, but then gave in, nearly collapsing into my hold. Her shoulders shook, and the room grew eerily quiet. I knew exactly what was coming. But that didn't help me prepare for it at all. The silence was broken by the most excruciating sound I'd ever heard in my life. It was beyond a wail; it was the harrowing outpour of sheer agony. Like the right pitch can shatter glass, my heart splintered into a million pieces.

"Don't cry, Nora. I love you. Please don't cry."

But she didn't stop. And neither did I. We stood in that kitchen for what felt like forever, bawling our eyes out. Eventually though, our cries quieted to sniffles, and the shaking of our bodies steadied. I felt like such a selfish bastard.

"I'm sorry I upset you. I just don't know how to get through." I forced myself to look into her pained eyes. "I'm sorry, Nora."

She swallowed and cleared her throat. "Did you mean it when you said you will do anything I want?"

"Of course."

Nora looked into my eyes. "Then I need you to let me go."

CHAPTER 28

Nora

"**Y**our heartbeat is slow, but that's to be expected with this stage of your illness and after what you went through last month. That's probably the reason you're feeling a little sluggish," Dr. Hammond said. "Well, that and the LA smog."

I smiled. "Okay."

"How long ago was the heart attack?"

"It'll be six weeks tomorrow."

Dr. Hammond scribbled notes in my new chart. When he was done, he closed it and looked at me with a smile. "You're really the spitting image of your mother."

"My dad says the same thing."

"How is your dad?"

"He's okay. He acts like nothing is wrong, but I know it has to be tough on him to watch someone who looks like my mother go through what she did."

Dr. Hammond nodded. "I'm sure."

He'd been my mother's cardiologist when I was a kid. While I wasn't doing any treatments, I still needed a refill of the dozen medications I took in order to keep breathing. I thought it might be easier to go to someone familiar with my disease. Not every cardiologist has experience with it because it's so rare.

"Everything else looks good." Dr. Hammond shut my chart. "Your lungs are clear, blood pressure is stable with the help of the medications you take, and your EKG was unchanged from the last one your doctor in New York sent over."

"Great."

"You can return to your normal activities. Keep your exercise on the light side, and be mindful of becoming winded. You can also resume sexual activity and return to work."

The mention of sex made my chest feel hollow. It had been a whole fifteen minutes since I'd last thought of Beck.

"Okay, thank you."

"And I'll see you back here in three months to see if we need any medication adjustments."

Three months.

Lately every reference to a date in the future hung heavy in the air. Would I still be around then?

Back at the house, my dad wasn't home from work yet. He'd left laundry in the dryer, so I folded it, then went to his bedroom to put it away. I looked around. This room hadn't changed very much from when I was a kid—same dark walnut furniture, same white wooden blinds, even a dark brown robe hung on the back of the door that led to the small, attached half bath. The top of the dresser was lined with framed photos that hadn't changed in twenty years. I picked up the first one that caught my eye. It was of my mom laughing, taken on her and William's wedding day. A small pearl crown sat on top of her head, the veil that had been attached long gone since it was the end of their reception. She had cake smeared all over her face. I'd gone through their wedding album dozens of times after mom passed. There were pictures of them cutting a three-tier cake and Mom smashing a giant piece into Dad's face.

Tears clogged my throat as I stared at the photo. So I set it back on the dresser and picked up another one. This one was of Mom and William walking on the beach, with two-year-old me on William's shoulders. They looked so happy. Growing up without a mother wasn't easy, but I was glad my mother had gotten to have a family—even if only for a short while. I'd always dreamed of having a bunch of kids, probably because I grew up an only child. But it wasn't in the cards.

"You peed on my neck that day." Dad's voice startled me. I hadn't heard him come in. He leaned casually against the bedroom doorway with a smile.

"I did not..."

"Yep, you did. We were walking along, and all of a sudden, I felt this warmth. At first I thought it was sweat. It was a pretty warm day out."

"Why have you never mentioned that before?"

Dad shrugged. "I'm not sure. I guess we never discussed that photo. But you were only two and a half and potty training early. It wasn't a big deal. I just went for a swim, and we finished our walk."

I stared at the picture for a few more seconds before putting it back. "Can I ask you something, Dad?"

"Anything."

"Have you dated since Mom died?"

He nodded. "Here and there. It's nice to have companionship once in a while, to go to a movie or a restaurant."

I smiled. "I'm glad."

I'd been thinking so much about my mom's death since I moved back home. But I'd also been wondering about the aftermath for William. I was so little when it happened. I didn't remember what it was like for him.

"It must've been tough for you after Mom died..."

Dad walked into the room. He took a seat on the edge of the bed and patted the spot next to him. "What's really on your mind, sweetheart?"

"What do you mean?"

He tapped his finger to my temple. "You've been moping around, lost in thought since you arrived. I know what you're going through is heavy and a lot to carry, but it's more than that. I can tell."

I leaned my head on my dad's shoulder. "You're always so good at reading me."

"Is this about that guy, Beck, you told me about?"

I sighed. "I miss him a lot."

"So go see him. Or have him out here. We have plenty of room. I think I might finally be okay abolishing the open-bedroom-door policy when a boy's over."

I smiled. "I can't. I don't want to make it harder for him."

Dad shifted and looked at me. "Harder for him? Please don't tell me you're keeping away from a man who cares about you because you think it will help him heal easier someday."

When I didn't respond, Dad shook his head. "Nora, I would take a lifetime of sadness for one minute longer with your mother. Life isn't a math equation that's simple to figure out. Sometimes forty-two good days outweigh hundreds of bad ones."

"I know...but if you and Mom had never fallen in love, you'd probably be married now and have someone to keep you company. You would have lived your life more fully."

"And if I could do it all over—make a choice today to have four years with your mother and some loneliness in the years after, or no years with your mother but never be lonely—I'd choose your mother. It's not even a question. I'd choose her every time. Your mother was the love of my life. Not everyone is lucky enough to find their person. I was, and for that, I feel lucky, not regretful."

"Oh, Dad..." Tears welled in my eyes, and I threw my arms around his shoulders and hugged him. "Your love for Mom has been an inspiration to me. It's beautiful."

"Then let the inspiration guide your actions, sweetheart."

"I can't. It's different with me and Beck. You were already married to Mom and head over heels for her when she got sick the last time. It was too late for you. It's not too late for Beck."

My dad shook his head. "I was head over heels the day I met your mother." He stroked my hair. "You've made some pretty tough choices and expected everyone to honor them. But you're not allowing this Beck to make his choice. You're making it for him."

∾

The following night, my phone rang at eight o'clock. I smiled at the name flashing on the screen.

"Hey, Louise. How are you?"

"My ticker is still ticking. So I suppose it's a good day." She had her usual spunk in her voice, but there was something else off. Louise sounded almost out of breath.

"Are you wheezing?"

"Just my allergies," she said. "Maddie and I worked on her garden badge today. The pollen count must've been high."

"Oh." I sighed. "How is Maddie?"

"Well, today she came home from school with a drawing. She'd drawn a bunch of people but only labeled herself, Princess Maddie. The teacher told her that for homework, she needed to label the rest of the people. So I was helping her. I pointed to the person standing next to her in the photo. The figure was twice the size she'd drawn herself, so I assumed it was her father. I said, 'If you're a princess, who might this be?' She said it was her daddy. So I asked her what his title was if she's a princess? Does that make him a king? She thought about it for a long time. And then answered with a dead-serious face. 'That makes him a servant.'"

"Oh my God."

"I laughed so hard, I nearly peed. Then I helped her spell *servant* so we could label him properly."

I chuckled. "Of course, you did." I was quiet for a few heartbeats. "And how is Beck?"

"He's hanging in there," Louise said. "Back to working too much. When he's not at the office or on his laptop, he's usually moping. I think he misses you more than he'll say."

The feeling was mutual. "I'm sorry he's hurting, Louise."

"No apologies necessary, sweetheart. I understand." She started to cough, a dry hack that went on for quite a while.

"That doesn't sound good, Louise."

"It's just allergies."

"Maybe. But if it doesn't get better by morning, I think you should go get it checked."

She changed the subject without agreeing with me. "I got an email from Frieda, our Bahamian friend. She was checking in, but she also gave me a recipe for the sweet biscuits we liked when we were down there. They're called Johnny cakes. You have to try them. I'll email you over the recipe."

I smiled. "Alright, I will."

We talked for another half hour, but by the time the call was ending, it sounded like Louise had run a marathon.

"I really think you might need to get that wheeze checked," I told her.

"We'll see. I do have lung cancer, you know."

"You might need something simple, like a steroid again."

It was hard to push someone to go to the doctor when you weren't getting treatments yourself. But I did my best. After we said goodbye, I was about to swipe to end the call, but I heard Louise yell my name.

"Eleanor!"

I brought the phone back to my ear. "Yes?"

"Neither of us knows when it might be the last time we talk, so I just wanted to tell you I love you."

I swallowed. "I love you, too, Louise."

The next morning, I decided to take a walk on the beach. I couldn't shake the melancholy feeling I'd had since I left New York, so I hoped a little sunshine and ocean might help. I walked a few miles before coming upon a jetty of rocks. It was time I turned back, but I thought I'd sit for a while first.

I stared out at the Pacific Ocean and closed my eyes, forcing myself to think of all of the good things I had in my life while listening to the ocean crash against the surf. Doing that usually helped, but today I couldn't shake the feeling of impending doom. After a few minutes, I got up and started to walk again. When I was almost back to where I'd started, my cell phone rang with a Manhattan area code. I didn't recognize the number, but I swiped to answer anyway.

"Hello?"

"Hi. Nora?"

The voice was familiar, but I couldn't quite place it. "Yes?"

"It's Jake Cross."

I stopped walking. "Hey, Jake. How are you? Is everything okay?"

He was quiet for long enough to make my heart race. "Jake?"

"Gram had another stroke, Nora. A bad one."

"Oh no." I clutched my chest.

"It's not good. The doctors said there's no brain function. They're basically keeping her alive so we can say goodbye. We're going to do it tonight, if she doesn't...you know. The priest will say a few words and then..."

Tears streamed down my cheeks. "Oh my God. I'm so sorry, so, so sorry."

"Thank you. I know things between you and Beck are...whatever they are, but I thought you might want to come, to say your goodbye and to be here for him. And her."

"Do you think Beck would be okay with that?"

"I don't think Beck is in any condition to know what he needs. He's the one who found her. He doesn't even

know I'm calling you, Nora. He's a mess, and I thought..."
He blew a rush of air into the phone. "I don't know what I
thought. But I felt like I should call you."

"I'm glad you did. What hospital is she at?"

"Lenox Hill."

I nodded. "I'll do my best to be there."

CHAPTER 29

Nora

Beck blinked when he looked up and found me standing in the doorway. "Nora? What are you doing here?"

I smiled sadly and slanted my eyes to his brother, who was sitting on the opposite side of the bed. "A little birdie called."

Beck raked a hand through his hair. "I didn't know."

I walked over and hugged Jake first, then went around to the other side of the bed. There was a moment of awkwardness, but then Beck let me hug him. "I'm so sorry, Beck."

"I'm going to run downstairs and get some coffee," Jake said. "You guys want anything?"

"No, thank you," I said. Beck shook his head.

When it was just the two of us, I looked over at the monitors. "Is there any change from this morning, when Jake called?"

"No."

I stared down at my friend. "She looks at peace."

Beck nodded. "She does." He glanced over and caught my eye. "How's California?"

I forced a smile. "Sunny."

"How are you feeling?"

"Pretty good."

He nodded again. A few long moments ticked by with us just staring down at Louise.

"When my mom passed away," Beck said softly, "I had a lot of pent-up anger. I wouldn't talk about it, so my way of letting it out became fighting. I got into four fist-fights after school in two months. Gram decided I needed an outlet. Most people would enroll their kid in karate or sign them up for boxing classes to channel their anger." He shook his head and smiled. "But not Gram. Gram brought home a tree stump and a hammer and nails. Looking back, I don't even know where she got that huge stump from— the thing had to be three feet around—or how she got it up to our midtown Manhattan apartment, for that matter. But she told me that if I woke up angry again, I should take a nail from the box and hammer it into the stump until I felt better. I think we went through three or four big boxes of nails. But eventually, I stopped hammering. One day I came home from school and all the nails had been pulled from the stump. Gram sat me down next to it and made me run my finger over the holes. She said that's what taking out your anger on others does—it leaves scars. And the ones on people don't go away so easily. This morning, she wasn't answering her phone, so I went to check on her. She must've had an idea this was coming, because when I found her, there was a Mason jar full of rusty nails on her nightstand, with a note underneath. *Just in case you need these again.*" Beck's eyes glistened. "There aren't enough nails in the world to help me get over her."

"Oh, Beck." I couldn't stop my tears. I laced my fingers with his and squeezed. "I've only known her a short time, but she's made a giant impact on my life. I can't imagine how difficult this is for you."

"I'm glad you came," he whispered. "She would've wanted you here."

I leaned my head on his shoulder. "I'm glad I came, too."

He smiled through the pain etched in his face and looked down at Louise. "The doctors and nurses all seem surprised she's hung on this long. Now I know why she did."

"Why?"

"She's been waiting for you."

∽

Less than an hour after I arrived at the hospital, Louise May Aster died at 10:04 PM. The doctors didn't have to intervene, Louise's breaths just slowed down until she had no more left, and she was gone.

The nurse suggested we each take a moment to say goodbye one at a time. I went first, while Beck and Jake stepped outside.

I said a little prayer, then held her hand while I spoke. "Death ends a life, not a friendship. So I hope I find you waiting for me on the other side, in a rubber wingsuit or with a parachute strapped to your back, ready to cause a ruckus. I love you, Louise."

Jake went next. Beck and I watched through the glass as he spoke for a while, then leaned down and kissed his grandmother's cheek before coming back out.

I knew Beck's turn wouldn't be easy. He was such a big, strong man, someone you couldn't imagine losing control. But he did. And I felt his pain in my chest as I watched through the glass. Beck's shoulders shook, but it looked like he was trying to rein it in, pull himself together. It was a battle he lost, and it all started to pour out. Beck leaned over and hugged his grandmother's body, sobbing for the longest time. When he finally stood and walked out, I felt as broken as he looked.

"Fuck." Jake pulled his brother in for a hug, and Beck was barely able to reciprocate. When they separated, it was my turn. I wrapped my arms around Beck and held him. He tried to break free a few seconds into it, but I refused to let go. Eventually he gave in, and suddenly he was crying all over again, all of his weight leaning on me.

I held him through it—held him like both our lives depended on it, until it was impossible to figure out whose tears had spilled onto the floor because we'd both cried so much.

"What can I do?" Pulling back, I used the sleeve of my shirt to wipe the wetness from his cheeks. "Do you want to go for a walk? Maybe some fresh air will help?"

Beck stared at the ground, shaking his head.

"Maybe a drink?"

"I'm fine."

"No, you're not, Beck. Let me help. What do you need?"

He kept his head down for a long time. When he looked up, his eyes were bloodshot and puffy. "Help me forget," he said.

We'd come full circle. That's what I'd told him the first time we were together, and now it would be our last. I nodded and took his hand. "Let's forget together."

Beck's apartment was dark when we walked in. He made no attempt to turn on the lights. Instead, he crushed his lips to mine while we were still in the foyer. He'd been quiet on the way here, and all I wanted was to make him feel better. So when our kiss broke, I sank to my knees. Beck surprised me by hoisting me back up.

"Not like this. I don't want a quick fix. I want to make love to you."

I took a step back. "Beck…"

He reached for me. "I know what you're willing to give me. I'm not asking for more. I just want to give you everything I have."

"Oh, Beck."

He reached out to me. I hesitated, but there was no way I could deny this man what he needed. Even if it would break my heart to take it and still walk away in the end. So I took his hand and followed him to the bedroom.

Beck never took his eyes off me as he peeled off my clothes. The way he looked at me—with so much intensity—I knew before we even started that tonight was going to ruin me.

He lifted me off my feet and carried me to the bed, setting me down gently in the middle. Normally, Beck was domineering, so unapologetically brazen, but tonight he was different. Soft almost. He climbed over me, kissed the scar over my heart, and looked into my eyes for the longest time before pushing inside. When he was fully seated, my eyes fluttered closed.

"No. Please look at me."

I opened.

Beck's eyes brimmed with emotion. "I fucking love you, Nora. I don't care how many days I get, or how much heartache it causes in the end, I will *never* regret loving you."

No one had ever said something so beautiful or looked at me that way. Tears prickled the corners of my eyes as Beck glided in and out, never breaking our gaze. I'd heard the words *make love* a thousand times in my life, but until this moment, I never understood them. Beck wasn't just inside my body, he'd reached into my soul.

The room was so quiet that I heard nothing but our breaths and the sound of our bodies slapping together. Pretty soon, Beck's jaw grew rigid, and I knew he was close.

"I love you," he gritted out. "I fucking love you."

That was it. I couldn't take much more. So I wrapped my legs around his waist and crushed my lips to his. Things grew to a frenzy after that. Beck picked up speed, bucking hard against me as his thrusts increased in intensity. My orgasm knocked the wind out of me when it hit. Muscles pulsing, I moaned through every wave, every ripple. Beck must've sensed I was on my way back down, because he began his own climb. His hips ground down hard and fast, and he let out a loud groan.

After, I was completely drained—emotionally, physically, and mentally. I couldn't imagine how much of a toll the day had taken on Beck. Yet he just kept gliding in and out of me, still semi-hard.

"Wow. That was..."

Beck leaned in and pressed his lips to mine. "Making love, to the woman I love."

I didn't know what to say, so I nodded. "Thank you. I don't think I realized how much I needed that tonight."

"Just tonight?"

"Beck..."

He smiled sadly. "I know. But can we just for tonight pretend you're not going to run out on me when daylight hits?"

CHAPTER 30

Beck

"**C**reeper..." A lazy smile spread across Nora's face before her eyes fluttered open. "You know the Bedroom Strangler used to watch his victims sleep, too."

"Who?"

"I've been binge-watching serial-killer documentaries."

"Sounds like a good use of your time out there in sunny California." I brushed my lips over hers. "Good morning."

Nora stretched her arms up and over her head. "What time is it?"

"A little after eleven."

Her eyes widened, and she pushed up to her elbows. "Really? I can't believe I slept that long."

"Well, it's only eight AM on the west coast. You probably didn't adjust yet."

"Oh, yeah." She nodded. "That's true. How long have you been up?"

I wasn't sure I'd actually slept at all. I shrugged. "A while."

"Were you just staring at me the entire time?"

My lip twitched. "I got up and made coffee and then talked to my brother about the arrangements."

"Oh." She fell back into bed and turned on her side, tucking her hands under her cheek. "Did Louise...talk to you about what she wanted?"

"No, we didn't discuss it. But she left Jake and me a letter. She said she doesn't want a wake. She thinks they're morbid. Instead, she wants us to throw a celebration-of-life party on the one-year anniversary of her death." I shook my head. "I think she knew I'd give her a hard time if she told me all that, so she saved it for when I couldn't argue anymore."

Nora's lip curved into a sneaky smile. "That's exactly why she didn't tell you."

"So you knew?"

She nodded. "Are you going to keep to her wishes?"

"Of course. What choice do I have now? Though it feels like I need to do *something*. I'm just not sure what yet."

"It'll come to you." She covered her mouth, and her cute little nose scrunched up. "I really need a toothbrush. And some coffee after. Is there more?"

I'd been worried that the moment her eyes opened she'd dart out the door. But it didn't look like she was in a rush. Not yet anyway.

"I just made a fresh pot. Extra strong, like you like it."

"Thanks."

"Do you have a return flight booked already?"

She nodded. "Nine PM."

Great, only ten hours to convince her to stay.

Nora brushed her teeth and downed two cups of coffee like it was medicine she needed to get better. After, she asked if she could use the shower. While she was in the bathroom, I sat down on the couch with the paper I'd taken from Gram's apartment yesterday. Her bucket list. It had been on her end table, next to the Mason jar full of rusty nails. I'm not even sure why I stuffed it in my pocket, but I'd read it five times since then. It was really no more than a bulleted list of things she'd wanted to do, all but one crossed out in pen.

Rainbow Falls in Watkins Glen

It made me sad that she hadn't gotten to finish her list, sad that after Nora moved back to California, I hadn't made the time to do it with her. I regretted that. But I'd thrown myself into my work to bury what Nora's leaving had done to me, and selfishly, I hadn't come back up for air soon enough. *You always think there's more time...*

Nora came out from the back of the house, all showered and blown dry. I still had the list in my hand. I looked up at her, then back down at the paper, and an idea struck me—one that would solve more than one problem.

"I think I figured out what I'm going to do to honor Gram's death."

"What?"

I held up the list in my hand. "I'm going to finish this."

Nora took the paper and scanned it. "Her bucket list?"

I nodded and stood.

"Oh wow. I think that's a great idea, Beck."

I smiled. "I'm glad you do. Because I want you to come with me."

She shook her head. "Oh. That's not a good idea."

"Why not? Is your health not up to it?"

"No, it is...but..."

"You were her partner in crime for everything on here. Don't you wish you could have finished it together?"

"Of course, but..." She motioned between us and sighed. "I don't want to hurt you, Beck."

"Why would you hurt me? I'm over you."

Her eyes narrowed. "Oh really?"

I shrugged. "You weren't so hard to get over after all."

"Is that so? Then what was last night?"

"I needed to not think for a while. To forget. You understand the need to do that, don't you?"

"You made love to me, Beck. That wasn't fucking."

"It was an emotional day."

She gave me the side-eye. "I don't believe you."

"That's because you're an egomaniac."

Her eyes flared. "*I'm* an egomaniac?"

"Well, you do think you're impossible to get over."

She shook her head. "Beck..."

I rested my hands on her shoulders. "Come with me. It's only a four-and-a-half-hour drive. We could go up one day and come back the next. It won't take long. This is what I feel like I need to do—for me and for Gram. But I think you should finish this list too, Nora."

She nibbled on her bottom lip. "I've never been upstate..."

"Then let's do it. We can leave tomorrow, or the day after."

It looked like she was considering it. "It wouldn't change anything between us, Beck. I'd go back to California when we returned."

I shrugged and lied through my teeth. "It won't be a problem."

Her lips twisted.

"I think Gram would be happy that we made the time to do this," I said.

Nora squinted. "That's playing dirty pool. You know I can't say no when you put it like that."

My smile stretched from ear to ear. I couldn't help it. "I'll make the arrangements."

CHAPTER 31

Nora

"This must be a very special waterfall to make it onto Louise's list."

Beck glanced over and back to the road. We were about four hours into our drive. "I think it's less about the waterfall and more about the memories she created there."

"I didn't realize she had been there before. We talked a lot about the other items on our list because most of those needed a lot of arrangements. Since this one was drivable and a quick trip, we never really spoke about it."

"Watkins Glen was a special place for my grandparents. They have a small cabin up there. That's where we're heading."

"Really? Oh my God. Why wouldn't Louise have put that at the top of her list then?"

"Because she hasn't been back since Gramps died. His ashes are in the waterfall. As much as it holds a lot of good memories, I think some were hard. Plus, I think she thought she had more time. I know I did."

I sighed. "Yeah. I get that."

Beck was quiet for a while. "My grandfather proposed to my grandmother at the waterfall. *Twice.*"

"She said no the first time?"

He shook his head. "Nope. She accepted his proposal twice. Once when they were twenty-two, and the second time when they were sixty-two."

"You mean he asked her to renew their vows?"

"I guess technically that's what they did. Though Gramps thought he was proposing for the first time. Gramps had early-onset Alzheimer's."

"I knew he died from Alzheimer's, but I didn't realize he'd had it so young."

Beck nodded. "He was only fifty-eight when he was diagnosed. By the time he was sixty-one, he was living in a facility because Gram couldn't watch him twenty-four-seven like he'd needed. He would wander off and leave their apartment in the middle of the night when she was sleeping, or leave the stove on. Gram visited every day and took him out often. When the fortieth anniversary of the day he proposed arrived, Gram took him up to the falls again. He no longer remembered that she was his wife, but he still enjoyed her visits. He used to tell people at the nursing home that she was his girlfriend." Beck stared off with a smile on his face. "Anyway, when she took him up to the falls, he told her he'd fallen in love with her. Then he got down on one knee and proposed."

"Oh my God, Beck." I held out my arms. "I have goosebumps. That is the sweetest thing I've ever heard."

He smiled. "I was only eleven or twelve at the time. But I remember Gram inviting all her friends and family up to the cabin the next day. She had a minister come, and the two of them got married in the gazebo in the yard. Gramps had no idea he was marrying his wife of forty years, but he didn't stop smiling the entire day." Beck chuckled. "I thought the whole thing was kind of strange at the time. Years later, I realized how special the day had been and how incredible their marriage really was. A man who didn't remember his wife fell in love with her a second time."

"Wow. That's an unbelievable story. Though if anyone could make the same man fall in love with her twice, it would be Louise. She was very special."

Beck nodded. "Yeah. She was."

We arrived at the cabin a little while later. It was rustic and small, actually made of logs, which I hadn't expected, but anything more would have felt out of place among the babbling brooks, tall trees, and lush surroundings. Beck said it had been a while since anyone had visited, which explained the shutter dangling from the house, two toppled rocking chairs on the porch, and a collection of vines starting to grow over the front door. The driveway was made of small pebbles, and it crunched beneath us as we pulled in and parked.

I took a deep breath of fresh air into my lungs. "It smells incredible up here."

Beck looked around and nodded. "I forgot how off the grid this place is."

Inside looked like something out of a movie. There were sheets over furniture and cobwebs growing from some of the tall beams. A giant stone fireplace took up almost an entire wall of the living room, and a ladder led to a second-floor loft.

"Guess it really has been a while," Beck said. "Are you up for going to see the falls today, or would you rather rest and go tomorrow morning?"

"Let's go today. Maybe we can take off the furniture coverings, wipe away the dust and cobwebs, and leave the windows open so it can air out while we're gone."

"Sounds like a plan."

Beck and I went to work. When we were done, we piled back in the car for the short drive to Watkins Glen State Park. It was a good hike from the parking lot to the waterfalls, but worth every step. I'd expected a waterfall, not waterfalls. Nineteen separate falls plunged through a breathtaking natural gorge. Stone steps wound their way to the bottom, and natural bridges connected different areas. It looked like something out of a fairytale.

"How you feeling? Do you want to stop for another rest?" Beck asked. He'd already insisted on two along the hiking trail to get here.

I wasn't tired, but I checked my heart rate on my Apple watch anyway. "I'm good. We can keep going."

Down at the bottom of the gorge, Beck pointed to a natural alcove. "There is where Gramps proposed the first time. The second time was up at the top. He couldn't make it down anymore."

"I see why this place is so special. It's magical, Beck."

He looked down at me and took my hand, weaving our fingers together. "It is. I'm glad we came."

I squeezed his fingers. "I am too."

"Come on." He motioned with his head. "Let's sit over there for a while."

We sat side by side on top of a stone wall, watching the falls and pointing out all different things to each other—until Beck looked at his watch.

"We should probably start the hike back," he said. "It's going to get dark soon, and I have no idea how late that little store in town stays open. We need to pick up something to eat."

"Okay." I looked around one more time, then saw my reflection in the water beneath us. "Wait. We have to make a wish."

Beck's forehead wrinkled. "A wish?"

I nodded. "Louise says you have to make a wish whenever water clears and you see your reflection." I pointed. "Look."

The main falls had slowed a bit, causing the water to smooth out. The bright sun beamed our reflection back to us, clear as day now.

Beck smiled. "That sounds like Gram."

I shut my eyes and took a deep breath, wishing for something I'd stopped wishing for a long time ago. When I opened my eyes, Beck was staring at me.

"You're supposed to make a wish."

"I did." He looked into my eyes. "I know exactly what I want, so it didn't take long."

My heart squeezed. I had a feeling we'd both wished for the same impossible thing.

∽

"What would be on your list?" I asked.

Beck had made a fire when we got back to the cabin. We were both sprawled out on the floor in front of it with our heads propped up on throw pillows as it crackled. He'd been pretty quiet since we left the falls.

"I'm sorry. What did you say?"

"I asked what would be on your bucket list, if you made one."

Beck sat up. He grabbed the bottle of wine from the coffee table and refilled our glasses. "I need another to consider that question."

I smiled. "It is a pretty tough one."

He sipped his wine. "I don't think mine would be quite as adventurous as yours and Gram's, but it'd probably have a lot of travel on it. I've been a lot of places for work, but not too many for pleasure."

I sipped. "Like where?"

"Running of the bulls in Spain. Greek islands. Tuscany wine tasting."

"Interesting. Go on."

"Floor seats at a Knicks-Celtics game, where the Knicks win. Preferably a playoff. Fifty-yard-line seats at a Giants-Patriots Superbowl, where the Giants win."

I smiled. "You're such a New Yorker. Basically you just want the New York teams to beat all the Boston ones?"

The corner of his lip twitched. "Pretty much."

"What else?"

"Road trip across America in an RV. See the Northern Lights in Iceland." He grinned. "Smoke a joint with Snoop Dogg."

I chuckled. "Do you even smoke pot?"

"No, but with Snoop Dogg I would."

"Anything else?"

He shrugged. "Safari in Africa. Take flying lessons. Hike the Inca Trail in Machu Picchu, Peru.

"Those are all good ones."

Beck looked into the fire. "But you know what?"

"What?"

"I'd give them all up to spend the rest of my days with you."

"Beck..."

"I know. I know. This trip changes nothing, and you're leaving when we get back. But you asked, and that's the damn truth."

I smiled sadly and leaned my head on Beck's shoulder. "I hope you find someone, Beck."

He leaned his head against mine. "Already did, sweetheart. Already did."

A little while later, he climbed to his feet. "I want to see something."

"What?"

"My grandparents wrote letters to each other the night they got engaged the first time. Gram read the one she'd written to my grandfather at his memorial service. They were hidden in the back of their wedding photo, which is hanging in the loft upstairs. I wonder if the one Gramps wrote is still there."

Beck climbed up the ladder to the loft and came down with a dusty, framed black-and-white wedding photo.

I took it. I'd never seen a picture of Louise so young. "She was beautiful. And you look so much like your grandfather—the same masculine, square jaw."

"Turn it over. Let's see if it's still back there."

I flipped the frame and bent the prongs holding the wood backing in place. Sure enough, there was an envelope with *Louise* written on the front. I picked it up and ran my finger across it. "This was written sixty years ago."

"Open it," Beck said.

"Should we do that? It's a private letter from a man to the woman he loves."

"I think we should. Gram read hers to a hundred people at his memorial. She'd want someone to read it if she couldn't."

"You sure?"

He nodded. "I'm positive. She was proud of their love."

"Okay." I held the envelope out to Beck. "But you do it."

He took a deep breath and nodded. Inside, the stationery was yellowed and the ink faded, but the letter was still legible.

Beck cleared his throat.

"My dearest Louise,

I tried to remember the exact moment I fell in love with you today. But looking back, I can't. Because it didn't happen just once. It happens every day, and I blissfully fall all over again. So rather than tell you when it happened, I'll tell you why I love you. I love that the only thing that rivals your big mouth is the size of your heart. I love that you are fearless and don't live life afraid of what might come next, but rather you look forward to conquering things that try to stand in your way. I love you because you're beautiful, but forget to look in the mirror some days. I love you because wherever we are, you make it feel like home. My love for you is so great that it spills over onto me—I love you because you make me a better man.

You are, my dear, everything. And even that feels like too small a word.

Yours always,
Henry"

I covered my heart with my hand. "That is so romantic."

"Yeah." Beck shook his head. "Damn. That was beautiful."

I looked up. "I hope Louise heard it."

Beck nodded. "She did. You know, before we came here, I felt bad that Gram didn't get to come one last time, didn't get to finish her list. But she could have come at any time. You know what I think?"

"What?"

"That she knew we'd come. And she wanted us to have this time. To remind us what love is. I know you love me, even if you refuse to say it."

An ache squeezed my chest. I wanted to tell Beck I loved him with all my heart, and that I didn't need the reminder. But how would that help? It would only make things more difficult in the end.

The end.

That was coming closer and closer each day.

Beck watched me with hope still in his eyes. It was physically painful to squash that hope yet again. But I did, because a little hurt now was better than him sitting by my side when I was on my deathbed. I didn't want him to end up alone like William—no matter what William said about having no regrets.

"I'm sorry, I don't love you."

"Yes, you do. You're just too much of a coward to admit it."

CHAPTER 32
Beck

Days bled into weeks and weeks into months. It had been eighty-four days since I'd seen Nora, since I'd heard her voice or even read a text from her. It still hadn't gotten any easier. But my loss was two-fold, Gram and Nora. Sometimes I forgot that Gram was gone. Only for a split second—like when Maddie did or said something I knew Gram would enjoy and I thought I should call and tell her. But then it would hit me, and I'd remember.

Every time, it left my insides feeling hollow in a way that couldn't be filled—no matter how much I buried myself in work or in the bottle when I finally got home in the middle of the night.

Then there was Nora, who had a grip on my heart so tight it felt like I should see a cardiologist. I'd moved on from being mad at her for leaving. Now I was just mad at the world in general.

My brother popped into my office. He had the strap to his leather bag slung diagonally over his chest, with the satchel resting behind him.

I glanced at the clock on the wall. "Early even for you, isn't it?"

He strolled in and leaned on the back of one of my guest chairs. "Heading to the printer."

I nodded. "Have a good night."

My brother didn't take the hint. He never did. Jake tilted his head. "You should come with me tonight."

My brow raised. "Come where?"

"For drinks. I'm meeting a few of my buddies from college. Ryan and Big Ed. Remember them?"

Vaguely. I shook my head. "Thanks. But I have a lot of work to do."

"You've been working eighteen hours a day since you got back from your trip upstate. You have to be caught up by now."

"It's a busy time."

Jake made a face that said *bullshit.* "One drink."

"I don't think so."

He sighed and pulled something from his back pocket. "I didn't want to have to do this. But you're leaving me no choice." Jake extended an unmarked envelope over my desk.

"What's this?"

"A note from Gram."

"What are you talking about?"

"You know those letters she left each of us?"

I nodded.

"Well, mine had one in it for you. She instructed me to give it to you if I felt it was necessary."

"What's it say?"

He shrugged. "I don't know. I didn't open it."

I tore open the envelope. Seeing Gram's slanty handwriting brought that hollow feeling to my chest again. The note was only a paragraph long.

My dearest Beckham,

Get your head out of your ass. If you're reading this letter, it's because you've been moping around, working too much, and probably drinking too much. In my seventy-eight years, I thought I'd learned all the lessons I needed to learn. But it turned out there was one I wish I'd learned earlier: LIVE. Shit happens. Deals fall through. People die. We only get one life, so it can't be wasted dwelling on the past. Suck it up and create a new future. No excuses. If you won't do it for yourself, then do it for me.

I love you, you stubborn bastard.

Now get up and go do something stupid with your brother. He's good at that.

Always, Gram

P.S. Seal this letter up and give it back to Jake. I have a feeling he'll need to give it to you more than once.

I shook my head when I finished reading, but I was smiling. *Even when she's gone, she's still busting my balls.*

Jake stood waiting. "What's it say?"

"It says she wants me to babysit your ass." I stood and grabbed my jacket off the back of my seat. "Come on. Let's go get drinks."

∽

All I wanted to do was go home and sleep, even after a gorgeous brunette sidled up to me at the bar and set her wine down.

"Hi. I'm Meghan."

"Beck." I nodded.

She tilted her head coyly. "Can I buy you a drink, Beck?"

I held up my full glass. "Got one. Thank you."

The woman looked down at my left hand. "Married, but don't wear a ring?"

I sipped my whiskey. "Nope."

"Gay?"

"Definitely not."

She frowned. "Oh...kay. Then it's just me. I can take a hint." She picked up her drink, and I realized I was being a jerk, so I stopped her from leaving.

"It's definitely not you." And it wasn't. She was petite with a tan complexion, big blue eyes, full lips, and loads of dangerous curves. "You're beautiful."

She turned back with a smile. "Thank you. That helps my bruised ego, a little anyway." Meghan sipped her wine. "I'm not usually the type of person who walks up to a guy in a bar. It tends to give him the wrong idea. But you look sad, so I figured what the hell."

"I'm sorry. It's been a rough go lately."

She leaned her elbows on the bar. "Recent breakup?"

I wasn't sure I'd ever *had* Nora to define what happened between us as a breakup. Yet I nodded. "Yeah."

"What happened?"

No way in hell was I telling anyone about Nora's illness. So I told half the truth, the part that wouldn't cause me to bawl like a baby. "She moved to California."

Meghan nodded. "Long distance is hard. My ex-husband tried it with his mistress. But eventually it got to be too much, so he packed his shit and moved to Miami." She winked, and I smiled.

"Sorry."

"Nothing to be sorry about. Our marriage was over anyway. But thank you." Meghan sighed. "My breakup was two years ago. How about yours?"

"Eighty-four days."

She arched a brow. "Not that you're counting?"

I smiled. "Right."

My brother Jake walked over. He perked up when he got a look at Meghan.

He slung one arm around my neck and extended his hand. "Hi. I'm the non-brooding brother, Jake. What's your name?"

Meghan chuckled and shook. "Meghan. It's nice to meet you, Jake." She looked to me. "I didn't realize you were here with anyone. Let me guess, he dragged you out?"

My lip curled. "Something like that."

Not long after we arrived, Jake and his buddies had joined a table of ladies who looked like they might still be in college. I'd declined to join them, hoping I could sneak out soon. I figured I'd complied with Gram's guilt-trip-letter request long enough.

"We're going down the block to The Next to go dancing," Jake said to Meghan. "Why don't you two come?"

Meghan's face was pensive. "I'm going to guess your brother isn't up for that?"

Jake slapped my chest. "Of course he is. Aren't you, Becksy boy?"

"Not really, *Jakesy boy*."

"Oh, come on. Don't be such a party-pooper all the time. *Remember the letter...*"

I heard Gram's voice in my head. *"Cut the shit and go. Stop acting like a spoilsport. We only get one life. Don't waste it dwelling on the past. Suck it up and create a new future."*

Fuck. I sighed. "Fine."

"Now that's not any way to invite your new friend, Meghan, is it, big bro?"

Meghan's eyes sparkled. She was enjoying the inter-action between me and Jake.

"Would you like to join us at some stupid club with my pain-in-the-ass brother?"

She grinned. "That sounds wonderful."

Ten minutes later, I was at a nightclub. The house music was so loud, I could barely hear myself think. Jake and his crew were already out on the dance floor, while Meghan stuck with me at the bar.

I pointed to the band of idiots and leaned in, but I still had to yell. "Go dance with them!"

"Will you come too?" she yelled back.

"Not enough alcohol in me to get my ass out there."

She smirked and raised her hand to the bartender. "Let's fix that!"

Meghan ordered shots called mind erasers. While the name sounded nefarious, they tasted like nothing but sweet coffee. Though after three, I wondered if maybe I should slow down. I liked to sip a whiskey, but I didn't usu-ally do shots or drink three drinks in one evening.

"What's in those things?" I pointed to the empty shot glass.

"Vodka, coffee liquor, and a bit of club soda. They're delicious, right?"

"Tasted good. But I think I'm starting to feel it. I'm not really a hard drinker."

She smiled. "Does that mean you're ready to dance?"

My initial reaction was to decline, but why the fuck not? What's one dance? So I nodded and took her hand. "Fuck it, let's go."

One dance turned into two, and two turned into more than an hour. Meghan and I were both laughing and sweaty by the time we got off.

"You got moves, brooder," she said.

"So do you." I smiled.

We'd grinded a bit out on the dance floor, but when we weren't out there anymore and she pushed her tits up against me, it felt different.

"I've always found that men who can dance are really good in bed." Meghan's tongue peeked out, and she ran it along her top lip. She really was sexy as shit.

"Oh yeah?"

She wrapped her arms around my neck. "You're fun when you loosen up. But I also kind of like the brooding side of you. Why don't we get out of here? I know you're not emotionally available, but I like you. It doesn't have to be more than a fun night."

An offer like that from a woman who looked like Meghan was nearly impossible to turn down. Six months ago, we would have been dancing in the sheets by now. And I *wanted* to want to fuck her. But it would have felt like I was cheating. It was dumb of course, because Nora wasn't even talking to me anymore. I had no idea what the hell she was doing out there in California. For all I knew, she was back to picking up Tinder dates for a one-night stand. But I still couldn't do it.

I took Meghan's hand and lifted it to my mouth for a kiss. "You're incredible. And if I wasn't still hung up on someone, I'd feel like I hit the lottery." I shook my head. "But I just can't."

"Wow." Meghan smiled. "This is the first time I've ever been turned down."

"I'm sure it is. And I'm also sure I'm a fucking idiot and will probably regret it." I kissed her cheek. "But I'm going home."

"It was nice to meet you, Beck."

"You too." I'd walked a few steps when Meghan yelled my name. I turned.

"If you're up for it then, I'll meet you back here three months from today."

I smiled. "Take care, Meghan."

A little while later, I climbed into bed. I'd just shut my eyes when my cell rang from the nightstand. It was one in the morning, so I figured it was probably Jake, busting my chops because I'd left without saying goodbye. Rather than getting guilt tripped again, I turned over and ignored it. But when it rang a second time, I grabbed it.

The number wasn't local, so I swiped to answer.

"This better be important," I said.

"Hi. Uhhh...is this Beck Cross?"

"It is. Who's this?"

"My name is William Sutton."

I sprang upright, my entire body on high alert. "What happened? Is Nora okay?"

There was a painful few seconds of silence where my heart stopped beating.

"She's in the ICU. I wasn't supposed to call you unless..." He paused again. "But I think she needs you."

I jumped out of bed and yanked on my pants. "Where is she?"

"At Cedars-Sinai, in LA."

"Will you stay with her until I get there? I'm not sure how fast I can get a flight, but I'm heading to the airport now."

"I'm not going anywhere, son. I'll see you whenever you arrive."

CHAPTER 33

Beck

A man stopped me in the hallway as I charged toward the ICU's double doors.

"Beck?"

"William?"

He nodded and extended his hand. "Thank you for coming."

"Of course." I stupidly hadn't asked for his number earlier when he'd called. I'd phoned the number on my caller ID, but he must've called from the hospital because it brought me to the Cedars-Sinai switchboard, and I couldn't get anyone there to tell me anything, no matter how many times I tried. Needless to say, I'd been ready to crawl out of my skin during what turned out to be the nine hours between William's call and my arrival. I kept thinking the worst would happen before I got here. And now that he was in the hall and not with her... I swallowed. "Is she okay?"

William nodded. "She's about the same as when I called. The nurses are changing one of her ports, so they asked me to step out for fifteen minutes."

I looked to the double doors and back to him, raking a hand through my hair. "Okay."

He gestured away from the ICU. "The coffee is drinkable in the machine. How about I grab us two?"

I nodded. It took every bit of willpower to wait while he punched numbers into the vending machine and got us two paper cups of coffee. But William looked as frazzled as I felt, so I thought he might need a few quiet minutes.

He passed one paper cup to me. "Here you go. Sludge with milk."

"Thanks."

"So..." He sighed. "Like I said on the phone, my daughter was very specific with her instructions when she gave me your number. I was only permitted to use it if she..."

I put my hand on his shoulder. "I get it. You don't have to say it. I don't think I could either."

He smiled sadly. "Thanks."

"What happened? Did she have another heart attack? Or has she just deteriorated over the last two-and-a-half months?"

William's brows puckered. "Do you not know about the surgery?"

"Surgery?"

He closed his eyes. "I'm going to kill my daughter."

"What surgery did she have?"

"Nora had a heart transplant four days ago. She told me before she went in that she'd told you. I had no idea you didn't know."

My brain was still stuck on the first sentence. "Nora had a transplant?"

He nodded.

"But she wasn't even on the list."

"She wasn't until a few months ago. One day she received a FedEx with a letter inside. She spent the entire day locked in her room crying, but the next morning, she came out and told me she'd changed her mind and had an appointment with her cardiologist to get on the list."

Gram. It had to be. "Do you know who it was from?"

"I thought it was from you. But obviously I was wrong."

It didn't matter now. "So they did the transplant? She has a new heart?"

William smiled. "A healthy one that's beating strongly. She made it through the surgery great, which was the riskiest part. Going in, her chances of pulling through were on the short side of fifty-fifty. The vessel reattachment was complicated due to where her tumors had been located. But she fought the fight."

"What happened then?"

"A blood clot got caught in the artery near her lungs. They kept her out for two days to let her body heal after the surgery. The afternoon they were going to lower the sedatives, she started having trouble breathing on her own. She's on a ventilator now." He rubbed the back of his neck. "And an infection set in. It's not looking too good."

Fuck.

Fuck.

Fuck!

"Do you think we could check if it's okay to go back in? I really want to see her."

"Sure thing." Her dad put his hand on my arm. "But son, I should warn you, she doesn't look so good. She swelled all over from the blood clot, and she's got machines with bells and whistles doing all of the work for her. It's a lot to see."

I swallowed. "Okay."

All the warning in the world couldn't have prepared me for what I found in Nora's room. If William hadn't led me to the bedside and picked up his daughter's hand, I probably could have passed right by and thought it was someone else. Nora looked terrible. Her skin was pale, there was a fat tube threaded down her throat and taped into place on her face, and another smaller tube ran up her nose.

I couldn't move from the doorway. Eventually, William came over. He rested his hand on my shoulder. "If it's too much, I understand."

"No. No. I'm sorry. It's just..."

"I wanted to speak to the nurses, anyway." He gestured toward the bed. "I'll give you a few minutes alone. They say she might be able to hear us, so I've been talking to her."

I forced myself to take William's place at Nora's bedside. What I wouldn't give to change places with her right now. Why did the women I loved always have to endure so much when I rarely got a cold?

Leaning down, I kissed her forehead gently.

"Hey, beautiful." I shook my head. "I can't believe you had the surgery and didn't tell me. I should be mad at you for that, but I'm too fucking happy you took the chance." I brushed hair from her face. "I knew you were fearless. You are the strongest person I know. A woman who swims with sharks and jumps out of airplanes is not going to let a little blood clot keep her down. You're going to pull through this, sweetheart. I'll be honest, I was terrified on my way here, not knowing what the hell was going on. I let my mind go to some pretty dark places. But you have an angel watching over you now. And even if I had doubts about the doctors' ability to bring you back to me, I have *no doubt* that Louise can do it."

William came back a few minutes later. "You good?"

"I am now." I smiled and took Nora's hand. "I've never been more certain of anything in my life. She's going to make it."

William smiled back. "She's going to kick my butt when she finds out I called you."

"It's okay. I bet you'd be really happy to have her pissed off."

He chuckled. "Yeah, I would."

"Me too."

For the following forty-eight hours, nothing much changed. Nora was on heavy-duty blood thinners to ward off additional clots and a heavy dose of antibiotics to treat the infection. At one point, she sprung another fever, but her medical team managed to work through it. The doctors had warned though, that her heart rate had grown slower—likely from the infection—and each day, the chances of her pulling through declined.

I'd convinced William to go home and rest for a little while, but only on the condition that I'd take a break when he got back. I didn't want to, but I also didn't want to go back on my word with her father, whom I'd only just met. I thought I might crash in my rental car for a bit, so I could still be nearby.

William returned, looking a little more awake, and just as I was about to go, an older woman walked in. She had bright makeup and the type of smile that showed on her whole face. It went with her cheery pink blazer and the stickers all over the cart she was pushing.

"Good morning." She stayed in the doorway. "I'm one of the volunteer angels."

William and I nodded. "Morning."

"I have a cart full of goodies, if you gentlemen would like anything. I have sample-size deodorant, toothbrushes, toothpaste, even a razor and shaving cream, if you need them. Also got some books and newspapers. We know family doesn't like to leave too often, so we bring the necessities to you. What can I give you today?"

William shook his head with a polite smile. "I'm good. But thank you."

"Me, too."

"Okay." She reached into a box on the top of her cart and pulled out something small wrapped in plastic. "But I'll leave you with this. We can never have too many people watching over us." She stepped into the room and held her hand out.

William took whatever it was. "Thank you."

"I'm here until three. So if you change your mind and need something, just press zero on any hospital phone and tell them to send Thelma up." She waved and pushed her cart away.

I looked at William. "What did she give you?"

He opened his fist. "A little gold pin. It's an angel holding a heart." He turned it over. "There's a prayer on the back, the prayer for the patron saint of the sick—Saint Louise."

"Saint...Louise?"

William nodded.

I looked up and closed my eyes with a smile. The angel pin would have been enough to make me believe, but Thelma and Louise? Now that was my grandmother's sense of humor.

CHAPTER 34

Beck

"**I** also don't like California. It's too sunny. It's like a person who smiles all the time. You can't trust someone like that."

Two days later, I'd decided to change my approach. Nora still hadn't woken up. They'd taken the breathing tube out and cut all the sedatives, but she just continued to lie lifeless. It was three in the morning, and I'd climbed into bed beside her and started to tell her all the ways I disagreed with her. Telling her how much I loved her didn't work. Begging didn't work. So I'd resorted to trying to wake her by pissing her off.

"And seventy-eight-year-old women shouldn't be *wingsuit diving*." I looked over at the monitor, hoping for I don't know what—a blip, a stutter...*something*. But nothing changed. "And the Yankees are the best team in baseball. Forty pennants and counting. The only thing your Dodgers are good for is that sexy little T-shirt you wear to bed."

I went on for at least an hour, listing things I knew would infuriate her. No change. So when I yawned, I let my eyes take a break.

I had no idea how long I'd been conked out when I woke to someone whispering.

"Candy fax," the voice said.

My eyes opened and nearly bulged from my head to find Nora looking at me.

"Holy shit. You're awake."

"Candy fax," she again whispered. "Do sider." She swallowed and touched her throat. "Dry."

"Of course. You've had a tube down your throat for almost a week. Holy shit. Am I dreaming right now, or are you really awake?"

The hand at her throat crooked a finger, so I leaned closer.

"Sandy," she whispered in my ear.

I pulled back to look at her. "Oh sandy, not candy. Do you mean your throat feels sandy?"

She shook her head and again crooked that finger. So I leaned again.

"Koufax."

My forehead wrinkled. "Sandy Koufax? The old Dodgers player?"

She nodded and whispered again. "Jackie Robinson. Duke Snider."

My jaw hung open. She was listing the greatest players from the LA Dodgers to counter my comments about the Yankees being the best team in history. *She'd heard me.*

She crooked her finger and whispered in my ear again.

"Wingsuit diving is safer than walking down the street in Manhattan at night."

I started to cry like a baby. "You're awake. You're really awake."

She smiled. "I'm not a coward."

"No, sweetheart. You are definitely not. You're the bravest woman in the world. But how do you feel? Are you in pain?"

"Like an elephant sat on my chest."

"I think that's probably normal, but let me get the doctor." I turned to roll off the bed, but Nora grabbed my shirt.

"Five minutes."

"You want me to wait five minutes to get the doctor?" She nodded.

I rolled to my side, facing her, eyes wide. "I can't believe you're awake. You made it through a freaking heart transplant."

Nora frowned. "A lot can go wrong."

"A lot can go wrong any day of the week. That's life. It's filled with chances and ups and downs."

"Even if I get through the rest of this, I'm going to die young, Beck."

I cupped her cheeks. "I'll take every day we can get. We'll make each one about quality, not quantity. I'd rather be happy for a little while with you than miserable for a lifetime without."

Tears streamed down her face. "That's what my dad said about my mother. I love you, Beck. I'm sorry I never said it back, but I've loved you since almost the beginning."

"I knew even without you saying it, sweetheart." I smiled. "But hearing it is pretty damn nice." I cupped my ear and leaned close. "Maybe you should say it again."

"I love you, Beck. I love you, I love you, I love you."

"It's definitely better hearing it."

"I'm sorry I hurt you. I really am."

"I don't care about that. But I wish you would've told me about your decision to go on the list and have the surgery. I would've been here the entire time."

"I know you would've. That's why I didn't tell you. I didn't want to get your hopes up and hurt you all over again if I didn't make it through."

"We're going to talk about this when you get better. If you expect me to accept your decisions, you need to accept my decision to be with you through thick and thin."

She smiled sadly. "My dad said that, too."

"William is a smart man."

She glanced around the room. "Is he here?"

"He left about midnight to sleep a little. He'll probably be back soon. We started taking shifts. But I should call him. He'd want me to wake him up so he can get back here."

"Okay."

"I should probably get the nurse now, too," I said. "One more thing though, what made you change your mind? To go on the transplant list?"

"Louise."

"Something she said?"

Nora shook her head. "Something she did. About ten minutes after Jake called to tell me Louise had passed, a doctor called from UNOS. Louise tried to leave me her heart."

My brows drew together. "What do you mean?"

"Apparently she went to a cardiologist to discuss the possibility of a directed donation of her heart. She had cancer, so it's not the ideal organ for a transplant, but she registered with UNOS as a donor, just in case we might be a match."

"Were you?"

Nora shook her head. "No. But the fact that Louise wanted to give me her heart really hit me. After I got back from New York, a letter came, too. She must've known the end was near, because she wrote it a few days before she died and had one of her friends mail it to me after she passed. Your grandmother literally and figuratively gave me her heart. That day, I called my doctor and went on the list."

"Holy shit."

Nora nodded. "I know. It's a lot to absorb."

"No, it's not that. I meant the candy striper."

"What candy striper?"

I sat up and reached for the portable food tray, which had become our makeshift nightstand. I picked up the little cherub pin the woman had left a few days ago. The tiny angel held a heart out in front of her. "A volunteer came by. I was really nervous that morning because it was the first time I was going to leave the hospital since I'd gotten here. But I knew if I didn't take a turn to rest, neither would your dad, and he needed some sleep. The volunteer left this pin for you and said we could never have too many angels watching over us. On the back is the prayer of Saint Louise. I had no idea Saint Louise was the patron saint of sick people. It gave me the comfort I needed to leave for a few hours. But this little angel is literally holding her heart out to you."

Nora held her hand over her mouth. "Louise gave me her heart when we met, and in the end, she tried to leave it behind for me. That's her. That's our Louise."

"Wow." I raked a hand through my hair. "If that's not a message from beyond, I don't know what is."

∽

Seven weeks later, Nora and I were headed to the doctor for another checkup. This was the big one—the *resume all regular activities* appointment. And there was definitely one activity I was looking forward to more than others.

Over the last couple of months, I'd spent three days one week and four days the next out in California, going home only on the days I had Maddie. Nora's doctor wanted her to stay close until she got the all clear, and the big day might be today. I walked Nora to the passenger side of the car and opened the door for her, then jogged around to the driver's side. As soon as I climbed in, I pushed the button to put the top down. A few days after Nora was released, I'd traded in my shitty rental for a convertible. She needed to rest a lot, but we both went stir crazy cooped up in the house, so we'd started to take long drives, and keeping the top down made us feel alive and free.

I slipped my sunglasses on, and Nora elbowed me.

"Someone is getting used to the sunshine every day," she chided.

"It's not as bad as I thought out here, but I like my city a little less cheery, more cynical."

"Like your personality." Nora chuckled.

Her doctor's office was at Cedars-Sinai, so I dropped Nora at the main entrance and went to park the car. The lot was packed, and it took a while. By the time I got upstairs, she was already walking toward the door that led to the exam rooms. I jogged to catch up.

"There you are," she said. "Thought maybe you ditched me."

"Nah. I don't miss these. My favorite part of the appointments is watching you change into the gown."

She smiled. "Perv."

I leaned close. "You have no damn idea. You should be a little scared if the doctor clears you for sex today. I have a lot of pent-up perverted things I can't wait to do to you."

A nurse walked by, so Nora shushed me. "Keep it down."

"That's what you'll be saying later, too. Because *it* isn't going down for a long time once I get you underneath me." I smirked.

In the examination room, a nurse hooked Nora up to a bunch of leads and did a quick EKG. Then her surgeon, Dr. Meachum, came in and did a sonogram of her heart, followed by a short exam. He spent longer than usual with his stethoscope on her chest, which had me feeling a little panicky. When he was done, he wrapped it around his neck.

"Everything sounds perfect. EKG is clean, sonogram shows no swelling or post-op abnormalities."

I let out an audible breath, and they both looked over to me.

"Sorry." I held up my hand. "I guess I was a little anxious."

He smiled and returned his attention to Nora, picking up her chart. "So, what are we, at seven weeks now?"

"Since release," I corrected. "Eight-and-a-half post-op."

Dr. Meachum smiled again. "Right. Okay, well, I looked at the reading from the heart monitor you wore last week. You did some walking and light exercise during that time, correct?"

Nora nodded. "I did."

"Great. Everything looked perfect there, too."

Nora liked to pretend I was the only one nervous at these visits, but I saw her shoulders relax. "So back to all normal activity?" she asked.

Dr. Meachum nodded. "I don't see why not."

They talked for a few more minutes, and then he asked if she had any questions. Nora shook her head no, but I raised my hand.

"Could I ask a few?"

"Of course." Dr. Meachum closed his file and set it aside.

"So, normal activity, that includes sex, right?"

He smiled. "It does."

"I don't mean to be graphic or anything, but I want to make sure Nora is safe."

"Oh Jesus," Nora said.

"There's no inappropriate question when it comes to a patient's safety. What's on your mind?"

"I was wondering if sex should be limited to the missionary position—you know, with Nora on the bottom and not exerting too much energy?"

"Nope. We've already tested out light activity, so it's safe to do whatever you might fancy. A little workout during sex is absolutely fine."

"What about boobs? Should I keep away from the chest area?"

Dr. Meachum smiled. "As long as Nora's not feeling any discomfort on her ribs or from her scar, you can visit whatever areas you like."

I smiled. "I really like them all."

"Beck!"

The doctor laughed. "It's fine. It's been a long eight weeks. I get it."

"Eight and *a half*," I noted.

"You two enjoy yourselves. A heart transplant is a second chance at living. Take advantage of every moment."

After the doctor walked out, I turned the lock on the door behind him. Nora looked up when she heard the clank.

"Oh no..." She held her hand out. "Don't even think about it, Cross. We are *not* doing it here."

I wrapped my hand around the back of her neck. "I just wanted a kiss, to celebrate the good news. But I like the way you're thinking, dirty girl." I crushed my lips to hers, forgetting where we were for a minute. It wasn't easy to control myself. But I pulled away before she did. I wiped Nora's bottom lip with my thumb and nodded toward the door. "Let's get out of here, so I can kiss you other places."

Nora's eyes grew hooded. She bit her bottom lip. "Would it be weird to get a hotel room half an hour from my house? My dad will be home soon."

I reached into my pocket for my cell and scanned through emails until I found what I was searching for. I handed my phone to Nora.

Her forehead creased, then smoothed when she read the message. "You already made a reservation?"

"Yep. A little place on the beach about a half hour from here. I figured we could have an argument on the way over as foreplay." I winked.

EPILOGUE

Nora
Seven months later

"**I** have a present for you."

Beck put down the broom and flashed a dirty smile. "Oh yeah? I've been looking forward to unwrapping it all day."

"Sorry to disappoint, but I have an *actual* present."

He pouted, and I had to laugh. "Wait right here. I'll bring it to you."

Beck and I had been working at the new office every night for the last week, getting it ready for the big day tomorrow. But he didn't know about the other project I'd been working on, for months now. What had started as a small idea had grown much larger than I'd expected, so my gift was resting on a dolly in the closet with a sheet over it, since I could no longer carry it. I tilted the steel carrier back and pushed the two-hundred-pound labor of love into the room next door.

Beck's brows rose. "What the heck is that?"

"It's your gift. Don't get too excited. It's homemade."

"I'm intrigued…"

Settling the dolly in front of him, I was suddenly nervous. What if he was upset that I hadn't asked him before using his things? I suppose it was too late to worry about that now. I pointed to the empty back wall. "I thought it could go there—that is, if you like it."

Tomorrow was the grand opening of Louise's List—a nonprofit, Make-A-Wish-type program that would offer funding and planning assistance to terminally ill adults who wanted to fulfill their bucket lists. Beck and I were hosting a fundraiser in the new office space tomorrow night. The following Monday, the website would go live and the office staff would start work.

"If you made it, I'm sure I'll love it," Beck said.

The funny thing was, there was a lot of truth to that statement. Beckham Cross loved me in a way I never knew was possible—selfless and with his whole heart. Sometimes it made me nervous, because while my health had been great since my surgery last year, I was already beating the odds.

I inhaled a deep breath before lifting off the sheet to reveal what I'd made. The sign stood up on its side, so it took a few seconds for Beck to read it and process everything. His eyes widened. "Are those the nails...?"

I nodded. "I hope you don't mind that I used them."

I'd taken the rusty nails from the Mason jar—the ones Louise had Beck hammer into a tree stump more than two decades ago to teach him a lesson—and used them to make a Louise's List wooden box sign. The rim of the signage and the large words spelled out in the middle were made of the rusty nail heads. It had a rustic look, but I thought it had turned out pretty incredible, if I did say so myself.

Beck teared up as he stared. "It's perfect. Her life lessons belong here on display. She would be so proud of you for everything you've done to open this place, sweetheart."

"She'd be proud of *us*. I couldn't have done it without you."

Beck cupped my cheeks in his hands. "My grandmother gave me many gifts during her lifetime, but the best one she gave me was *you*."

⁓

The following evening, we opened Louise's List with a big party. Beck went to the office early with Jake to hang the sign before people started showing up. It took me forever to get an Uber a little later, so I wound up arriving at the same time as some of the guests. Since the grand-opening party was also a fundraiser, Beck had invited some of his clients. That must've been who he was talking to, holed up in a corner with two older men I'd never seen before when I arrived. I stole the moment to appreciate my man in a tux before he noticed me. Considering we'd been pretty much living together since my surgery, I would've thought checking him out would've grown old by now. But somehow it never did. Beckham Cross still took my breath away.

From the outside he was eye candy—sharp, angled jaw; full lips; tall, dark, and undeniably handsome. A true ten at first glance. But it was everything else that elevated him to a twelve—the way he stood so tall and confident, the refined way he spoke during the day at work, the dirty mouth he had only for me at night. And the way those two melded together in the bedroom—I had tingles thinking about it.

As if he felt eyes on him, Beck turned from the conversation he'd been engrossed in. He scanned the room until his gaze locked with mine. I watched his eyes dip down to my royal blue dress and caress their way back up. His lips turned up in a devilish grin, and I knew he was silently telling me I'd worn this dress for him. Of course, I had.

Beck excused himself from the conversation and strode across the room. The way he walked with such purpose, zeroing in on me like no one else existed, was always foreplay for me. Especially when he cupped his big hand around the back of my neck and brought my lips to meet his.

I was dizzy by the time our kiss broke.

"You look gorgeous." Beck leaned his forehead against mine. "Thank you for wearing that color, today of all days."

I smiled. "I figured you couldn't be blue when I was in blue. Especially when I have nothing on underneath."

Beck groaned. "I knew I should've soundproofed the bathroom."

Luckily, we were interrupted. Jake slung his arm around his brother's neck, uncaring that we were still pressed together intimately.

"What are you guys up to?" He wedged his grinning face between us.

"Go away. I'm busy," Beck grunted.

"That doesn't even work in the office." He chuckled. "It's definitely not going to work here."

I laughed and took a step back. "Hi, Jake. You look dapper this evening."

He showed off his signature crooked, dimpled grin. "Better than Beck, right?"

"You know I'm not going there. Though, I will say, Maddie's Brownie leader stopped me when I picked her up after the troop meeting yesterday to ask if the gorgeous uncle who picked her up last week was single."

After twenty-six badges on her own, Maddie had finally decided to join Brownies a few months ago. As much as she'd enjoyed earning badges with her dad, she was really loving doing it with girls her own age.

Beck rolled his eyes, and Jake's chest puffed out a little more. "The redhead?"

"Yep. Miss Rebecca."

"Guess I'll be picking up my favorite niece from Scouts next week."

"Your *only* niece," Beck grumbled.

Jake slapped his brother's shoulder. "Sounds like someone is jealous that the pretty Scout leader doesn't check him out. Don't be bitter. It'll cause more wrinkles, old man."

A few more guests arrived, and before long, the party was in full swing. I was glad I'd assigned Jake to coordinate the entertainment, because a DJ and some young dancers were exactly what was needed to keep the vibe upbeat on what could've otherwise been a down day. By ten o'clock, the alcohol was flowing almost as freely as the pens on the checkbooks people had brought. I couldn't believe how much money had already been donated. Earlier in the week, Beck had asked me if I wanted to make a speech this evening. He was much better at that type of stuff than me, so I'd declined and suggested he do it. So when the music cut off and Beck stepped to the middle of the room, I thought that's what was about to happen.

"Can I have everyone's attention, please?" Beck asked.

Guests formed a circle around him, and the rumble of voices quieted down.

"I want to thank everyone for coming tonight. As most of you already know, Louise's List was inspired by my late grandmother, Louise Aster. When she found out her cancer was back and treatment would no longer be able to cure her illness, she decided to spend the remaining time she had living life to the fullest. That was my gram. There was no stopping her." Beck looked over at his brother and smiled. "Lord knows I tried, right, Jake?"

"That you did," Jake said. "And for a while there, I enjoyed being Gram's favorite because of how annoying you were."

Laughter echoed around the room.

Beck nodded and thumbed toward his brother. "He's not kidding. Anyway, when Gram passed, she left my brother and me a note saying she didn't want a wake or any sad funeral services. Instead, she wanted a party in her honor—a celebration of her life on the one-year anniversary of her death." He paused and smiled. "I believe her exact words were, 'When you're able to get your head out of your ass and remember me without a pity party.' Well, today is one year, and I don't think there's any better way to celebrate Louise Aster than with the opening of this foundation you have all so graciously contributed to tonight. But I'm not the one responsible for bringing this to fruition. A very special lady is." He turned to me. "Nora, would you please come over here?"

I hated to be put in the limelight, but everyone was watching, so I stepped into the center of the room with Beck. He took my hand. "Thank you for creating this beautiful legacy for my grandmother. I know she's looking down right now and smiling. Actually, come to think of it, she's probably not. She's probably wondering why the hell I didn't do this sooner..."

Everything after that seemed to happen in slow motion. The crowd of people around us faded into the background as Beck bent down on one knee. I covered my mouth with a trembling hand, realizing what was about to go down.

"Eleanor Rose Sutton, you came into my life during a time when I was intent on being miserable. I wanted nothing more than to wallow in self-pity and sulk, but it was impossible when I was near you. Even a text would cheer up my day and put a smile on my face. And that... Well, that just pissed me off even more."

I laughed. "It really did."

"You are the kindest, most loving and passionate person I've ever met. You're as beautiful on the inside as you are on the outside. You've made me understand what life is, and now that I understand what's important, I don't know how I got through my first thirty-four years without you." He reached into his suit jacket and pulled out a black velvet box. "I spent a few weeks looking for the perfect ring for you. I wanted the biggest and best diamond I could find. But nothing felt right. And then I realized it was because nothing was right. You were meant to have *this* ring."

Beck opened the box, and I immediately recognized what was inside. *Louise's engagement ring.* Tears welled in my eyes.

"You are my best friend, my lover, and my universe, Nora. I am absolutely positive I don't deserve for you to be my wife, but I promise that if you marry me, I will spend every single day trying to be a man worthy of you. You've taught me how precious life is, and I don't want to waste another minute without you by my side. Will you marry me, Nora?"

I leaned down and pressed my forehead to his. "I don't know how long we'll have."

"If we both live to be a hundred, it won't be enough," he said. "An eternity with you wouldn't be enough. But I'll take whatever I can get."

Tears rolled down my cheeks as I nodded. "Okay."

"Okay, you'll marry me?" The smile that lit up his face might have been the sweetest part of his proposal—my always-confident man needed reassurance.

"Yes, I'll marry you. How can I not? This is the *second* heart that's fallen in love with you."

OTHER BOOKS BY VI KEELAND

The Game
The Boss Project
The Summer Proposal
The Spark
The Invitation
The Rivals
Inappropriate
All Grown Up
We Shouldn't
The Naked Truth
Sex, Not Love
Beautiful Mistake
Egomaniac
Bossman
The Baller
Left Behind
Beat
Throb
Worth the Fight
Worth the Chance
Worth Forgiving
Belong to You
Made for You
First Thing I See

OTHER BOOKS BY VI KEELAND & PENELOPE WARD

ACKNOWLEDGMENTS

To you—the *readers*. You have given me a career I could only dream about years ago. Thank you for more than a decade of support and enthusiasm. I'm honored so many of you are still with me and hope we have many more decades together!

To Penelope – The woman who puts up with my neurotic side more than my husband! Thank you for being the yin to my yang.

To Cheri – Thank you for years of true friendship and laughter.

To Julie – Paint your toes! Fire Island here we come! Finally!!

To Luna – Thank you for your friendship and unwavering loyalty.

To my amazing Facebook reader group, Vi's Violets – more than 25,000 smart ladies (and a few awesome men) who love books! You mean the world to me and inspire me every day. Thank you for all of your support.

To Sommer –Thank you for figuring out what I want, often before I do.

To my agent and friend, Kimberly Brower – Thank you for being my partner in this adventure!

To Jessica, Elaine, and Julia – Thank you for smoothing out all the rough edges and making me shine!

To Kylie and Jo at Give Me Books – I don't even remember how I managed before you, and I hope I never have to figure it out! Thank you for everything you do.

To all of the bloggers – Thank you for always showing up.

Much love

Vi

VI KEELAND is a #1 *New York Times,* #1 *Wall Street Journal*, and *USA Today* Bestselling author. With millions of books sold, her titles are currently translated in twenty-six languages and have appeared on bestseller lists in the US, Germany, Brazil, Bulgaria, Israel, and Hungary. Three of her short stories have been turned into films by Passionflix, and two of her books are currently optioned for movies. She resides in New York with her husband and their three children where she is living out her own happily ever after with the boy she met at age six.

Connect with Vi Keeland

Facebook Fan Group:
https://www.facebook.com/groups/
ViKeelandFanGroup/)
Facebook: https://www.facebook.com/pages/Author-
Vi-Keeland/435952616513958
TikTok: https://www.tiktok.com/@vikeeland
Website: http://www.vikeeland.com
Twitter: https://twitter.com/ViKeeland
Instagram: http://instagram.com/Vi_Keeland/

CPSIA information can be obtained
at www.ICGtesting.com
Printed in the USA
JSHW022239210523
41991JS00001B/3